# UNDERTHINGS

Bikini wearers favor phosphorescent colors. They will buy panties patterned with spiders or eggplants or pigs or skulls. She's learned to pick them out, those women. They dress conservatively enough on top but underneath there's more to be found than flowers or polka dots. And for a while slogans were big. *Peace. Make love, not war.* Arachne never liked selling those; she thought they were in bad taste.

She made up a list of her own and sent it in to head office. *I have a headache. Eat sh\*t. Go for it. Chew nails. Try me. Don't miss.* Ladies' Comfort didn't respond.

And when a store owner's wife asks which line she recommends, Arachne always gives the same answer. The white cotton. Cool, easy to care for, inexpensive. The bottom line is, her advice has to match her image. She can't go around wearing bikini panties printed with alligators. Still, it is fortunate no one ever checks.

On principle, Arachne wears nothing at all.

Seal Books by Aritha van Herk

NO FIXED ADDRESS
THE TENT PEG

# Aritha van Herk

# No Fixed Address
*an amorous journey*

**SEAL BOOKS**
McClelland-Bantam, Inc.
Toronto

NO FIXED ADDRESS
*A Seal Book / March 1987*

*Financial assistance of the Canada Council and the Ontario Arts
Council toward the publication of this book is gratefully acknowledged.*

ISBN 0-7704-2149-0

*Seal Books are published by McClelland and Stewart-Bantam Limited.
Its trademark, consisting of the words "Seal Books" and the portrayal
of a seal, is the property of McClelland and Stewart-Bantam Limited,
60 St. Clair Avenue East, Suite 601, Toronto, Ontario M4T 1N5, Canada.
This trademark has been duly registered in the Trademarks Office of Canada.
The trademark, consisting of the words "Bantam Books" and the portrayal of
a rooster, is the property of and is used with the consent of Bantam Books,
Inc. 666 Fifth Avenue, New York, New York 10103. This trademark has
been duly registered in the Trademarks Office of Canada and elsewhere.*

PRINTED IN CANADA

COVER PRINTED IN U.S.A.

U     0 9 8 7 6 5 4 3 2 1

*For Paul Adams*
*For Heidi and Thomas, my Swedes*
*And for Bob/who saw her.*

*Notebook on a missing person*

*You discover in your search that the fashionable woman's shape has always been in a state of constant change. We have come to be what we are after years of changes in cut and color, drapery and form adapted and re-adapted in variations on camouflage. At any given moment, the garments covering it have determined the contours of the body; but the final appearance of the outer costume was inevitably controlled by a supporting apparatus beneath. This combination of garment and underpinnings reduced or expanded the natural female shape in an often remarkable manner, the goal, it is important to remember, to aid physical attractiveness, a standard inevitably decided by men.*

*For centuries women have suffered the discomfort of corsets, padding, petticoats, girdles, bustles, garters and bust pads. The trimmings too contributed: buckles that chafed the tender skin of the ribcage, hooks and eyes of dubious connection, front-closing snaps on uplift bras that released at inappropriate moments; the sucking rasp of elastic, spandex that relaxed too soon, itchy lace. Only recently have we come to enjoy some freedom from clothing designed to create an aesthetic of beauty based on physical impairment, elongated waists, squeezed breasts, and bound stomachs and buttocks. It is a wonder* we can still walk. And who will be responsible for what those tortures have created? The existence of smelling salts, hysteria, frigidity and shrewishness can all be attributed to uncomfortable underwear.

It was for a long time taken for granted that woman's body should be prisoner, taped and measured and controlled. Some fashions literally demanded that women walk within the wooden and metal hoops of cages, their progress a gently swaying bell and the body within an unclamorous tongue. How small their heads seemed by comparison, and at night, the voluminous nightdresses that their husbands' hands encountered were like the drapery of prudish angels.

All that has changed, and now, if we wear satin and lace, we do so desirous of the proper consequences. We have forgotten our imprisonment, relegated underwear to the casual and unimportant. In cheerful androgyny young women stretch boyish cotton briefs and undershirts on billboards. No art, no novel, no catalogue of infamy has considered the effect of underwear on the lives of petty rogues.

## Comfort — or to stay amused

On a blue glazed June morning Arachne bumps off the road onto the gravel shoulder and parks. She has managed to convince the general store in Cluny to try her new Princess line: full nylon panties in galvanic colors. Cobalt green, honey bee yellow, congo rose and zaffer blue. The new line is not doing well. Women who buy waisted panties prefer pastel colors, nothing exotic. The pale tones eventually wash to pinkish gray, Arachne knows, because they are the kind she used to wear. Bikini wearers favor phosphorescent colors. They will buy panties patterned with spiders or eggplants or pigs or skulls. She's learned to pick them out, those women. They dress conservatively enough on top, but underneath there's more to be found than flowers and polka dots. Animals are popular, especially reptiles, turtles and alligators. So are cars, racers and antiques. And for a while slogans were big. *Peace. Make love, not war.* Arachne never liked selling those; she thought they were in bad taste.

She made up a list of her own and sent it in to head office. *I have a headache. Eat shit. Go for it. Chew nails. Try me. Sing high. Don't miss. Go home.* Ladies' didn't respond.

She has a continuing dispute with them about the boxed sets of Sunday Monday/Tuesday/Wednesday/Thursday

Friday Saturday panties. Saturday is always red with black trim. Sunday is virginal white. The rest are a mixture of pastels. They are a big seller, have been a steady item for years. Even though they are poor quality, which Arachne is quick to point out. She can afford to be honest about the sets because the stores order them anyway. And if Arachne says that the elastic around the legs is cheap and that the waist will sag, that the machine-stitched embroidery will ravel, it gives her more credibility; the buyers believe what she says about other lines. Arachne counts on the sets as a barometer for sales. The number of boxes sold equals roughly the number of birthday parties that month, except around Christmas when — a natural choice for the Sunday School name draw — there's a run. They are a seasonal indicator too. Farmers' wives buy them in the spring after the wheat is seeded, and in the fall after combining. Not like the combed white cotton that dominates winter's coldest cold, summer's hottest heat, something to do with the effect of extremes, a religious awareness that white cotton must be healthier if it's unprovocative. And when an owner's wife asks which line she recommends, Arachne always gives the same answer. The white cotton. Cool, easy to care for, inexpensive.

The bottom line is, her advice has to match her image. Although she might sell them, she can't go around wearing bikini panties printed with alligators. Ladies' Comfort cannot afford aberrance, so she has to be dead ordinary. Still, it is fortunate no one ever checks. On principle, adamantly determined not to be her own best advertisement, Arachne wears nothing at all.

But she is the regional sales representative for Ladies' Comfort Limited, a Winnipeg-based firm specializing in women's underwear. She travels to all the towns and villages and hamlets where general stores still carry rubber boots and writing paper and bolts of cotton and Kotex and socks and underwear – both women's and men's. The stores are not as messy or dark as they once were, but they carry the same cacophony of goods, they still have glass candy cases and old coke coolers, the smell of dead licorice behind the screen door's bang, the extract of bewilderment that permeates all rural commerce usurped by the city.

Arachne travels light. One gouged suitcase with the tidy dresses that she sells in, a pair of shorts if she has time to run at the end of the day, very tight blue jeans and a sleeveless T-shirt. No underwear. She piles her sample boxes on the back seat of the Mercedes. The trunk is no longer sealed and the panties get sifted with a layer of dust from the gravel roads. The cardboard boxes jounce and rattle with the car and if she hits a particular rut, fly open to spill their juicy contents over the wide back seat. Ladies' has a catalogue, but Arachne finds the real thing more persuasive. "Feel this," she says.

Arachne is perfectly content with her job. She even enjoys it. When she has completed an order and pulled over to the shade of some fence-line poplars to eat her packed sandwiches, she is happy. She can prop her rump against the edge of her open car door and stare at the sky. She can squat to pee. She can crawl through a barbed-wire fence into blue alfalfa.

When she gets the job she rushes over to tell her only friend, Thena.

Thena is blunt. "You're bonkers," she says. "You've finally gone mad."

Thena's reaction is Arachne's measurement of success. "Why?"

"It's grotty," she pronounces with relish. "I thought traveling salesmen were obsolete. I thought that's how the telephone improved civilization."

"Women's underwear is too touchy for a telephone. If

some man's running a store he'd have to phone an impersonal voice long distance and rattle off his list. Can't you just hear him? ' 'Er two dozen full panty, assorted pastel colors; three dozen brief, with cotton gusset; a dozen bikini prints. And uhm, uh, about that there midnight line . . .' "

"What on earth is the midnight line?"

"Black panties, all sorts. And he's got to stock them because they sell. He's cutting himself out of business if he doesn't."

"Well, don't say I didn't warn you," says Thena. "You'll be staying in grotty motels and eating greasy food and driving country roads that are either washboard ruts or snowbound. I hope you asked for a mileage allowance."

"All the upkeep of my car. Come on, cynic. I'm getting paid to explore all the weird little towns in the West."

"You're giving up a perfectly good job driving a clean, warm, city-maintained bus in order to be an underwear salesman," Thena says flatly, knowing there is little hope.

"Right. No squalling kids and mothers wielding strollers, no ten-cent hoods, no traffic jams on the freeway, no passenger with a ten-dollar bill when the fare is sixty cents and the sign's already told him I don't give change. I'm my own boss. I am free of the shrill and the halt purveyors of public transport."

Admittedly, they have been drinking Beaujolais, but Arachne would never have said it that way. More likely, "I never have to put up with the assholes who ride the bus again." And if Arachne is elated, Thena is cynical. She suspects that the distaff side of Arachne's character, which she knows well, will have far more opportunity to experiment now that Arachne has managed to get rid of what form and structure there was to her work, if not her life. Arachne's main difficulty lies in keeping herself amused.

Thena is right. Arachne has represented Ladies' Comfort for four years now, and although she isn't sick of the job, she sees too many grotty hotels and greasy restaurants and bad roads. The work isn't demanding because the product sells itself. Covering her territory two times a year is more tedious than difficult. Each year she trades in one old region for a new one. She whips through townships and counties. With three regions, she is the most productive of the Ladies' Comfort reps; management is careful to agree when Arachne Manteia asks for a specific area.

Still, she has to keep herself amused.

## The buried

When she sees the roadside sign slide past her window,
Arachne slams on the brakes, backs up and pulls into
the parking bay. The old highway is deserted, and up
the hill to the southwest she can see the dominoed map
of a graveyard. Arachne is particularly fond of graveyards;
they are her ideal picnic grounds. She slides down from
the car's high seat and stretches her arms. Tracing a finger
over the dusty fender, she walks around to inspect the
plaque. Chief Crowfoot: his dates and a generalization
on his life. Arachne kicks the marker; she hates the way
they minimize everything, reduce even enormous people
and events. The graveyard should be better.

She takes her thermos of coffee and her ham and pickle
sandwich and heads up the hill. An orange camper van
is parked there, but Arachne knows the limits of sightseer
patience. After taking pictures and seeing that there is
little to see, people are quick to leave. Especially graveyards,
such aloof places.

She walks up the hill slowly, breasting the solid heat.
Grasshoppers startle from her feet, the smell is of sage
and damp earth. She stops at the top of the hill, the river
a flung silver chain below. Beyond it, dusty jade trees
conceal what Arachne knows is a golf course, a private
resort with a gate and a guard fencing out the Indians
who sold the land.

She walks between the graves, swinging her thermos and reading the names on the scattered markers. There is something dreadful about marching lines of granite and marble, about slabs of rock marking the positions of expensive and disintegrating coffins. This graveyard is comfortingly neglected; the graves are shallow and the dirt is piled in untidy heaps, unmarked. No neatly trimmed grass, only rain-stained ribbons and mutilated plastic flowers, toppled glass jam jars. These graves shiver on the hill crest overlooking Blackfoot Crossing, the flats across the river.

At the very lip of the valley is Crowfoot's grave. It is mercilessly rigid, surrounded by an iron fence. Chips of colored glass embedded in the heavy concrete tablet chill the sun. Arachne reaches out and closes her fingers on a rusty spike. She knows the old man doesn't like this, can't possibly appreciate that weight holding him down. She wills him to push it aside and stand; arms folded, look across the river and join his voice to the lizard whir of the afternoon. Sixty-nine when he died. Could he still harden, snag a woman against a tree? Arachne's sexual fantasies are incorrigible. She hums. She pushes the heel of her hand against her crotch.

"Hey, come up here," calls a voice. She turns into the advancing voices, the three campers.

She could leave. There is a field of rape down the road. Let the yellow close over her and imagine Crowfoot. But she decides to wait. They are tourists, they will fidget and speculate and then go looking for another site. Too hot to stay here long. Three of them – an old man, a woman and a teenage boy. Arachne eyes the boy, the worn crotch of his jeans, but his face is pimply and squinting, and she lifts a mental shoulder. Too young.

"Well, at least *this* one has been taken care of," says the woman, the untidy graves a direct affront to her. She is large, solid, with a pleasant face that contradicts her tone. "Imagine burying them so carelessly. The bones are hardly covered."

"Chief Crowfoot. Died April 25, 1890. Age sixty-nine years," the boy reads the limestone marker aloud. "He must have been important."

The man, a gangling figure shrinking within his clothes, waits apart and says nothing. His eyes are hooded and the joints of his fingers knobbed. What makes Arachne stare is his hair, a spun floss of white, thick and wild, with a beard like it. She has never seen such a skein of hair – Albert Einstein hair. Curious how many bald, thinning men the world allows. She knows she is staring but when the old man swings around and stares back, she doesn't blink. Arachne has a needling gaze; she uses it with a disregard that has always gotten her into trouble. It is the man who shifts his eyes away first, while Arachne kicks at the cement base of a mutely self-righteous cross and waits for them to leave. She wants to jump graves and shout her name into the river's echo.

The clodded rows of dirt breathe quietly, distinguished only by shades of black, from ash to a fresher slate. One mound, huddled close against the side of Crowfoot's grave, is very dark. It is unmarked and unsurrounded, the piled-up earth still damp. Arachne wonders who would be allowed to lie so close to the old chief, but even though she circles to the grave's head, cannot find a name. The teenager is still discussing Crowfoot – a high school textbook – and Arachne, dirt sifting into her sandals between her toes, spits. Oh yes, she has bad habits. The old man glares at her, but she is oblivious, shaking one foot stork-like beside the mound. And she is about to turn away, retrieve her thermos and brown bag from the foot of the cross, when the bone appears, shoves itself to the surface, clamps her eyes.

The bone. More than bone, it is clearly the bottom half

of a skull, sharp jaw and cheeks, teeth worn but alive. Arachne cannot pull her eyes away from its angular emergence, she has to touch, feel its rough biscuit texture under her fingers, probe the hollow scoops of eyes. She stretches out a hand. She stiffens. If she gives the skull away, if she reveals this fleshless bone, the tourists will lay hands on it, hold it up in the sunlight and put it on the dashboard of their van, or in their rec room, brag to their friends, "This skull is famous, we found it next to Crowfoot's grave – isn't it nifty? Remember the summer we camped around Alberta, visited all the gas stations and historic sites, those cute local museums. . . ."

Arachne looks at the campers across the mound and tries to pretend indifference. If they leave, she can cover it up. But they are curious too. Finished with Crowfoot's grave, they inspect the one beside it while Arachne fumes and tries to block the skull with her body.

"Wonder who it is," says the teenager.

"It's not marked," replies the disapproving woman. "Not even a small cross." She glances surreptitiously at Arachne, who stands, arms folded, scowling, horny, mad about the heat, mad about Crowfoot, damn mad about campers and high school boys in tight jeans.

"Must have been a warrior," says the teenager.

Arachne makes a face and turns to her lunch. She is waiting too obviously. If she stands there, they'll notice the skull. The woman and the boy are watching her. Only the man stares away, telescoping the flats across the river. He seems to be trying to plumb distance, mesmerized by the haze. When the woman says, "Come on, Papa, let's go," he pulls his gaze back musingly, following the body of the landscape. His rheumy eyes cross Arachne's absently, dismissing her – a cold stick for such bright hair, she thinks – and drop to outline the mound of black dirt. He sees the skull. Arachne knows he sees the skull. He starts

19

and moves forward, but then stops himself, legs tensed inside baggy trousers.

Arachne almost chokes. Damn tourists, they should be licensed, snooping around where they have no business. She's ready to howl; she knows he will take the skull.

The woman and boy have already turned away. "Are you coming?"

He half turns after them. "You go. I come." It is the first time he has spoken and Arachne is surprised not only by his accent but at the reed of his voice, its unsteadiness. She expects a man with hair like that to sound dark chocolate. It only makes her despise him more, and she glares at him, hoping he'll be too ashamed to take the skull while she is watching.

Immigrant, she thinks. Arachne does not bother with delicate insults.

He ignores her and scuffs at the broom, hands in his pockets. But he does not go.

# Mad

Arachne will stay as long as he does. He will not touch the skull, not without her say. Old buzzard. She hovers on the edge of the grave, looking at the clumps of dirt, the patterns traced by rain. She spears the man her blackest stare. He squints across the river. But Arachne knows he is waiting. After a few minutes his eyes return to the skull, he wants to reassure himself that it is there. She will not leave before the man does. She will camp in the graveyard all night to make sure the van does not return to pick up *her* treasure. She scowls. She puts her hands on her hips. She swats mosquitoes. All this he ignores, even daring a tuneless whistle.

The man has seen the skull. He has seen it clearly, a bone flint reaching out of the grave to his own settling bones. He blinks and hesitates, steps back as if addressed. He sees it alive; like his middle-of-the-night awakenings when everything is larger than its daylight size. The girl has seen it too, he is sure of that. Dark, chin-length hair and tanned arms against a white but curiously severe summer dress. She glares at him with narrowed green eyes. He can smell her hostility. If he goes, she will take the skull. He is determined that she will not have it. He will not go until she does. He waits, staring at a mirage of trees across the river.

The solid, ten-foot cross is useful. Arachne settles herself on the cement base with her back against it, opens her thermos and spreads out her ham sandwich. She could just as well say, See, I have a reason to be here.

She munches down one sandwich, then the second. She drinks coffee. She screws the lid back on the thermos. The man does not move. Both pretend to ignore the other but they are choking; if one of them shifts, the other does too. Neither dares to move closer to the grave. Neither will leave.

Still, the man is at a disadvantage. The woman and teenager have long ago reached the Volkswagen van and are looking back up the hill. Arachne watches them talking and gesturing. Yes. Come and get him, thinks Arachne. But they decide against the walk and the boy only shouts, his voice strangely thin in the green air, "Grampa!"

The man turns and waves his arm as if to say, I'll be there right away. But he stays. He bends and scratches a mosquito bite. He picks a long spear of grass and puts it in his mouth.

Arachne crosses her arms. The sun makes her want to sleep, there above the river. Damn that man, he won't go, watching her from the corner of his eye, the kind of man who will not look directly at a woman, who always averts his gaze, as if his eyes will reveal something. She sneers at him. Try me, old man. Think you're up to it?

But his family is getting impatient and finally the woman tromps halfway up the hill, hands on her hips. "Papa," she calls. He is going to get it.

Still he waits, jacket belling, legs apart, stubborn, white hair pushed flat by the breeze.

"They're waiting," Arachne says.

His eyes, hooded, evil old magician's, fall on her before he replies. "Does not matter. I have the keys."

They wait. Arachne settles herself against the splintery

cross more solidly. The tension between them feeds itself on the heat and the wavering grass. She knows that nothing will move him. He is as unshakable as she is furious. She thinks of reasoning, explaining why he shouldn't take the skull, but even as she frames hostile sentences, she sees the woman and the boy toiling up the hill. She tries not to smile.

"Papa, what are you *doing*? Let's *go*!"

He hardly turns, and again Arachne is struck by the tight restraint of his body.

"We've been waiting for half an hour."

"Yeah," says the teenager, "it's hot, can't we take off?"

The man spins around and glares at the two of them. "You pester an old man to death," he shouts, and his voice breaks. "Can't I have peace?"

The woman recoils. She casts a frightened glance at Arachne. "All right, all right, just hurry up."

The man stands looking at the ground. Arachne throws silent malevolence at his head, wishes him warts and diarrhea. They wait.

His family sit on the open side door of the van, peeling oranges. They have turned on the radio and a faint jump of music filters up the hill. He pretends not to notice, but it's getting harder to ignore the girl's eyes. He shifts from the shimmering river to her face and suddenly returns her stare, the two of them unblinking twins of rage. They tense, almost crouch.

They are saved by voices, other visitors. Although they haven't moved, their bodies shift and they both glare at the new arrivals, a middle-aged couple in tennis shirts and expensive sunglasses. The strangers dally through the graveyard. They stop to point. They peer at a tilted wooden marker.

Mad, Arachne gets to her feet, dusts off her dress, steps down from the base of the cross. Mad, the man turns until he is standing beside Arachne, close beside her. She can smell his sweat, his old breath. The tourists amble closer to Crowfoot's grave, oblivious to the two watching their progress. At its foot, they push their sunglasses up to read the tablet.

"Look at that, Ron," says the woman. "Something, eh?"

He is chewing a golf tee. "Yeah, old days they just left the bodies. Didn't even bury them. Used to be saddles and blankets and food lying all over the graves here." He glances at the immovable old man as at an ally. "But they buried this one, eh?" And chuckles.

"Yah," says Arachne's guard. "They did." He sounds mad.

"Did you see the golf course over there?" The man waves his hand across the river and whistles. "Some layout! Wouldn't mind owning a piece of that little property."

"No," Arachne's companion speaks quietly, but the tension in his voice vibrates under Arachne's skin.

They are both rigid, straining to will all sightless, by some power blindfolded. What if one of them sees the skull, what if they — ? The notion is unthinkable. Arachne and the man breathe myopia.

The woman poses with one hand on a spike while her husband takes a lengthily adjusted Canon shot, then they drift away, wrinkling their noses at the graveyard. When the tourists climb into their car, Arachne and the man dare to look at each other. They are still mad. They are still suspicious. But Arachne nudges him with her elbow. "Did you see that? Dumb golfers."

"Blind," he growls.

Together they kneel at the mound and they touch the bone. Arachne rubs her fingers over its grain, the man cradles it in his palm. Together, dry fingers touching, they scoop a hole in the mound and bury the skull, cover it after its brief gleam in the sun, pat the earth firm and scratch the surface with a twig. Without a word, they walk down the hill. The man crosses to the van and Arachne slides into her Mercedes and they drive off, one east and one west, each disappearing over the hill at the same instant.

## Order out of chaos

In her motel that night Arachne listens to the dolorous rattle of the air conditioner and scowls. Stubborn old bastard, standing there waiting. Huh. Old guys like that — no juice — she can't do a thing with them. Unless they've had a chance to like women. Some storekeepers are tickled when Arachne comes in, start thumbing their suspenders and clearing their throats. She doesn't mind. The least she can do twice a year, bend over their counters filling out her order form, give them a chance to rub up against her. No harm in that. Besides, their orders are sizable, worthwhile. It's the ones who look at her like she's sour milk, who keep the cash register between them. He belongs with them. When he was young, he'd have been the kind of man she could hate. Just consolidates when they get old. Arachne makes small distinction between young men and old. They're not so different, sexually at least.

She and Thena talk about men a good deal, mostly their failings, although Arachne always cites Thomas as an exception. Thena agrees but declares, exception or no, that she's through with the bastards. "They're too much trouble for too little return."

Arachne is inclined to agree. Still, there are certain men she likes very much, most particularly the teasing, bear-like type who have somehow managed to avoid falling into the clutches of hockey and beer. There are more of them than Thena would imagine, undemanding men that Arachne can burrow into, men who do not mind her muscular solidity. They are neither possessive nor promiscuous and they almost always have a wife or a steady girlfriend who is as easy-going as they are. She is convinced that they are best for two reasons. One, they never talk. More important, unlike other men, they are able to make love to a woman without in some minuscule but thwarted way subduing her. Pleasure with them is exactly that, not something won or held back.

Thomas is this kind of man, and Arachne is grateful. She knows her inclination for cynicism would probably swamp her if he weren't around. And Thena always confirms it, shaking her head and saying, "You hang onto him, Arachne. There's damn few of *them* in the world." But a lot of others, Arachne knows. They're everywhere. In the government, in schools, in business. They occupy upper management at Ladies' Comfort.

She has spread her receipts out over the bed and is recording the week's sales. The too-small motel desk wobbles under her hand. She works steadily, separating the orders into piles according to district, checking colors and sizes and quantities. The window above the desk faces west and the June sun slides down the border of the sky until it hangs brassily, just above darkness.

Arachne likes the ritual of compiling her orders, sitting in a T-shirt, naked from the waist down.

Barker's Home and Handy Store, Gem
1 dozen full panty — assorted colors
Mi-Lady 100% nylon (73-1) Size S

3 dozen full panty — assorted colors

Mi-Lady 100% nylon (73-2) Size M

2 dozen full panty — assorted colors
Mi-Lady 100% nylon (73-3) Size L

Countess Co-op
4 dozen full panty — white
Modesty (503-B) Size M

She wriggles her toes on the raspy nylon carpet. She'll go for a long hike when she's through, wander down Bassano's dog-barking streets in the twilight. She is almost alone in the motel, June still too early for tourists. She has stayed here before. The beds are lumpy but it's quieter than the motel at Brooks. Arachne has learned that it's better to be carefully ignored in smaller towns than carefully watched in larger ones. No matter where, the Mercedes draws attention; there is always one car-loving teenager who can't believe what his eyes tell him when she drives down the street. She curses the way people stare after her. Someday some smartass will try to steal it. But she answers their questions straight-faced. "It used to be a hearse. I got it cheap."

"Wow, lady, if you ever want to sell it, let me know." Their longing makes her smile.

# A social call

Her neat list shadows. It must be getting late, she should go for a run now. Arachne rubs her eyes and finishes an order. When she glances up, she sees against the reddened haze the charcoal shape of a man standing flat outside her window. For a wild moment she imagines it's the ghost of some man she once laid and has forgotten. But the form is familiar in resistance – she is staring straight into the face of the man from Crowfoot's grave. From her chair, looking up at him through the glass, he seems giant. She can discern his shape but not his features; he is all menacing silhouette. It's the hair that distinguishes him. Looking with the same inflexible patience he showed at the grave, waiting without tapping on the glass.

He can see her plainly. The low sun washes the motel room as it does not at any other time of day. They stare at each other and then Arachne shrugs and shoves back her chair and goes to the door. He stands on the threshold as if giving her a chance to change her mind before he steps inside.

"How did you find me?"

"Your car." He bends, slides one arm between her bare legs, the other around her shoulders, and picks her up, holding her above that taffy hair in an iron embrace. The rough wool of his checkered jacket chafes her legs, her crotch, but she allows him, she lets him tumble her down on the arranged piles of orders. He slides both hands up her thighs, reaching to her belly and her breasts, his face so closed he seems blind.

Arachne feels no fear, only rage, rage at his shuttered face, rage that he handles her like bread and butter, rage that he dares to think that he can follow her. "Stop it," she says. "Stop it." Actually punches him, draws her knees up and kicks into his chest.

He pulls back, stricken, holds his open palms at his sides. "I'm sorry," he says. "I am sorry. I – "

Arachne sits up, props her back against the wall, paper crackling under her crossed legs. She folds her arms. She glares. "What's your name?"

"Josef."

"Josef."

He nods. "And yours?"

"Arachne." She feels the last slice of sun strike her arm, turns her head to look out the window at the highway.

"Arachne," he says awkwardly, pronouncing it wrong.

She doesn't correct him, just looks at him standing there, arms helpless at his sides, face locked as a brass box under that spun hair. She pats the bed beside her legs. He sits hesitantly, stiffly, as if he might have arthritis.

"You are alone?" The rasp of his voice makes her frown. "I don't mind."

Although he will fit in with all the stories Arachne saves for Thena, she knows that she will not tell her about this man, at least not for a while. He doesn't belong in her gallery of pickups.

While the sun lowers itself further, the room no longer red but dim and submerged, they breathe shallowly, looking not at each other's faces but at their legs, parallel on the chenille bedspread. Hers tanned and solid, his encased in brown twill cotton, the kind of pants older workmen dress up in. Two pairs of legs. On his thigh is a spot where he has spilled something. Head still lowered, he reaches out one hand and touches Arachne's right knee with the tips of his fingers. She looks at his hand, five points balanced around her kneecap. It is large and moderately clean, only one noticeable callus along the edge of his forefinger. She takes the hand and holds it between both of hers, the hand of a man who has been alive a long time. Here is a small scar and there, on the back, a few dark age spots. The joints are enlarged – he has done some manual labor. Experimentally, she turns the hand over, but it tenses within hers, and when she looks at his face she sees that the hand's momentary revelation is denied, he will not allow more.

"They'll be waiting for you," she says.

He nods and lifts his head, looks not only at her face but down her halved body, deliberately, not hesitating at her dark, bushy crotch. He pulls his hand away and touches her knee again, then shuffles to his feet.

"I have to go. They wait for me."

She looks for some trace of unsteadiness, a crack of disappointment. There is none.

"Fine," she says. "You go."

## Deprivation

Arachne's summer continues, a litany of small towns. They are all the same, with individual scars or decorations. It is a choking summer. The brick-faced farmers clogging in the post offices are full of doom and pessimism. Drought, they mutter, and hail. Nightly, thunderstorms rattle the darkness but only a few unsympathetic pellets strike the ground. Arachne's orders are low. When she asks about business, the store owners shake their heads. Even though the names of the towns are airy and genteel – Countess, Rosemary, Duchess, Millicent, Patricia, Princess – the people wear a coarse, gritty look.

Arachne pursues her customers with cheerful viciousness but the roads have holes, signs are changed, her maps are out of date, towns she remembers from three months ago have vanished, new ones have sprung up in unexpected places, large and ugly. Where there were once bridges, there are ferries; where there were once ferries, the road runs itself into a muddy flat of river. Arachne begins to spit out the window, to squat and pee without bothering to look for a decent clump of bushes. The Mercedes boils over. Arachne swears obscenely. She gets motel rooms next to drunks and lovers, but she herself finds no lovers. No, not one; in all the stretches of road she drives she finds not one man interested in lust. What has happened to

them, all the men so quick and comfortable and undemanding? The gas station attendants yawn and scratch
themselves, the telephone linemen cling to the tops of their
poles, the cowboys have taken to pickups that pass her
in a cloud of dust, and the grader operators aren't operating.
The holes in the roads show it. She picks up a hitchhiker
outside Drumheller, but he smells so bad she goes out
of her way to get rid of him quickly. Arachne develops
an ache between her legs from abstinence.

She has never told Thena the extent of her operations.
Thena would be more disapproving than shocked, would
flinch at Arachne's lack of discrimination. And Arachne
is not unselective: she has an instinct for men who are
clean, residually polite, who are decent lovers without being
nasty or dangerous. Some of them she even sees again on
return trips. They are easy and cordial; she may or may
not take them back to her room, it's no matter. They follow
her no further. If they even recognize her again, it's because
of the Mercedes. Arachne jokes that the car is better than
any aphrodisiac.

At which Thena snorts, "I hope you don't screw the
guys you're selling to."

"Oh no, that would be bad for business."

"So you practise some continence."

Arachne just laughs. She doesn't share Thena's fastidi-
ousness. And she doesn't tell Thena how useful it is to
the order list to let them, as she would say, "cop a feel."

"How can you, Arachne? Farmers and truckers."

Arachne shrugs. "They're just bodies, you could put
a paper bag over their heads."

"But how can you — just like that without — "

"I like men."

"All the time," Thena says sarcastically.

"Sure," Arachne grins. "I'm good."

The first time she says this, Thena laughs, then looks

at her doubtfully. "You don't come every time you screw one of these – road jockeys."

"Sure."

"Aargh. I don't believe you."

"Look," Arachne says, "it's easy. You don't have to love them. You just come – fast. Make sure you beat them, and don't count on having time for more than one."

But this summer there is nothing. The road jockeys have vanished or retired. After Rosedale, Aerial, Verdant Valley and Rainbow, gritty dust has crept into everything – Arachne's clothes, her eyes, her car. The lace edging on her sample panties is gray.

She can't picnic in the graveyard at Rosebud because there is a burial. And trying to find her way cross-country back to Rockyford, she gets lost. She asks directions from a promising-looking farmer, bare to his muscled waist, tightening a barbed-wire fence. He waves his hand carelessly and doesn't return her smile.

"Keep going till you come to the next corner, turn left."

Standing in her sundress on the edge of the ditch and looking at his hands on the wire stretchers, she asks how the pasture is.

He stares at her insolently. "You come all the way from Calgary in that buggy? You better head back before it gets dark."

She drives away furious at the rebuff and, following his directions, runs into a town cowering in a low valley. Redland, the sign says. It isn't on the map, it isn't on any map she has in the glove compartment, it isn't on the Ladies' Comfort list. She's been through here six or seven times and never heard of it, never seen it. She parks in front of the post office and studies the general store. She can't tell if the blinds are drawn against the sun or because it's closed. Nothing stirs. She opens the car door; she should try to persuade them to carry some stock. She gets a bonus if she enlists a new place. But even before she can reach for her catalogue, a German shepherd braces himself in the middle of the road and starts to bark. Down the street a woman, hugely pregnant, turns. She too stands watching Arachne, her face expressionless, her hands resting complacently on the shelf of her belly.

Arachne hesitates. She throws her catalogue back on the seat. "Damn," she says, then returns the stare of both dog and woman, takes a box of sample cotton briefs from the back seat and slams defiantly into the shuttered store. The interior is ill lit and ill smelling. The vegetables in their cooler case have a blackish tinge.

"Hello," she calls.

The blinds seem to sigh and Arachne turns, looks over her shoulder before taking a few steps forward. "Hello?"

A blurred face appears above a shelf at the back of the store, rises slowly to chin level and stares at Arachne.

"I'd like to speak to the manager."

" 's me."

Arachne takes another step. "I'm the sales representative for Ladies' Comfort. We represent quality women's items — briefs, panties, ladies' underthings of all types . . ."

"Don't want any. You sellin' panties?"

"Well — yes."

"Joe Parker from Tri-line stocks us. What are you doing in these parts?"

This is news to Arachne. It is *her* district. So far as she knows, she's the only sales rep in the country. "Who did you say?"

"Joe Parker."

"What company?"

"Tri-line." The woman has not raised herself above the shelf. All Arachne can see is a disembodied head floating above a stack of canned tomatoes.

"Where are they based?"

The woman shrugs. "Damn if I know. He supplies us. Don't need more underwear."

Arachne has never heard of Joe Parker or Tri-line. "Can I see your stock?"

"Help yourself."

The stock consists of a dozen grayish nylon briefs, clearly collecting dust for some time. "Can you tell me – " She stops. She'll get no information out of this pygmy. She turns to the door. "Thanks."

The woman stares after her, head raised an inch higher, as Arachne slams out into the gravel street. The pregnant woman and the dog stand in the sun, waiting. When Arachne emerges, the dog begins to bark and the woman slowly turns her back and rotates away.

She spins gravel and circles until she finds the 840, then heads south to Standard and west to Strathmore and Calgary. She never sees Redland again. Next time she passes that way she tries to find the town and can't.

## Progenitors

She phones Ladies' Comfort and asks for a week off, explaining that the Mercedes needs to be tuned up. Winnipeg must be suffering from heat too. Alf sighs and says that as long as she does some paperwork, she doesn't even need to call it a week off.

"Go to the Stampede," he says. People who have never lived in Calgary always say this.

Arachne is patient. "The Stampede's not on."

"Well, take a few days. The summer can't stay like this."

But Calgary, usually so insulated by urban privilege, is brown and defensive, worse than the road. The handsome young men driving convertibles have all gone to Banff or Vancouver. In Arachne's Sunnyside house the oak floors are filmed with dust. Thomas is away mapping at White Lake Observatory. Thena is in a bad mood. The sky is numb.

Arachne makes the best of it. She works on her suntan. She drinks gin and tonic and walks on Nose Hill without thinking of the next day's stops, without having to ignore the dun colors of motel rooms.

Arachne is perfectly capable of domesticity. She deprecates it – "who'd waste their life cooking and cleaning?" – but there are days when she can be caught and held by the probity of sink and stove, of market and vacuum cleaner.

Thomas usually takes care of that angle of life, but when he's not around, Arachne can experiment, refresh her sense of the horror of what she calls house arrest.

She finds two cotton dresses for her selling wardrobe. She gets her hair cut. She takes the Mercedes to Angelo, and it seems less capricious. She even convinces Thena to spend a day sunning. And she answers her telephone, thinking it might be Thomas. She misses him.

"Darling, you're home — "

"Lanie."

"I thought I'd come out for a visit. Vancouver is awful, the streets are flooded with tourists, it's wet and — "

"Lanie, are you in some kind of trouble?"

"No."

"You're sure?"

"Yes, of course. Don't lecture me, dear."

Arachne does not relish Lanie's visits. "I have to go out again on Monday."

"Well, maybe I could go with you."

"You'd hate it. You get car sick, remember?"

"That's true. Well?"

Arachne gives in. "All right, come and stay for a few days, but I do have to leave Monday."

Arachne acknowledges Lanie, but she doesn't endorse her. She isn't convinced that she has a mother; Lanie's connection to her feels tenuous and unproven. But once or twice a year Arachne will submit to biology. She is without a scrap of motherly feeling herself, that's what Thena says, glaring at her over a stack of ironing, a stack of sandwiches. "No heart."

"Hah," says Arachne. "I save it for other things." Motherhood rouses no idealized sentiment in her. That is something socialized, something incubated in a girl child with dolls and sibling babies. Arachne had neither. Her dolls were clothespins divided into two armies who alternately attacked and decimated each other. Toto played with her on the ripply linoleum floor, shouting "advance" and "retreat."

Lanie never played. Once she discovered there was no romance in being Arachne's mother, she simply backed away. And Arachne did not follow, never bothered to plaster herself to Lanie's stockinged thigh. She picked her scabs and stayed out of reach.

She has only one image that does not fit with Lanie's bullying and that she has never known what to do with. She is almost convinced she made it up. She was small, she must have been, she felt the slats of the painted crib under her bare feet as she clambered down. Bad. She wasn't supposed to climb out. Although she could not reach the knob, she could pull the door open with her fingers. Everything was dim, the television in one corner of the living room radiating gray. She toddled toward the only edge of light, another door ajar, and pushed it farther open, rocking on unsure feet.

Toto was kneeling in his work pants beside the claw-footed tub. He was washing Lanie. Sleeves rolled to his elbows, he rubbed a washcloth across her shoulders, down her narrow back. Lanie's hair was wrapped in a yellow towel, the stem of her neck bent under the purling cloth. They said nothing, there was only the faint splash of water, the tap's staccato drip.

The child turned and staggered to the living room where they found her sitting in the middle of the floor. Toto Manteia laughed and threw her back into her crib. But the image stayed, the blurred icon of Lanie's skin under the rough sweep of the cloth in Toto's knuckled hand. Arachne actually tried to ask Lanie, reconstruct the image some twenty-five years later, but Lanie only raised one plucked eyebrow, shrugged. And Arachne did not push her; would herself deny such a scene.

There is nothing soft or yielding about Lanie. She is a pragmatist, without sentiment, although she likes movies where the right people kiss at the end.

Arachne waits for the security doors to open and Lanie to trot through, clutching her oversize bag in both hands. Lanie's small obsessions have had their influence on Arachne; she refuses to carry a purse, she refuses to wear a nightgown, she refuses to thin her rather shaggy eyebrows. She refuses and refuses all the impositions of childhood and mothers. She is still refusing now, even though she has learned to smile at the same time.

Lanie comes out in a clump of people from the tourist section and begins to scan heads for Arachne. Their eyes meet and before they show recognition, each reads the other: What would we think if we were not supposed to be mother and daughter?

Arachne moves forward. "Hi, Lanie. How was the flight?"

"Bumpy. And they didn't give us a bite to eat." Lanie expels words between breaths, tries to inhale and speak at the same time.

"How's Toto?" Arachne marshals her downstairs to the luggage carousel.

"Same as ever. Sleeps all day and works at night. Watches TV until three or four in the morning. I hardly see him." And she laughs. "Hold my purse, dear. Those cubbyholes on the plane don't give you room to lift your skirt."

Arachne watches her zigzag toward the women's room, a short, barreling woman who scans the crowd with a pigeon's eye. She opens the purse. Inside are several packs of cards, a rat-tail comb, a Bingo boinker, a hammer, some crumpled pages torn from a telephone directory, a large change purse and a small billfold, Lanie's ticket folded twice, a compact half open and leaking powder, several toffee bars. All Arachne's measly, scrubby childhood returns, the smell of Vick's Vaporub, chapped knuckles, Toto's large red handkerchiefs — "snot rags," he called them. She snaps the purse shut, wonders if he and Lanie still make love and if that too is accomplished silently, taken around their dovetailed jobs. Lanie is a sales clerk for Woodwards; after his accident, the mill made Toto a night watchman. They seem to fill their own hours. Toto does the shopping and Lanie has joined a poker club. They live together, Arachne thinks, in silent amicability. She does not imagine them old and lonely; if that were suggested to her, she would be incredulous. But then, she does not think of them as hers. They are Toto and Lanie, two people she lived with as a child, people who occasionally insisted on oatmeal and bed at nine, but never often enough to make a difference.

She and Lanie wanted the same thing. Arachne began to understand this when Lanie locked her in the high-fenced backyard while she went off to a Bingo or a shoe sale. She heaped the unplanted dirt in the garden, smeared worms against the garage wall. And screamed raucously, hoping someone on the sidewalk would stop. Her dark face peered between the boards of the fence like a watchful fox, an insistent "hi" for every passerby. No one stopped.

Lanie did her best to avoid watching. If Lanie was not working, she was connoitering, gone out the door with her fingers fluffing her hair and her lipstick like a slash. At three Arachne climbed the fence. She fell on her descent, but heaved to her feet and trotted off. She was sick of waiting for Lanie to tap her way up the front walk, rattle the mailbox, flush the toilet in the bathroom, then unlock the back door and call, "Raki, time to come inside."

But when she saw Lanie coming down the street with her hands on her hips and her pocketbook swinging, Arachne took one look, turned and ran. She was prepared. Lanie was huffing before she caught up, before she could smack the side of Arachne's head with her heavy purse. Arachne sprawled into howls, her knees grating on the sidewalk.

"You brat."

Arachne screeched.

"I can't turn my back for a minute. What would I of done if you'd got lost?"

Lanie complained to Toto about Arachne running away.

"All kids do that. If she didn't try things out, she'd be dead."

A snuffling Arachne was taken out of bed and fed weak tea and a jam sandwich at the kitchen table. She showed Toto her bleeding knees, but he just shrugged. "That's what you get when you don't listen."

Still, Arachne climbed the fence again. She learned the duration of Lanie's expeditions, developed an inner clock that listened for the passage of time. She knew that Lanie's unerring arm would descend, a swat, a smack, a quick box on her ear. She couldn't grow up too fast for Lanie. Her forays beyond the fence helped to shape her solitary observant life. People looked away when they encountered the stubborn-looking little girl on the street singing under her breath, a monotonous refrain of "running away from home, running away from home." It was the fifties, the baby boom, people loved children, someone was looking after her, surely someone knew where she was. She must be all right, she was playing happily. And she was.

Now she is able to edge Lanie in the right direction, to pick up her bag from the carousel and talk to her without the choking love of most children.

She swings the suitcase into the trunk while Lanie settles herself in the front seat.

"Gabriel's car," she says, wriggling her feet in front of her. "At least *you* got something out of all that. Remember when he bought it? He took us both for a ride in Stanley Park. Remember?"

"No," says Arachne sulkily. "I don't."

"Oh, it was that fine. All the Japanese cherries in bloom."

Arachne is sure Lanie is making it up, she wasn't along, more likely it was just Lanie and Gabriel.

"Have you gone to visit lately?"

"Oh dear, no. What's the point? And it's so hard to find."

"You could bring some flowers."

"Why? It's a waste."

Lanie only seems callous, Arachne knows, she is nothing more than practical.

"He was good to us."

Lanie sighs. "I know. But it takes so long to get there on the bus, and Toto won't take me. Besides I'm sure *he* doesn't know the difference."

It is true that Gabriel alive maintained pristine indifference to all that he encountered when he sat at Lanie's arborite table. Crouched under the table, Arachne could see his hands lying open and empty in his lap. The dangling toaster cord, the stray crumbs, were nothing to his military back and alert knees. Squatting there beneath the subdued clink of teaspoons, Arachne never quite dared to nudge his toes, although she did reach a tentative tongue to lick the rough fabric covering his shins.

Lanie's speculations required lengthy pauses, then clattering shrieks. Gabriel never twitched.

Lanie continues to believe that noise is a measure of enthusiasm. Although she has visited Arachne in Thomas' home before, she trots from room to room, sniffing, with the interest others reserve for museums. Her trodden heels clack the hardwood in the living room. "You'd think he'd put in wall-to-wall. So much work, polishing this floor. I wouldn't have it myself." Lanie refers to all men, like a collective breed of dogs, as "he."

Arachne does not say that Thomas does the polishing.

She thumps Lanie's bulky suitcase up the stairs, wondering if it contains the same assortment as the purse. She knows Lanie will have brought her "something for the house," an egg timer or a picturesque placemat. Given sufficient time, she even manages to return some of these things.

She leaves Lanie strewing clothes and shoes around the spare room and pauses outside the door to Thomas' study. She always enters with hesitation, as if his room holds something uncertain. The blinds are drawn, it is dim, cooler than the rest of the house. The blue walls reflect gray; the finger she runs along the edge of the drafting table comes away with a print of dust. Thomas knows what to do with Lanie and Toto. He is ironically polite, assumes a family unity that never existed. Lanie and Toto credit Thomas with saving her. And maybe he has. Who can say? But Lanie knows her duty. If she doesn't remind Arachne of her good fortune, Arachne will never appreciate it sufficiently.

Despite herself, Lanie is impressed with Thomas' Cuisinart and Microwave oven. She enters the kitchen on tiptoe and walks around it holding her arms close to her sides. "I might set one of those machines off."

She will not even get herself a glass of juice. The ice-cube maker in the freezer startles her. She follows at Arachne's heels, adding up changes and gloating. "All this new-fangled stuff. You are a lucky duck."

Arachne grins weakly. She has heard the words often. It is her mother's favorite line for positive signs in the tea leaves.

But Lanie halts in the middle of the kitchen and points to a bread knife. "I almost forgot. Lottery night tonight. If I don't get my ticket I can't win."

Arachne rests one hand on the cutting block. She nods. "You find out where they sell them and I'll drive you." Her mother is here all right.

She finds Lanie's monitoring of life's jackpots, her careful selection of lottery tickets, utterly puzzling. Perhaps fallen arches and restrained angina give rise to a belief in the fortuitous. Arachne can see Lanie's attraction to chance, but she treats it as an illness rather than a symptom. When Arachne thinks of luck, she sees the bruised edges of over-shuffled cards. This week, she knows, will be full of game shows and lottery draws. If only the races were on.

Instead, they do rummage sales. August is the right time, the contents of basements and garages spread out on driveways. Arachne is forced to recognize that Lanie is a pro, she zeroes in on a seller's weak spot in minutes.

"I'll give you ten dollars for that lamp. Do you need a new garden hose, dear?"

"No. Thomas just bought one. Lanie, how are you gonna get this stuff home?"

"I'll manage."

She buys a stack of old records, a pair of winter boots with pompoms on the toes, a set of flowerpots. Arachne tries to keep a straight face, tries not to groan. She sneaks upstairs while Lanie watches *Win a Mile*, sits under Thomas' drafting table with her knees pulled up and her eyes closed. The weather is hot, torpid, Calgary jagged and cardboard under the sky's glaring disk. She can't sleep, she can hear Lanie snoring down the hall.

Every morning over her tea and toast Lanie says the same thing. "Don't let me bother you, dear. You just carry on."

Arachne decides to sort her samples. She spreads them out on the dining-room table, checks her list to ensure she has everything in the catalogue. Lanie watches from the doorway, her eyes bright and disapproving. Arachne goes through sizes, XL, L, M, S. She mutters under her breath and ignores Lanie.

"Did you pick out that china?" Lanie points to the cabinet behind Arachne.

"No. Thomas did."

"Just like a man. So plain. I like a bit of flower myself."

Arachne begins to fold the bikini prints, flip the crotch up, double under, a neat square. "They're just dishes. So what?"

"Something fancier be nice." She runs a practised eye over the panties on the table. "You've got a bigger line."

"Nope."

"Never had those before."

The truth is, Lanie loves looking at Arachne's stock. She sneaks into the boxes without asking and Arachne discovers her neat stacks pawed and jumbled. Lanie assumes that Arachne's job will get her a lifetime of free underwear. "Just order some extras."

"I can't. Really, Mother."

"Well, who gets these?"

Arachne always gives in, lets her choose from the accumulated samples. "Here," she says, shoving a multi-colored pile toward Lanie. "These are going out this fall."

Lanie holds up a pale-blue lacy pair and a black bikini, a cream-colored cotton. Tomorrow Arachne's list will be meaningless. There will be a dozen missing and Arachne will have to raid Lanie's suitcase before she goes. Having Lanie around involves playing a complicated game of trumps and Arachne saves certain moves for just these moments. "Okay. Do you want to go to a Bingo tonight?"

Lanie puts her head on one side. "Only if it's air-conditioned."

## *Eastward*

But it seems that spending three hours in a smoke-fugged room listening to the rancid voice of the caller, "Under the N," is only a preamble. Lanie is determined to get her money's worth out of any vacation, and winning fifty dollars for a blackout is further incentive. On the way home from the Bingo, Arachne yawning and horny – she cruised up and down the tables and saw not one acceptable man, but that, she thinks, is typical of *her* intercourse with luck – Lanie begins to talk about driving to Banff.

Arachne has not seen Banff since she passed through it with Thomas. She refuses to drive west, circles north and east and south from Calgary but never west, hardly even looks in the direction she came. She would not be able to tell why, is unprepared for Lanie's insistence, for Lanie's planning.

"No," she says.

"But, Raki, I've never been there, and this lady sitting across was telling me that you haven't seen anything until you been to Banff."

"No," says Arachne.

But in the car the next morning Lanie rummages through her purse and hauls out a deck of cards held together with an elastic band. There is a hole punched through the middle of the deck and they are embossed with the name of a Reno hotel. She shuffles them against the dashboard and begins to lay them out across the wide front seat.

"Mother," says Arachne. "Look at the scenery."

"I can see it, dear." She has seven cards face up. "Oh, you are bad. An all black hand. Spades and clubs."

"Mother, I can't concentrate."

"We're meeting someone there. I have to get some idea of what to do."

"Meeting who?"

"I don't know yet."

Arachne grips the wheel. The car humps itself over the road's curves too effortlessly. She can see how she'll have to exert control, make sure they turn around, or she'll be driving all the way back to Vancouver, Lanie's plan for saving air fare.

"Pleasure," mutters Lanie, turning up a face card.

Arachne listens to the hum of the motor; the car's life vibrates through her feet and up her spine in palpable massage. She does not think of it as a post-Hitler car, as a car built in Stuttgart – she has never heard of Stuttgart – but she is certain that the car's past resides somewhere in its bones, a quiet knowledge of speed and drift and wind resistance the only talisman she needs.

"Virtue," says Lanie triumphantly, laying down the two of spades.

"Forget it," says Arachne. "I want to be rich." And catching the wink of her mother's rhinestone glasses in the corner of her eye, remembers that Gabriel was rich.

"You'll never have his kind of rich," says Lanie complacently, peeking at a joker.

"Don't read my mind," says Arachne crossly. "And put those cards away – I want to open the window and they'll blow everywhere."

"Virgin," says Lanie with satisfaction, and fans the cards together.

Arachne cranks down the window and rests her head against the airy rush.

"You're in trouble," says Lanie. "When are you going to marry Thomas?"

Arachne scowls and pretends not to hear.

"Pleasure, virtue, riches, virgin . . . watch the signs for what's emergin'."

"Cut the hocus-pocus, Lanie. I don't believe that crap."

"Too good for it. Those are the people that always get caught. Mark my words."

Far down the road, Arachne sees a hitchhiker caught in the familiar posture, legs braced, thumb turned out at the end of a cocked arm. She pulls over and reaching for the handle of the back door, says to Lanie, "Tell this guy's fortune, okay?"

Which only makes matters worse. When they let him off in Banff, Lanie is buzzing with portents.

He wasn't much but Arachne cannot help but see that the streets are crowded with beautiful fuzzy-legged men. She has to get rid of Lanie. "Where do you want to go?" she says, formulating escapes, ducking down back alleys.

"Lunch," says Lanie, playing with the chain attached to her glasses. "At the Banff Springs Hotel."

Arachne groans but obediently turns up the hill.

They are early enough to get a good seat by the window overlooking the golf course. Arachne orders Lanie doubles — gin with only the faintest color of tonic. And after they have consumed a huge clubhouse sandwich each, she says, turning her head east, for beyond those mountains is Calgary and Thomas, "Lay out the pleasure, virtue stuff again, Lanie."

Lanie gives her a sharp look. "I already told you."

Arachne shrugs. "Maybe it'll turn out different." She hopes Lanie can't see her gritting her teeth.

But Lanie dives into her purse. The elastic band around her deck of cards has broken and they are jumbled in its bottom – she has to count them twice to be sure they are all there. But happily, the noise and scurry she makes in the process, bouncing on the low couch, is beginning to draw sidelong glances from the other patrons.

Arachne orders another round of gin, settles her bottom deep and ready. She takes a breath and while Lanie shuffles and folds and shifts and pins her glasses on her nose and begins to spread a complex line of clubs and hearts and diamonds on the table between them, Arachne thinks of maps, their legends, their size, their measurement of distance. She sits through her mother's expostulations on her past and her future by imagining the shape of the map that would lead her straight home to the house in Sunnyside, the crow's journey between where she was this morning and where she is now. And it works. Lanie has barely begun virtue when the waitress bends from the waist and says softly, "Excuse me, ma'am, the lady over by the pillar asks if you could do her next."

"Of course," says Lanie brightly, "just let me finish this one." But she speeds up, and when another drink arrives from a table of golfers who want her to predict an improvement in their handicap, she skips the virgin part completely and says to Arachne, "I can finish you later, dear. Let me get on with these other people."

Arachne sees her pull one of the high-backed arm chairs close to the pinched lady's table before she runs lightly down the staircase, before she turns the Mercedes back toward Banff Avenue. She cruises. There are men on the street, there are men in the bars, men up the hill at the School of Fine Arts. She wants to leave the car parked under the pine trees for shade. On the sidewalk, sounds clatter, lids of garbage cans invaded by black bears, violin squawks from the music students. She settles on the museum.

The curator eyes her suspiciously. He thinks he has seen

her before, at a nasty cocktail party where he was not the centre of attention. Or else she is a thief, the kind who likes to slide small curios into a side pocket. That is why glass was invented, to cover the displays of the past, prevent the present from touching. Arachne sniffs the air, the neat, recycled air, and falls in behind a tall German tourist. She does not know he is a German tourist, but he has a very large camera. He wants to take pictures of the pictures on display here, but the light is wrong, fuzzy and gray. Arachne brushes his thigh. He moves away. She follows, close behind. He can feel her breath on the back of his neck.

They reach a door marked PRIVATE, a door that Arachne tests with one hand while she beckons him with the other. When it opens, he follows her, rising on tiptoe in conspiracy. Beyond is a workroom, tables, shelves, littered with books and papers. Somewhere farther is a murmur of voices, confidential. Arachne looks around, then stoops and crawls under a table against the wall. She turns, peers up at the tall man from under the edge. "Come."

His lanky height and complicated camera are a disadvantage, but he crouches and squirms in beside her. He cannot sit upright, so he sprawls on one elbow. The table's cave smells of floor polish and dusty paper, and when Arachne turns toward the man, she has a sudden image of the curator coming in and trying to shoo them out from under, of how safe they are.

She tries to take the camera from around the man's neck, but he shakes his head and only moves it under his arm before he begins to unbutton her light blouse. The camera and the table are bumps and angles striking at her from all directions, so much so that the man's skin reminds her of wood and plastic, and it is only his breath in her ear, murmuring over and over, "Du bist ... du bist ..." that reaches through the telephoto lens poking against her ribs and the man's belt buckle somehow caught under her thigh. When he pulls away from her, he does so too quickly and strikes his head on the table top above them. "Shit," he says in clear, perfect English, and rubs his head. Arachne slides out, stands, pats her skirt. He tries once more. "Du bist . . ." But she leaves him to straighten his parts and goes back through the private door before he can follow.

The shadows have moved so that the leather of the car's seat is unbearably hot. She sits carefully, lifting her legs away from the sticky burn, and drives back to the hotel. Lanie is at outraged attention on the front steps. When Arachne pulls up, she marches to the car and jerks open the door. "Where have you been?"

Arachne hopes Lanie cannot see the red mark on her neck, smell the damp between her thighs. "I went to get the car."

"They — " Lanie settles the glasses around her neck, "threw me out. Just because people wanted to give me a small appreciation."

Arachne giggles, and Lanie glares.

"You were gone for hours."

"I went to the museum. I didn't want to sit here while you were casting fortunes for everybody in that place."

"Humph. Fat lot of good you are. Never around when you're wanted."

"What could I do? They'd have asked you to leave anyway." And she smiles to herself. The summer has resumed. Lanie will leave. The men have reappeared, she is already on the road, into Calgary, the road east. The drought is over. Lanie will leave.

# The fortunes of tea

Although Lanie insists on telling Thena's fortune the last night. They eat together in the backyard, picking up the chicken bones with their fingers, opening yet another bottle of beer in the long August twilight.

Thena smooths Lanie, indulges her tendency to embroider a life already thick with ornament. And Arachne is saved from both, can tip her chair back and observe the window of Thomas' room.

Lanie pats her lips after a restrained burp. "In those days," she says, "you took your chances. If you got knocked up, there wasn't a thing you could do."

Thena grimaces. "Don't I know it. I'd never have gotten married otherwise."

"No wonder you're divorced. At least I didn't have to get married." Lanie cocks her head and laughs. "I was a war bride. Did she tell you?"

Thena smiles. Arachne tells her everything, lays out the intricate spirals she lives, so that Thena probably knows more about Arachne than she does herself. But she enjoys Lanie's version, its modified text.

Lanie was a shopgirl sitting behind a counter filing her nails in a sooty English town when she looked up into Toto Manteia's smile. Both parents killed in the

London blitz, technically an orphan, she was seventeen, too old to be adopted. It was 1945, plenty of uniforms around, but most of them ignored her for the older girls. And this one was Canadian. She straightened up and put the nail file down and smiled back.

Authorities be damned. Once she married Toto there was nothing they could do. Besides, they had too many other things to think about, and Lanie became a war bride, dry-eyed among her weeping companions when the ship pulled out of Liverpool. What was there to cry about? Being married to Private Toto Manteia was better than serving customers needles and thread in her foster parents' poky shop. They had neither wanted nor liked her, with her London street talk, but felt that they should help an orphan for the war effort.

"I was a war bride," she says again and laughs, as though she had played the ultimate joke on herself. "I came with three dresses and one pair of shoes. I hated the old stuff they gave us, I left it all behind. When I stepped off the train at Vancouver, I think I was the only one who was glad to be there." It was true. The journey had made the rest doubtful, but Lanie was gay.

Her expectations were hardly met. Toto Manteia had been transposed from a good-looking soldier in uniform to a shy young man with little education and no special skills. He'd landed a job in a sawmill on Mitchell Island and he was proud of himself for having accomplished that, just as proud as he was of the two-room apartment he'd found on Thurlow.

Lanie did not cry, nor did she try to return to England, as so many others did. Besides, she had nowhere and no one to go to. She bit the bullet, as she was fond of saying, and made the best of it. She was somewhat disappointed. She'd expected that a Canadian soldier would be better off. But after six weeks of hustling she came home one day and announced that she'd landed a job at the Fisherman's Café reading teacups at fifteen cents a shot.

Toto was delighted with her spirit, and only after going out for fish and chips to celebrate did he raise a doubt. "But you don't know anything about teacup readings."

"Oh," said Lanie airily, "me mum used to do it. I figure I'll catch on quick."

There was a great enthusiasm for fortune-telling then, as if tea leaves and tarot cards would balance the uncertainty and hesitation of the war. It was fashionable for people to stop for tea and a reading on a Saturday outing.

Lanie caught on quick. Most of the teacup and card readers were older women, puffy and dyed blond and too cheerful. There was something about Lanie that drew people. Gaunt and sullen, she looked as though she had suffered some unmentionable misfortune and her disguised accent enhanced her mystery. The wheezing, middle-aged readers didn't stand a chance. If people were going to cross a palm with silver, they wanted to cross a suitable palm. Before long, Lanie had captured most of the teacup business at Fisherman's. Of the fifteen cents for the reading, Lanie got ten cents and the café got five, but she was allowed to keep tips, and on the day she came home and counted out all of two dollars and fifty cents, Toto was full of admiration.

"Gosh, you really cleaned up today."

The money helped but the marriage slid a little. Evenings and Saturdays were the busiest and Lanie was not one to let opportunity escape. She relied on fortune to help her finances but left little else to chance. With the assistance of nefarious concoctions like vinegar douches, and capricious bouts when she refused to have anything to do with Toto, she managed to avoid getting pregnant. She always monitored him to make sure he used a safe, which he futilely protested was "kid stuff."

"Lanie, we're married now. We don't need to act like we're not."

Lanie was stubborn. "I ain't getting stuck at home with any brat."

And for four years she circumvented the inevitable, working the teacups at the Fisherman's Café for all they were worth, enticing tips with dark-ringed eyes and a pouting bottom lip. Even businessmen who laughed at superstition would drink a pot of tea and turn their cup over in the saucer for her. Fisherman's was popular, the food cheap and quick. Office workers took it over at lunch, then gave way to the afternoon's influx of matrons and young wives shopping downtown.

If Lanie had heard some of the remarks about her, she might have been tempted into something beyond teacup reading. Still, she didn't. She observed each customer's future with an intensity that was a lure in itself.

Whatever the war had done to Lanie, it had taught her the value of security. She was determined to buy "one of them cute little houses on the edge of town." She thought no further, but that was typical of Lanie. Her first goal had been to escape her flaccid, gum-sucking foster parents. Her second was to learn the business of teacup reading. The third was to get out of that two-room apartment into a house, some kind of house. She did not imagine something large and suburban. She thought, with her English girl's limitations, of a house as a bit of lawn and a bathroom of your own.

They made little enough. Toto was unskilled labor, a body to muscle green wood around. A stint overseas meant nothing. Everyone had been overseas. They made do, Lanie undeflected, Toto drunk no more than once a month. Both of them were satisfied, Lanie by tea leaves and Toto by boards. Until the day Lanie came home from Fisherman's early, not even eight o'clock. She flung her shabby coat

56

over the ironing board and announced to Toto, who was sitting in his undershirt, trimming the hair in his nostrils in her magnifying mirror, "I feel sick. I'm knocked up, I know it."

He swung around, scissors in hand, and watched her kick her shoes to the floor. "Nah, Lanie, you just got the flu."

"Nope," she said, lying back on the couch and crossing her arms over her stomach. "I'm knocked up, I know it."

Toto looked at her flat, thin shape. He didn't know what to do, rejoice or comfort her. She was in many ways still formidable to him. He approached the couch. "Lanie?"

She opened one eye, cocked her head up at him.

"Are you sure?"

"I know it. I'm knocked up."

He stood looking down at her. "Can I get you something?"

"Nah. I'll just lay here till I feel better."

He went back to his mirror, surprised at her compliance. He expected protest, anger and recrimination. It showed how little he knew her. He should have realized by then that once the inevitable struck she did not resist.

Still, she knew the score. "Lord, Toto," she said one morning, clutching the chenille housecoat at her throat, "I'm going to lose my job. Nobody wants a pregnant teacup reader. I can't look like I know something they don't if I'm sticking out a mile." She dropped her hand open on the table and for a moment he glimpsed that hopeless waif who knew she had no one to rely on but herself, a repeated shutter of the look he had surprised one graying London dawn in a cheap room with the pigeons pecking on the roof outside, a look instantly wiped away but that had made him say, gruff, reaching across her flat breasts for his cigarettes, "Here. We'll get married."

He dumped his oatmeal bowl in the sink with a clatter.

"Why'nt you take it easy." And he shrugged into his jacket and out the door.

Five months later Lanie left Fisherman's without expecting them to ask if she would come back, without thinking of the array of people whose lives she had divined through an arrangement of sodden leaves in the bottoms of crockery cups.

Occasionally a customer, gazing around the café, would recall, "There used to be a teacup reader here, young, quite good. She could really tell you about your life." Although she always told them what it was, they didn't remember her name. They had thoughts only for themselves and the picture she drew of their future.

"I should never have given up fortune-telling," Lanie says to Thena. "I was good, I had a gift, everyone in town knew me. I just couldn't do it while I was pregnant, so I quit. I should of gone back."

Thena looks at Arachne to see if Lanie's resentment stings, but Arachne's face is impassive. She knows Lanie didn't want her, she's always known that. She's surprised Thena's so sensitive.

"It was a passing fad, Mother." She stretches her legs out in front of her with a tingle of satisfaction. They are hers, they belong to her, she can take them anywhere she pleases.

"I was so good at it, Gabriel came back for years."

"To get his teacup read?"

Lanie flushes. "Yes. He – Anyway, if I'd gone back, I would have done all right. Better than serving people. 'Can I help you, ma'am?' I'm sick of it. At least teacups took some imagination. I could still – Here," she says, standing abruptly, "where's the tea? I'll do yours, Thena."

"I don't have any loose tea." Arachne's tone is blank but warning. She does not want Lanie fortuning her friends.

But Lanie is determined and, scorning tea bags, goes off to the corner store for real tea. Thena and Arachne eye one another, then clear the dishes.

"Don't blow her cover," says Thena.

"I've lasted this long, haven't I? Good thing she's leaving tomorrow."

When Lanie returns, she says to Thena, "Turn your cup over," and takes it between her palms. Frowning, she turns it this way and that, the black leaves mesmerizing, Lanie forging a mystery in the flocked pattern. "You live alone."

Arachne snorts but Lanie ignores her.

"You live alone not out of choice, but you will stay alone out of choice. You are a mirror for others, they—" She stops. "I see a man, an older man—"

Arachne laughs again but Thena is bent toward Lanie's performance.

"...there are three people grouped together." She brightens. "Your children, of course. It seems you will make a move, or get a job, and something else . . . A candle. That means you'll reveal something—That's it! You're going to meet a man who will change your situation."

"Lanie!" Arachne bursts out. "Really!"

"I wouldn't mind," says Thena. "Somebody else could take the little buggers to horror shows."

"Where are they now?" asks Lanie.

"With their dad. But his new wife hates horror shows."

Lanie reaches for Arachne's cup, but Arachne snatches it up and takes it into the kitchen, rinses it under the tap.

"Come on, dear. I haven't read your teacup for ages."

"I'm afraid you'll read me a fortune I don't want."

Lanie waves a pudgy hand. "Oh, I know, she's afraid I'll tell her that she'll lose the Mercedes or Thomas. She thinks saying it will make it happen. No imagination.

Besides — " She aims at Arachne's back. "Why don't you marry him? Sew him up?"

"Marriage, *Mother*, is not the haven of refuge for me that it was for you." No — what she really said was, "I don't want no ring in exchange for screwing."

Lanie shrugs. "You'll lose him," she sings. "He wants a proper life and all you do is run off."

"Of course. You never did."

Thomas is a sign they are ready to quarrel. Thena leaves and Arachne can only hide in his room, curl up in his armchair and rub her face against a sweater he's left that smells of his skin. She ignores Lanie's dulcet "good night" and falls asleep on the floor of the study, above her the cylinders of map tubes and rolled charts ghostly curled worlds.

Sunday Arachne is glad to be driving Lanie back to the airport. She taps her fingers on the wheel and dodges in and out of traffic. Tomorrow this drift of breeze through the open window will be a road, she will be barreling down a secondary on the way to Three Hills.

Arachne turns onto McKnight and speeds up, then has to shift again, caught behind a left-turning car.

"Lanie," she says, and in her rearview mirror sees an orange van gaining on her.

"Yes."

"Hmm. Nothing." A coincidence, she thinks, remembering so distinctly the orange vehicle, her last glimpse of the bright color in the rearview mirror as it dropped behind the hill west of Crowfoot's grave.

She changes lanes, dodging trucks and campers, threads the Mercedes through traffic so skillfully that the van is left far behind, blotted out.

"Will Toto be there to pick you up?"

Lanie laughs. "Oh no. I'll take a cab home, it's easier."

The van reappears in the left lane. Arachne frowns,

checks again. The same indelible color. But surely that isn't the only orange van in southern Alberta. At the next red light it pulls up beside her. Arachne cranes her neck at the passenger side. Sure enough, it is the tight-lipped woman. Arachne studies her profile, turns to check it against Lanie's. They are the same generation, but Lanie is chubby and relaxed, pouting. The woman is just reproving. She senses Arachne's eyes and looks down but her controlled expression does not change. She gives no hint of recognition.

Arachne shrugs. Fair enough, she thinks. So we live in the same city. The light changes, the van guns ahead and Arachne hesitates before lifting her foot off the clutch. The old man's hands were so still, open.

Lanie is discussing Thena, pointing out that she needs to forget her husband. "Can't you introduce her to another man, maybe one of Thomas' friends?"

"She doesn't want to be introduced."

"Sure, she does. She just won't admit it."

"She hates men."

Lanie snickers. "I doubt it."

"Well, you can't blame her."

"Her husband, you mean?"

"He's horrible."

"Ah," says Lanie, checking her lipstick. "You have to learn to work around them." And snaps the compact shut with finality. "Thomas has certainly done wonders for *you*."

To which there is no retort.

## Driving, driving

Credit Thomas with saving Arachne, with preventing her from becoming an escapee. At least he has given her some structure. She has a schedule of sorts. She has a telephone. She is inclined to return home. She even leaves the road jockeys where she finds them, although she wouldn't give them up. Arachne is not unkind to Thomas. She is only consistently unfaithful. She is also unwilling to indulge in the polite rituals that are expected when a woman is connected to a man. She refuses to accompany him to topographical survey parties and she will not provide him with even a minimum of domestic service. He is the one who hangs clean shirts in her closet, he is the one who does the marketing, who stands with a fork lifted beside the stove. It is true that Arachne is often away, but even when she is home she is absolved; he brings her beer in frost-cold glasses, he follows the roar of the vacuum, while Arachne tracks in air and dust, litters the living room with her samples, her order forms, her road life.

He saved Arachne.

Arachne, twenty-three, driving the Number 17 bus. The drivers lowest on the totem pole get the electric buses, converted trolleys. Over the Cambie bridge you have to slow to three miles an hour or the trolley lines will disconnect and you'll be outside in the drizzle trying to poke them back, the bus black inside, the passengers muttering, late and resentful.

Arachne's right leg shifts: accelerator, brake, accelerator, brake. Always someone running for the stop, should you wait or go, always the pensioner who will topple over in the aisle the minute you pull into traffic, the children who ride alone. They are all running away and the bus goes by the door, will take them to the strip where they can buy candy, coke, grass, where they can sell themselves. Arachne learns to keep her eyes to herself, look in the rearview, look ahead, check the side mirror, cars don't slow down for buses – Why should I let that bastard in ahead of me? She has learned to be cautiously aggressive, to watch the road and the traffic and to stay on schedule, given no disconnected poles, no heart-attacked Chinese gentlemen.

She knows the movement of human flesh at different times of day. First the early shift going to the factory district, then the office secretaries and clerks always half an hour before management's briefcases and Italian shoes, then the school children on their way to French immersion or uniformed private school, then the salesgirls and cashiers, and by eleven the waiters and cooks, before the wives going downtown to shop, before the theater ushers for the two-o'clock feature, before the afternoon shift, before the early-evening cocktail waitresses, before the clients of entertainment downtown to listen to a concert, to eat out, to slum, to pick up a girl or a bargain. Arachne's doors open on the world's schedule and she has only to drive down there and back, down and back, four hours and she can go home and sleep, always blind tired after driving, traffic swirling behind her eyes until she wakes again to proceed with a normal day, take the bus herself, do an errand, walk down to George's to work on the car.

Arachne has learned not to look at them. She answers

questions, checks the change that rattles into the fare box, but never looks into faces. She cannot bear it, that stream of stumbling features: foreheads, eyes, mouths, the ears hidden or not, the hands reaching. She shrinks from them. The road, her windshield, her mirror, the sound of the bell telling her to pull over at the next stop, press the door release, all the gestures automatic but deliberate, a silent voice saying, "Now."

She will not make conversation, even to the large women who plump themselves down in the seat by the door, who draw their feet back from the boarding passengers and inevitably begin to relate habits, dreams, affairs. Opening innocently with the weather, but Arachne knows what will follow, what will spill out on the rubber-ribbed aisle. She keeps her eyes ahead, she refuses to respond, so the habitual ones give up. "Cold fish, that one, why don't they put a man on this time of morning?" Only the occasionals try. She will not answer. If she does, their leaking, thinned-out lives will overwhelm her, she will be sucked down. And so she refuses to raise her eyes, refuses to look beyond their hands or beyond the street.

When she first starts to drive, she is nervous about handling the bus in traffic that is smaller and faster and more maneuverable, so she has to ignore the passengers. The practice helps later. Still, she is surprised at her own callousness. One day a man sits in the front seat by the door and begins to cry, begins to relate to her an unstoppable story. His wife has died. Has, it seems, killed herself. The man, distraught with grief and guilt, does not understand why, cannot believe that the woman he lived beside would do something so final without him having an inkling of her intention, that they have been strangers sleeping together, locked one from the other. Arachne hears it all and feels panic rising. Her hands clench the big wheel. She cannot stop her ears but she stares straight ahead down the street. "Please," she says, "don't talk to the driver."

The man's voice falters but he continues to weep, rubbing his sleeve across his face, the anguish that he needs to spill winnowed against her cold back, her indifferent profile. When he gives a choking cry and stumbles up, hand flailing at the pole, Arachne pulls over at the next stop and opens the door, although he has not rung the bell. He crashes down the steps, a hobbled, shambling plunge toward despair, and Arachne has to sit at the stop for a moment before she pulls out into traffic again, continues as if she has heard nothing. But at noon, she bends over the toilet, retching. She cannot get the man's hopelessness out of her nostrils; its reckless smell rouses nausea.

That is the last time she thinks about what they say. Oh, she still hears shuffling words, tears, but she filters them. They are without meaning or influence. Pull up to a stop, open the door, watch the change, the passes — you can do that out of the corner of your eye, peripheral vision enough to police fares — close the door, signal, check the mirrors, pull out, slide down the street until you see bodies at the next stop or until you hear the bell. Ting, ting, ting. Don't distract the driver.

The seat next to the door is called the pickup seat. The other drivers joke about it, the pickup seat. They talk to the women who sit there, eye their legs, yes, try to pick them up if they have nerve and time before the women get off again. Two or three years before, Arachne herself noticed handsome bus drivers and plopped herself down to make edgy conversation, but she never chose the right ones, had never gone so far as to let herself be picked up. She enjoyed the game because when the men proved stupid or hopeless, she could get up and say, "Here's my stop." It wasn't usually that easy to escape. Parties and dates you were stuck with them, you had to wait until you got home. And once they had a hold of you they didn't want to let go, they knew their advantage. Although Arachne never indulged in much conventional dating.

Now she is tethered to that pickup seat. It isn't only the talkative and the sorrowful who use it, who think the presence of her ear proof of a listener. Itinerant men eye her, remark, "Hey, what's a girl doing driving a bus? I didn't know the Greater Vancouver Transit System hired women. Hey, you're pretty cute for a bus driver. Are you busy tonight, would you like to get off at my stop?" Arachne ignores it all.

Until the huge – what would she call him? – Black. He sits, arms folded, until the end of the route, and when she announces, "End of the line," to the empty bus, he chuckles.

She looks at him. That is her mistake, she looks at him. An outsize frame with muscles gathered around it, his black skin a texture she has never seen before. Like taffeta. Black taffeta, enough to make her forget that his body promises he won't be much good at conversation. And he might be violent, a man that brute size.

Arachne stands up and shakes her head. "Come on, fella," she says. "Don't make me call in help."

He smiles at her. "You're tough."

And curiously, sitting, he opens his palms, lays his hands open and upward on his knees as though to reassure her that he knows nothing of fists, as though asking for a chance. She finds herself staring down at his open, peach-colored palms, one hand as big as both of hers, the map of lines innocent and unrelenting.

She changes the number to 23 and sits down again, does not look at him.

"I'm patient," he says. He rides the next two and a half hours without talking, watching the boarding passengers with the exact attention that she refuses, reacting to them, a smile, a shrug, a language in the way he turns. And he watches her, unnerving, while she drives.

At the stop where her replacement waits, she lifts one shoulder. "All right."

He gets off and takes a few steps while she collects her thermos, her hat, says, "See you tomorrow, John," to the new driver, who immediately begins to adjust the mirrors, muttering, "Damn women."

On the ground he seems even taller, but graceful, more graceful than a large man has a right to be. "Coffee?" he says. "Lunch?"

"I usually go home and sleep."

"Sleep better with some lunch."

He takes her to a small downtown restaurant that is busy but informal. Arachne is thankful; restaurants make her nervous. She hasn't learned how to use them. Her childhood had no linen napkins and hors d'oeuvres. The most Lanie and Toto went out was on a summer day at Kits beach, when they bought fish and chips from the concession and ate with their fingers, sitting on a bench strewn around with wrappers. Arachne remembers those few occasions as ecstatically balanced and happy, remembers the greasy cardboard boat of chips with a spurt of saliva.

It is worse that she is wearing her blue-gray bus-driver's uniform, absurdly formal in its muted color with a darker stripe down the leg; that she is carrying her cap, her thermos, that she is without makeup. She never puts it on to drive, one of the rules: "Women drivers will not drive wearing makeup."

"They want us to look like men," complains a woman who is hired and trained with Arachne. "They've got to hire us, but they'd just as soon if the passengers couldn't tell us from men."

Arachne wishes that she looked like a man. Indeed,

Arachne wishes that she were a man. Driving seems so much easier for them, reaching, turning the wheel. She wants to drive a bus because it is safe. She's no powdered frill trapped behind a typewriter and unable to get away when the need arises; she is up high behind a thick wind-shield, she wheels away from bus stops, no one can close in on her. Arachne loves to drive, she lives to drive, it is the only activity that convinces her that life is not static and fuzzy. The whir of tires, the flash past peripheral vision, objects receding in the rearview mirror. That is why she wants to be a bus driver, driving seems the only sensible way to deal with the world. She'd made a list: cab driver, truck driver, bus driver. She is infatuated not with machines but with motion, the illusion that she is going somewhere, getting away.

He watches her eat. It makes her uncomfortable, some dish weighed down with cheese, so she lays her fork prongs in the middle of the plate and looks back at him under that lambent skin. She has to know if it feels like it looks, she needs to touch. So she sits. To his amused questions she gives answers. She has an apartment in the city but she has a roommate. (This is a lie.) Has she always lived in Vancouver? Yes. (This is the truth.) What is it like to drive a bus? Just like any other job. She doesn't ask him questions and he tells her nothing, only his name, Basilisk, which doesn't even make her blink, since he tells her to call him Bas.

They walk together to a West End apartment, a high rise overlooking the bay, uncannily empty except for an enormous stereo in the view-obsessed living room and a mattress on the floor in the bedroom. He lets her touch his skin, lets her finger him in doubtful pleasure. He feels the way he looks, yes, he does. But although he lies beside her on the mattress, although they shed their shirts and pants, Arachne's uniform undignified on the floor, he makes no move to take off his shorts. He seems only interested in looking at Arachne, while she touches him speculatively, as though stroking something that might bite.

"I never seen a black man before," she says.

He grins at her and rolls onto his stomach. "Am I that different?"

"No, but you feel different."

"Oh," he says, and he isn't being vain, "that's just me."

So she touches and he looks, and eventually Arachne falls asleep and dreams about driving across Canada. The cities are strung out in a straight line and she has to stop for gas every few minutes. In between are highways so narrow that when she meets an oncoming car she has to pull into the ditch to let it pass.

When she wakes up, he is crouched against the wall, still watching her, still in his shorts. Arachne reaches down to check if they haven't made love after all, but her body is quiet and dry.

"I have to drive tonight," she says.

He nods.

"What do you do?" She can only ask such a question with her back turned, with her legs stepping into the restrained trousers of her uniform.

"I play."

Arachne adjusts the tie around the collar of her shirt.

"Piano."

"Oh," she says, thinking that she understands, fitting him into the scheme of stereotypes she has absorbed, seeing him picking jazz in a café, like Sam in *Casablanca*.

"Can I call you?"

Arachne dusts her hat lightly against her leg. "My room-mate . . ."

She doesn't have a roommate, he thinks, and he is pleased with her caution. He puts on his clothes, nondescript pants, a sweater, a nylon windbreaker, and walks her back down to where she picks up her bus, waves solemnly as she drives away. And goes to practise.

Next morning when he gets on the bus almost at the end of her shift, she isn't surprised, she's even been expecting him.

He grins and bobs his head at her, his hands on his knees flexed and patient. This time they don't bother with lunch but go straight to the apartment and repeat the day before, trying it on as though it might become a soothing habit.

Arachne is hypnotized. She agreed the first time because she really did want to touch his skin, but now it is different, she doesn't have that excuse, yet here she is. She has always subscribed to the practice that once you decided to sleep with a man, you might as well go ahead and get it over with. There isn't much point in playing around, waiting for an appropriate moment, because it never comes, it's never the right time. Arachne has learned to get her pleasure fast, catch what she can, has trained her body to pleasure itself. The man can be anyone as long as he's half decent. Think about yourself or you're doomed. Men don't think about you.

But this one, Basilisk — and she would not know how to spell his name — doesn't charge at her, barge into her. He just looks, as if he gets more pleasure looking at her body than he would handling it.

Arachne goes to sleep on the mattress trustingly, lets herself sink down to a place under sleep, and when she wakes he is there, open-eyed, lying on the floor listening to Schubert.

She thinks they might go on like this forever; she discovers that she doesn't mind the idea at all. He is a perfect man, large and indifferent and quiet, and he does not interfere with her.

## Audience

Still, she is not surprised when a week later he says, "Tonight is the last concert. I'll be leaving tomorrow."

Arachne could weep and grizzle, but she doesn't. She thinks it's a waste of time to trail after men with tears and lamentations. She shrugs and takes the week for what it has been, nothing beyond a chance to touch his skin.

He is more sorrowful than she. He's never found a woman quite so perfect for practising. His concerts in Vancouver have been masterpieces; even his admirers are not prepared for the performances he gives. He's surprised at what the odd little bus driver evokes, her face as stubbornly oblivious, blind and continuous as a score. He would like her to be at the last concert even though she confuses classical music with the homogenized stuff piped into elevators and dentists' offices. She is fiddling with the silly tie they make her wear, adjusting the knot to sit properly under her collar.

He pulls his ragged sweater over his head. "Look, would you come?" He trails off nervously, while she frowns at him with those curiously depthless eyes.

"I mean, come to the concert." His words are thick.

"I have to drive this afternoon."

"It starts at eight-thirty."

Arachne watches him alertly. If it hadn't been for the

way he'd acted all week, she would sense a trap much more dangerous than sex.

"You'd rather not."

She shrugs. "What is it?"

He almost laughs, the women in the orchestra hovering outside his dressing room, the women in the audience straining forward, reaching despite the decorous way that they sit beside husbands and boyfriends, he can feel when he plays how they want him. And she stands blank-faced, shrugging, telling him she has a bus to drive.

"Have you ever been to a symphony?"

She shakes her head.

He feels a sudden remorse. "Look, you don't have to come."

But her face has cleared. "Will I be able to see you?"

He arranges a good seat, close to the front and at an angle where she can see the keyboard clearly. He takes her there himself, settles her with a program. It is a cold night and she is wearing a shapeless duffel coat over her uniform.

"We can leave at intermission. I play just before."

Alone, she feels queerly naked. Don't talk to the driver, she thinks. Here they are, the people who never ride the bus. Funny, she knew they existed, but hasn't thought of them as real, and now they are around her, talking about this man she's spent most of the week with, speculating on his technique, his expression.

The lights dim, the crowd quiets and the maestro strides out to conduct the first piece, an overture by Mozart, pleasant and short. Arachne does not applaud with the rest of the audience; she watches the ritual being acted out as though she is not sitting in the middle of it. The orchestra's finesse does not interest her; she looks at the musicians' faces one by one and hardly hears the music.

In the pause before the second piece, the stagehands

wheeling out the huge Steinway, she remembers the black man lying naked beside her on the mattress in that otherwise deserted apartment, and all her scraped and greasy childhood, her ragged and layered survival returns. The first notes he touches, delicate as they are, lash, and she shrinks in her seat, knowing he is performing those intricate motions for her, that the stretching of his fingers and the half smile on his face are for her, a way of watching her, an invasion. It is unbearable, so thin, so brilliantly cruel, he is skinning her with the razor blades of his damnable breeding, his culture, his learnedness, the fact that he can lift and fall his giant hands over those black and ivory keys and bring out such perfect sounds. She keeps her eyes fixed on his hands.

After the explosion of applause, she waits for him outside, under the sticky light hanging below the street lamps. Still in the swallow coat, his throat polished stone against the white shirt, he touches her sleeve. "I was afraid you would have gone." They turn toward the West End, toward the apartment. On a quieter street he stops. "Thank you," he says hoarsely. "Thank you."

She pulls her clenched hand out of her pocket and hits him, once, twice, as hard as she can, before shoving her hand back in her pocket.

He bends and pulls her against him, her solid bulk inside the duffel coat, then lifts her and carries her through the streets.

In the dark he fumbles a huge hand over her face. "Forgive me."

Arachne rips his shirt open, tears his clothes off. She rides him, hammers and gallops and clenches above him until her knees are raw, the insides of her thighs are bruised, both of them are sobbing.

Lift me, she screams, take the driver, give me music lessons and evening clothes, give me ears. And he shouts, take it, take my skin, take all the notes, give me a bus and a uniform and a closed face and oblivion.

For days Arachne is shredded. She drives the bus. She eats, she sleeps with frozen limbs, knowing that she has been snatched from the edge of a chasm with nothing to spare, that the looseness in her stomach is the closest she will come. To what? Dissatisfaction? She is perpetually dissatisfied, she has always been dissatisfied. Ambition? To better herself, to culture herself? What good. would it do? She only knows that she has stepped perilously close to another knowledge. And that it is dangerous.

She will drive the bus and stay out of trouble.

## Savior

She drives. Through months of seasons, through a dark winter and a pale spring, through streets that spill together into one stretched asphalt. She hears nothing but the ting of the bell, she feels nothing but the wheel under her hands. The gray triangles of faces not faces themselves, never features. Even if they are regular riders, she makes no sign. She has learned the trick of looking past people, seeing them only as shapes.

In that winter following Basilisk, she concentrates on the car, puts everything she has into the Mercedes. Eats, sleeps, drives the bus. Double shifts, she asks for them and gets them. Who wants to drive two four-hour shifts a day? Looking for trouble, that's when drivers start to have accidents. But aside from disconnected poles, aside from one sleet-cursed day when the bus can't make it up a hill, Arachne has no accidents. She pours all her money into the car. She counts on the car; it is a blessing from the past, one talisman against her uncertain future.

She is thinking of the car the day Thomas gets on the bus, she is thinking of its six-cylinder overhead cam inline water-cooled fuel-injected engine. Its attributes soothe her, must make her face relax because he grins at her as he drops his fare in the box, before she has time to neutralize her expression.

"Nice day," he says.

She nods and edges the bus into traffic and he moves up the aisle and sits down.

Careful, she thinks to herself. Wipe that look off your face. But she has noticed him.

He catches the 17 every morning at exactly seven-thirty, gets on at the Oakridge corner and rides downtown. When he gets off he walks toward the old Sun building, unhurried, thoughtful. Arachne finds herself watching him; the fourth day he is on, she earns a sarcastic comment from the transit supervisor for being half a minute late.

He carries a briefcase and a bright orange tube that must contain charts of some kind. His face is smooth, youthful. He stretches his legs across the sidewalk gladly. His change rattles into the box with a firm conviction that it is morning; he knows exactly where to go and what to do. His regular and quiet smile at her stings. He has, she knows, the telephone numbers of blue-eyed young secretaries who wear confident skirts and whose teeth have been straightened to tongue-tempting lines. He does not hesitate before he calls them up, they do not hesitate to accept his invitations; and he can take them anywhere, without having to think if the restaurant or theater is suitable, without having to think what to leave for the waiter.

Arachne knows she is working-class. She has never thought of her narrow life as disabled. She is concerned with survival, self-protection. She knows what pleasure is: the coil of urgency in her breast when she's driving, when she first settles behind the wheel of a vehicle. All the other urges in her life have come from hunger: to be fed, clothed, loved, to possess this thing or that.

But there, locked into a schedule of stops, fixed to her seat by invisible lines, she watches him one morning walking away in the group that threads from her bus — she sits behind her huge wheel and feels a choking lust. Not

76

for him, oh no, but for an indefinable quality that he represents, conveyed in his walk and the angle of his head and the surety of his hands. Not the same as the bayonet thrust of the first notes that lifted from under the black pianist's fingers. That pain was defined, isolated; it was the lunge of something hopeless, not to be resolved, ever. You can pierce yourself on the impossible but the impossible remains impossible. This is different, a sharp gnaw of discontent, a sense of something graspable brushing past. If she can only force her hands into the right shape, she can have it too.

This idea is insidious as disease. What does she think? That she can become middle-class, respectable, a wife, a mother, a keeper of clean tea towels and hot casseroles? With her inclinations? With her background? Toto resting his greasy head against a cushion while he lies watching the gray flicker of the television, Lanie tottering in from Bingo or shopping with that half-derisive giggle of hers, tilting the gin bottle above her cup of tea.

"Eh, Raki, how's transport?" Toto's question is always the same.

"Fine." Her answer is always the same.

And Lanie. "Mrs. Carling died, she must have fallen. The ambulance was here for hours and in the end they couldn't do a thing, just let her lie there, then bundled her up like a sack. Give you the shivers."

"It's a good job, Raki. Hang onto it." Always the last thing Toto says. She takes his words at face value.

Now she is mooning after the back of an ordinary man wearing a suit and tie, attending an office from eight to five, all the respectable trappings she knows she does not want.

It is spring, the car is almost completely overhauled. She should take a holiday, drive somewhere. She debates that with herself, where to go. She has never been out of Vancouver. She knows this city beyond all possible knowing, she is as familiar with its bridges and streets, its habits, as she is with her own. She has inhaled it growing up.

She is driving double shifts, morning and night, from six to ten and then again from eight to midnight, the first bus and the last at night. Between shifts she sleeps, eats. Sometimes she rubs a washcloth under her armpits, or irons her uniform, waiting for the wheel's urgency. High above traffic, she is calm, in its stream, yet separate. Some afternoons she stays downtown and goes to a matinee, hidden in the close, musty theaters. Or she goes down to George's, allows herself the sensual luxury of helping him with the car, its fat black body sitting above the pit, waiting.

Her petty discontent is stilled by the car. George works out of his lust for the car. The money she pays him will go toward his own, she knows that all the while she asks him questions and all the while he's injecting the car's needs into her, prenatal classes on maintaining this relic of Gabriel's wealth. In the four years since she got it, Arachne has just about run the car into the ground; now she will take better care.

Arachne has nothing to do with the pleasure George derives from the car. He knows her allegiance, has known her since she was a snot-nosed kid running around the neighbourhood after dark, when she should have been put to bed at seven like any other kid. Still, she turned out all right, changed from being a foul-mouthed teenager to someone surprisingly patient, quiet-voiced, polite. When he thinks of Arachne Manteia, he gets a reflex image of her kicking over garbage cans, a fight that is still neighbourhood legend.

Now she bends over the hood beside him with an intensity he wonders at, and when the alley kids straggle up to the garage door, she talks quietly to them, gives them the change in her pockets. Only occasionally does he surprise the thick sullenness that he remembers, and once she is aware of being watched, she wipes it away, presents an expression as blank as her color. But her short nose and wide mouth do not permit disguise. She looks insolent, George thinks. There is something curious in the bones around her eyes that needles people. He knows it is dangerous to get on her bad side. But here's the Mercedes and Arachne asking him to work, offering him good money to fix it over the winter. He can come home from the shop at three and keep his overalls on, have a cup of coffee and go out to the garage, fill in the hours until supper with the beautiful old car under his hands. He worried that Arachne would be a nuisance, but after the first month he relaxed into the seduction of that intricate engine. He knows her pleasure when she slides into the leather seat and rests her palms on the steering wheel; he does that himself when she isn't around. He'll be sorry when she takes it away.

Gabriel's car. And Gabriel always there, beyond Arachne's memory, his visits strokes of passage. "Don't bother Gabriel," said Lanie, Gabriel sitting upright in a chair waiting for the tea water to boil. Lanie bustling, pouty, her made-up mouth moued. She drew a careful face before he came, standing on one foot in the bathroom, with eyebrow pencil and a fat pot of rouge. As if he noticed. He was gravely polite, spoke to her over a fence. Attentive, watchful.

Lanie's command. "Don't you bother Gabriel." So Arachne slid past a doorway or crawled behind the couch. He watched her, his eyes followed her. He did not bring her presents, he did not coo and jabber. He watched her. And he held out his two hands in a gesture not of welcome but of knowledge, held both hands parallel and open, without smiling, without asking. She sidled toward them, between them, let herself be lifted to his bony knee, into his formal posture, his creaking shirts and stiff-moustached breath. He held her as though they were watching a ceremony together, pedantically, until the brown betty teapot and the clicking cups appeared. "Go play," cried Lanie, lifting her away. "Git."

Yet the perch on his knees was always repeated, the same gesture of his age-spotted hands drawing Arachne between them. He held her no more than enough to balance her, did not cuddle or touch her beyond impersonal steadying. Gravely they sat for the few minutes Lanie allowed them, without speaking and without ornament.

Only once, Arachne sick and screaming with a sore throat, a cough, unable to breathe, did he take her forcibly into his arms, took her up from her crib and clenched her flailing.

"I don't know what to do," said Lanie. "She got medicine but she can't sleep."

"Take her for a drive."

"How'm I supposed to do that?"

"I will."

He walked out of the house with her, without Lanie. Set her in the front seat beside him and drove, one hand holding her. Arachne gave up screaming and curled against his thigh, the rhythm of the car wheeling her into a long cry and then sleep. She woke hours later to his fingers stroking her back under her sleeper, a friction steady and relentless, his hand down and back, down and back. When she finally moved, he started the parked car and drove her home, put her into Lanie's hands without comment. And had his teacup read before he left.

That was early, before he bought the Mercedes. Lanie gushed about the new car, went on to Toto for days. As if the car finally let her know how well off Gabriel was, as if he were identified at last.

## Arachnid

While Lanie waited for Arachne to come out and be born, she sat by the apartment window and watched the street. The light that winter felt bluish-gray, muffled. She liked the way it crept over the body, the way it swam around her swollen lap and collected at her feet. Despite the wait, she felt strangely content, caught in a web of quiet before she had to get on with the noisy impatience of living. She watched the street and played solitaire against herself. She ignored the child inside her.

The street was typical of that neighbourhood, a mixture of seedy shops and run-down walk-ups like Lanie's and Toto's. A few doors down was Silver's Confectionary, where they could get milk on Sunday mornings. Lanie laughed at the word "confectionary." To her it should have been a shop that sold a mixture of exquisite candy and billowing, old-fashioned hats. Instead, it was just a grocery store, dark and rather smelly. Directly across the street was a café, inexplicably called the Orange Café, run by a scowling Chinaman who would come to the doorway and scream, "Shoo, cats." There were no cats around, but yelling seemed to satisfy him and he would disappear back inside to serve tepid coffee to the neighbourhood's old men. Sometimes Lanie and Toto went over for Chinese food; it was cheap.

The street Lanie watched was aimless, crossed rather

than crossing, close to downtown yet with an air of being on the fringe. People who walked it were only passing on their way to somewhere else. Lanie looked up from her cards into desultory life; only in movies did characters long for adventure, follow it, seize it.

In Vancouver spring brings rain and with it the insects of rain. Early one morning Lanie caught a flicker of gray on the window's outer edge. She leaned over the huge mound in her lap, so close that her breath obscured a patch of glass, and when it cleared, the spider had already anchored its first thread diagonally across the window. It was a large spider with a belly as rotund as Lanie's. Her legs were swift and hairy, seemed almost to dance, drawing the silvery filament out from her anus, weaving with her hind legs. Lanie saw that the spider had been injured; it had only seven legs. But that did not hinder her design or ambition. The silken web grew while Lanie watched.

"What is it?"

She turned sharply in her chair, glared at the man standing in the door. She'd opened it, trying to air the cooking smell that hung, that made her stomach clench in the mornings.

"What do you want?"

"You're Lanie?"

She looked down at herself, her only-too-obvious pregnancy.

"I'm from — I used to come to Fisherman's every couple of weeks."

Fisherman's seemed another lifetime, like England. He was stocky, dark, with a toothbrush moustache. She could not remember him at all.

"Gabriel Greenberg."

His brown oxfords were polished and his pants sharply

pressed. The topcoat was new.

"I wondered," he took a step forward, "if you still do teacup readings."

Lanie shook her head.

"Could you do a reading for me? I'd pay you five dollars."

Lanie stood up, balancing her stomach. "How'd you find out where I live?"

"Fisherman's."

"How'd they know?" She didn't wait for him to answer. "Well, come on in then. Shut the door."

She and Toto had never had a visitor and she hardly knew where to put him, but he stood by the window while she rattled the kettle on the gas burner and rinsed the teapot.

"Arachnid," he said softly.

"What?"

"Spider." He smiled at her and she noticed that his teeth were false, they didn't fit properly. "Arachnid."

"Oh." She flung a handful of tea leaves into the pot, hoped they weren't too stale.

"A good thing it caught something. Spiders are rogues. They eat each other when there's nothing else to catch."

But Lanie was busy ignoring the elbows and knees of her kicking baby.

Across the arborite-topped table, the brown teapot between them, neither mentioned Lanie's pregnancy or the impending child. Lanie agreed that he could come on Monday afternoons every two weeks. Except for the five dollars, it made no difference to her. Nor was she curious about Gabriel. He had money and he was willing to give her some. That was all she cared about.

When Lanie went into labor, it was Toto who panicked, who flung articles into a Woodward's shopping bag, who hurried her to the hospital and then went home and played checkers against himself until they called him. When he went up to see her, he couldn't think what to say, she seemed the same, although she pulled a face at him and said, "Christ, Toto."

It was a girl with brown fuzz and a squeezed face. When the doctor told her, Lanie frowned. "I wanted a boy," she said and regarded the infant critically.

"We'll call her Arachne," she told Toto.

"What?" He wanted Sue or Mary, something easy.

"Arachne," she said stubbornly.

It must have been Gabriel's five-dollar bill. Toto tried to accommodate himself, but no matter how much he twisted his mouth, he couldn't pronounce Arachne. He ended up calling her a combination of nicknames, usually Raki. Or Rach when he was angry with her.

Now that her body was her own, Lanie was determined never to give it up again. She refused to breastfeed the child, but bottle-fed babies were not unusual in 1950. She handled Arachne with calm aloofness, changed her and bathed her and fed her, but separate, out of range.

A month after Arachne was born, Lanie made sure the baby was asleep, then put on her coat, walked across the street to the Orange Café and asked if they needed a waitress.

The scowling Chinaman was suspicious. "Got any experience?"

Lanie looked him straight in the eye. "I worked at Fisherman's Café downtown for four years." It was like Lanie not to mention that she had been a teacup reader rather than a waitress.

Toto was, for once, aghast. "You can't just leave the baby here alone!"

"Why not?"

"She'll choke or she'll smother or something."

"Nah," said Lanie. "She just sleeps all day. I got nothing to do but wait until she wakes up, and then I feed her and then she goes back to sleep. Anyway, I'll be right across the street. I can come home at coffee breaks and lunch."

"What if she cries?"

"I'll leave the window open so I can hear her," Lanie said reasonably. "Besides, she don't cry much."

So Lanie became a waitress, and Arachne slept and grew without a mother hovering over her progress. Lanie did not neglect Arachne, she just ignored her. She refused to let a baby interfere with what had once again become her ambition – to buy a house. Arachne was fed, washed and changed, but according to the whims of the schedule the Chinaman, Louis Chan, imposed.

When Louis Chan found out that Lanie left her three-month-old baby alone in the walk-up across the street all day, he would have fired her if she hadn't been so good. Instead, he worried. He would go out into the street and stand looking up at the apartment window, listening, only as an afterthought saying, "Shoo, cats," before he went back inside. When there was a lull, he would tell Lanie to take a break. "It's not busy now, go see if that baby's okay."

At night Toto came home shedding a smell of sawdust and tree sap. He played with Arachne, tossing her in the air and making train noises. Lanie, ironing her uniform or curling her hair, watched but did not join in.

Gabriel still came, and when he did, Toto made himself scarce. They'd met while Lanie was in the hospital. Toto opened the door to what he angrily referred to as this topper who put out his hand and said, "Has she had the baby?"

"What's it to you?" Toto was happy for an excuse to get mad.

"What the hell is going on?" he growled at Lanie during visiting hours.

She yawned. "I forgot about him. Jeez, Toto, I couldn't

turn down five bucks every two weeks. I saved it all."

"Well, who is he?"

"I don't know. Some rich guy who wants me to read his tea leaves. He just asks if business is going to be good, should he invest more money. Sometimes I say no, but mostly I just tell him yes. He's a smart guy — he knows what he's doing without asking me."

"Well then why is he asking you?"

"Hell, Toto, I don't know. It's nothing. I just give him a reading and then he gives me five bucks and leaves."

"I don't like it."

"It's nothing, honest. An ugly old guy like that? Come on." And she giggled.

Gabriel kept coming. He was the one Arachne smiled for. And Lanie's purposefulness paid off, although Arachne got the car.

## Surfaces — a chart

Arachne thinks of the car, sitting at the downtown stop at twenty to one, her last run that night. In thirty minutes she can leave the bus at the garage and walk home in the warming air, can even sneak by George's and look at the Mercedes. If she walks all the way home, she'll sleep, really sleep.

She checks her watch; half a minute to go. The few passengers on the bus shuffle and yawn, mostly cleaning people who work in the business towers. What was it like to do that, swim through deserted offices emptying waste-baskets and tidying washrooms, whispers silent under the hum of fluorescent surveillance, eerie evidence of people the janitors never see? Only a half-open drawer, a cardigan dangling crookedly from the back of a chair, a book of matches, a torn kleenex. Do they make up stories, read futures in the paper crumpled in the garbage, do they see blood, tears, anger in the position of a chair, the attitude of a typewriter, the angle of a wife's picture? They know the inhabitants of offices more intimately than we imagine. They are the ones who catch the smell of sweat and lust and worry, they see the come stains on the director's large chair, they find the frenzied love letters shredded in the bottom of wastebaskets, they wipe phlegm from the water fountains. Work, work, there is evidence of work but it is peripheral among all the other clues: this man will lose his job next week, this girl will kill herself, this man is passing out cigars to celebrate a baby. It is an immense burden to clean these offices without letting them infect you, shouting ghosts that will return in the flesh next morning. The cleaning people doggedly avert their heads, shift an ashtray, absently dust a telephone. Even go so far as to lift a plastic cover, try to fathom a computer or a teletype before they put it back and go on to the next office, the next revelation.

Sometimes they sigh and an accountant fighting afternoon drowsiness will hear, lift his head and listen for a moment. Of course, daytime people do not think of the cleaners; they take for granted their spotless floors and dusted shelves. After all, they are the ones doing the work. And the janitors climb wearily onto Arachne's bus, huddle against a window and stare into the dark; they are tired of disinfecting other people's dirt, they want to go home to their own untidiness and sleep.

Arachne is driving a diesel tonight, a treat not having to worry about losing the lines crossing the Cambie bridge. It is a Friday, that's why; weekends there are fewer runs and they all drive diesels, most of the electrics sit idle. No one wants to work Friday or Saturday nights, but Arachne likes those evenings, they're quiet. Besides, she makes time and a half. Hissing the doors shut, she checks her mirror before pulling out. Down the street comes a running shape. She's the last bus, better wait. Opening her door again, she barely glances at him before she pulls away.

The passenger she has waited for is the neat, enviable young man. He sits five seats from the front on the right-hand side with that orange tube propped between him and the window; he's clearly visible in her mirror. Arachne cannot stop herself from glancing at him, taking in his well-cut suit, but face less smooth, eyes tight and tired. He is staring straight ahead, impassive. What makes him so desirable? The fairness of his skin? The manicured hand that curls around the metal seat frame? Arachne feels again a surge of lust. What is he doing riding the bus at midnight on a Friday? He should be at a party or a restaurant, dancing, engaged in effortless social exchange.

The last janitor tugs the bell and gets off and he's left, alone. Arachne considers asking him a question, tossing out a comment, but decides not to. He would respond in a kind but diminishing way; she already knows how these perfect men speak to secretaries, waitresses, bus drivers – polite but distanced, raising an eyebrow.

The Forty-first Avenue stop is coming up. He seems oblivious, yet this is where he has gotten on all week. Arachne comes up to the light, slows, brakes. He sits. She watches him in the mirror, then calls, "Oakridge."

He jumps up so hastily that Arachne almost chuckles. Not so sure and composed tonight. The door hisses closed behind him.

She is seven minutes early. It doesn't do to arrive at the garage so fast; the supervisor accuses her of leaving people on the street. Arachne pulls over at the bottom of Cambie and goes back to the seat where the orange tube still leans against the window. She opens it, slides the curled paper out and unrolls it between her hands. It's a map, a beautifully drawn and colored map of southern British Columbia, twisting roads around the names of hesitant towns. Under the gray light in the bus, the elegant lines convert those curves into longing.

Roads, she thinks. There are roads out there.

A fist pounds the glass door.

Still holding the map, Arachne walks to the front, opens it. On the sidewalk stands the man, wet with sweat, his tie twisted. "My maps," he gasps.

"Yes, they're right here."

"I chased you all the way from Forty-first."

This is Sixty-fifth.

"You're lucky I was early." Arachne smiles. She has him now, the little prig. "Most drivers just head for the garage."

He comes up the stairs toward her. "My maps, what are you doing?" To his credit, he is still gasping. If he were breathing easily, Arachne would hate him for his tennis/squash/golf-player's body.

"I thought," she says carefully, "there would be a name or something on them. Things tend to disappear in Transit's lost and found."

His face clears. "You would have tried to return them to me?"

She shrugs. "There's nothing on them."

"Yes, there is. Geodetic Survey. And there's my seal."

She squints at the raised bumps. "Thomas Telfer, cartographer."

"That's me."

"All right, Mr. Telfer, here are your maps, safe and sound. I'm sorry you had to run so far."

"At least I caught you."

Arachne nods. She wants to look at the map again, but he's rolling it, his hands on the paper almost tender. He must spend hours, she realizes, hours. He loves the map, he could have shrugged and gone home, phoned Transit in the morning.

"Where do you live?"

He looks up, startled. "I don't live here. I'm staying with – a friend." That's the thing about these well-bred men; they are always completely honest.

"I mean," Arachne is careful, "where are you going?"

"Oh, about twelve blocks from Forty-first. I usually transfer to a 36 but I guess I've missed it."

Arachne looks at her watch. "You have."

"Well, I'll walk a bit. Cool myself off." He dabs at his sweaty forehead.

Even before, she knows she will be surprised to hear the words. "I'll take you home."

He laughs. "You can't use a city bus to take me home. It's not exactly your car."

"Doesn't matter. Here." She closes the door, swings the bus onto the empty street and at the next crossing lumbers a wide U back the way they have come.

He's grinning. "Isn't this illegal for a bus driver?"

"Yes."

"Then why are you doing it?"

"I was planning to quit. Now I'll have a reason."

"Then what will you do?" He sits in the pickup seat leaning toward her, the tube upright in one hand.

"Well, I thought I might do some travelling."

"Where will you go?" He expects her to say Europe or South America. Thomas is a civilized snob; he cannot conceive of a woman who has never been away from the city where she was born.

"I thought I would explore B.C." His map has made Arachne bold.

"Good idea."

Eyes on the street, she gestures at the map tube. "You should know."

"Most beautiful place in the world. Wish I could live here."

"Where do you live?"

"Calgary. I only come here once in a while if there's a job to do."

"What do you do?"

"I'm a cartographer with the Geodetic Survey." That civilized, amused look.

"But — what do you do? I'm sorry, I don't get it."

"I make maps — maps of anything that the survey wants.

I put it all on paper. Think of me next time you use a road map."

Arachne turns onto Forty-first. "Where now?"

"My friend's house is just this side of Oak. Turn left at the next light."

"Why don't you take the Oak Street bus?"

He looks at her; she asks too many questions.

She pulls up outside of the house that he indicates, the brakes squealing even though she eases them down gently. "Sorry. Don't want to wake everybody up." She has her foot on the door release. When he stands up she will have to open it. But he sits.

"Thank you. I would have gone berserk if I'd lost these."

"How long are you staying?" She says this too quickly.

"Oh, another week. I've got a lot left to do. That's why I work so late." He hesitates. Is he as reluctant to get off the bus as she is to drive away?

"How are you going back to Calgary?"

"I suppose I'll fly."

Of course. Arachne has never been in an airplane, but people take them all the time. Just because she has never left Vancouver does not mean that everyone else stays in one place.

"Why?"

Arachne imagines a note of hopefulness in his voice, a note of curiosity.

"I was thinking of driving through the mountains. I hate to drive alone, I wouldn't mind having someone along."

"Just like that?"

"Well, I want to go to Calgary." She improvises, feeling her way.

"Really?" He fumbles in his jacket pocket, pulls out a pen. "Here's my card and my number. I'd far rather drive through the mountains than fly, and if you'd like some company . . ."

Arachne takes the card. "All right." She opens the door to let him out. "Good night."

"You mean it?" He is so damnably polite.

"Yes."

On the sidewalk he turns and waves the tube at her.

## Without farewell

Driving now she sees fine black lines on cream-colored paper webbing their way through the mountains and east. All the rises and dips were colored, their shapes indicated by shading; those colors had lifted the tracery of roads above map. Under the metallic light they glowed orange and pale blue. Arachne thinks about the maps. She thinks about Calgary, about mountain roads, about the Mercedes. She goes over to see George. It's late February, almost March.

He rubs a rag over a small patch on the fender. "Purring like a baby. If you take care of it, this car will last you for years."

"Thanks to you." Arachne lays her hand on the roof.

"You don't have a garage at your apartment, do you? Want to leave it here? I'd let you if I could drive it now and then."

"Drive it as much as you want to this week. I'm going to Calgary."

George keeps rubbing at the spot. "Oh, holiday?"

"No. I'm driving to Calgary on Friday."

He looks at her. She is wearing her defiant face. He doesn't ask if she'll be back, although he already misses the car.

It occurs to Arachne that she shouldn't need a man as

an excuse to leave. If he wants to come, fine. She's going anyway. She tells Transit she's quitting – sorry about the short notice, but she has to leave town immediately, and can she use them as a reference?

She calls home. "I'm going to Calgary."

"Oh," says Lanie doubtfully, "why?"

"I'm moving there."

Lanie sniffs. "It's such an awful city, dear."

"Have you ever been there?"

"No, but everyone knows – "

Toto is upset. "You've got security, what are you giving it up for? You could be a senior driver in five years the way they turn over. What'll you do in Calgary?"

"I guess I can drive a bus."

He snorts. "Serve you right if you couldn't get a job."

Arachne packs her clothes and her Melmac dishes and her tools in the trunk of the Mercedes. There's nothing else to take.

# The road

She phones the number he jotted on the back of the card.

"Can I speak to Mr. Telfer."

"Tom! One of your girlfriends," a voice brays.

"Do you still want to drive to Calgary?"

He didn't expect her to call. He hesitates, as if he knows she's trouble.

"When are you leaving?"

"Friday morning."

"All right. I have to be back by Monday."

He comes out of the house lugging a leather garment bag and half a dozen orange tubes, lays them carefully across the back seat, reverential.

He is too polite to remark on the car, but his friend, who comes out to say good-bye, is not. "Jesus, Tom, how do you do it? Driving to Calgary with a woman in a goddamn antique Mercedes."

All the way down the 401 Thomas watches her surreptitiously. They hardly speak. Arachne caresses the Bakelite wheel; he slouches with one elbow on the black leather armrest between them. In Hope they stop for coffee, and the awe that silences them in the car is broken when they face each other across the table. They eat double portions of whole wheat toast dripping with butter and jam.

Arachne is giddy with travel. She has never driven the Mercedes on a highway, always in town, always shifting the manual on the steering column down instead of up. She is wild. If it weren't for the presence of this polite young man, she would explode, drive faster and faster until she vanished.

In Vancouver she bought a gas station map and tucked it in her pocket. Now she hands it to him. "Which way should we go?"

"The fastest way or the most interesting?"

"The most interesting."

"Let's take highway 3. There aren't as many tourists."

"Tourists?" She laughs. It is the first of March, they might need chains through the mountains.

Along the Similkameen they travel a black plunger of secret elation, safe in an oak and leather incubator, pleated map pockets and the white punctuated liner above, the oval back window receding their past, the big high tires urging a suspension of everything they know and trust. Can it have anything to do with choice that they find themselves driving toward Princeton together, wet and aching?

Thomas is too well-bred to show a visible erection, Arachne too shy to wriggle and burn, so the Mercedes drives and they sit on the verge of squirming, faces flushed and averted.

The road demands attention, slows them down. On the bridge at Princeton, Arachne touches the shift. "Should we go in?"

"No. Let's keep going. The best place to eat around here is in Hedley. Home-baked bread, half a barbecued chicken, a great restaurant for a deserted town."

"Tourists," Arachne says and chuckles.

"I think it's run by a bunch of hippies who decided

to sink into nowhere, but they have wonderful food. And they might as well make money from the tourists. There's not much else."

Talking of tourists and food only makes them ache more. Arachne is having trouble driving; Thomas feels he ought to cover his face. Surely she can see how much he wants to touch her, and he isn't even sure of how to say her name.

He can see the sheer wall of Nickle Plate mountain ahead; they are moving toward Hedley like an inexorable dot. How can he sit through a lunch across from her? Perhaps the restaurant will be closed, he thinks, perhaps he will be spared having to sit in one spot and eat lunch without touching her, without staring at her too much. But then he thinks of staying in the car, exquisite torture in this confined and subtle space, and when they pull up, he almost lunges for the door.

The restaurant is closing, but Moses agrees to serve them lunch. Thomas knows Moses from working in the area a few years ago; they catch up while Arachne escapes to the washroom.

She curls her fingers around the edge of the cold sink and tries to think reasonably. It's ridiculous, she knows better than to choose someone so patently unsuitable.

"What's the matter with you?" She shakes herself and looks at the face reflected in the mirror. Thomas must like women who look *cooler* than she does. Her dark hair and wide-set green eyes, wide cheeks, this strange pronouncement to her bones, a wide mouth, broad shoulders even. She looks like a person who will speak ungrammatically. True enough. She does not mind dirt under her fingernails, she does not feel that deodorant is necessary every day. It shows on her face. Rebellion. Dissention. Trouble. Respectable men hesitate. The other kind are attracted.

But she has already decided to trust him, when the only man she ever trusted before was Gabriel, and he's dead. And she will always return to a string of men, bar pickups, road jockeys. Even though she'll want to keep Thomas, have her cake and eat it too, as Thena would say.

She smooths her hair and walks out of the bathroom and sits across from him at a rickety wooden table. She does her best to eat carefully, actually thinks about using her knife, while Thomas looks down at his hands with a curious dismay. He's certain she won't react the way that other women do. When he makes love to them, those girls in sweater sets and good woolen skirts, always well-cut, he gets the feeling that even under questioning, they would not admit to anything.

He and Arachne eat and discuss the car and the weather through the pass and getting to Calgary around midnight. It is a lie. They both know they will never get that far, nor do they want to. When Moses comes out and joins them for a cup of coffee, they are relieved to concentrate on him, but in a few moments they want to be driving, alone again.

They leave Hedley, trembling with desire. Put them alone in an enclosed space and they begin to leak, to steam, to breathe shallow and unsteady.

Thomas is furious with himself for what he perceives as lack of control, an uncivilized reaction. You don't just jump women without the ritual of social foreplay. Or so he thinks. But the more he tries to distract himself, the more he wants to reach for her. It's the car. He blames himself but the car contributes, having to sit with her in this enclosed space without hope of relief for hundreds of miles. She is tantalizingly close, he is saturated in her smell – what is it? Not the smell of women he is familiar with; they exude perfume and anti-perspirant, the faint turpentine of expensive makeup.

She too is sticky with anticipation. It is all she can do to grip the wheel and watch the road. She is sure that if she pulled over and tore her clothes off, flung herself at him, he would recoil. He doesn't associate with women who haul off their sweaters at a few hours' notice.

They've driven only half a mile. Thomas thinks that if he can step out of the car into the brisk topaz air, he will be all right, he'll regain his better judgment. "There's an interesting graveyard along here. Would you like to stop?"

"Sure. Tell me when."

"Here," he says a few miles later.

She turns left, up the lane to a gate, and they are released from the car, buttoning coats against a knife-like wind.

He shows her his favorite stones, tells her about the valley and the mine, points out the tumbled buildings that still cling to the side of the mountain, refusing to be shaken off.

"Too bad it's winter. There's an old road up to the top that you'd like." He doesn't hear himself, but he is right, he knows already what she likes.

In the cold they can breathe again. It freezes their wetness, but at that moment they prefer discomfort. They need to give their scruples a chance, and the cold, the ironic tombstones, help. Twenty minutes later they feel they can drive miles together, calm and civil.

It is the car. How else can they account for their behavior? The minute they get back in the car, she behind the wheel and he in the passenger seat, their desire is worse than before. Arachne puts the key in the starter on the dash at her right-hand side; she even ventures to turn it, get moving quickly, but before she releases the clutch she makes the mistake of looking over at him.

The car is in first. Unforgivably, she lets it lurch and stall. She takes only enough time to turn the key off again before they lean together over the leather armrest, before she holds his body between her hands. And he holds hers. Not the texture of the women he has always known, but the darker glaze of those who keep their skin as substitute for fur.

It should be a disaster. The front seat of a car is, no matter how you use it, uncomfortable. But they are carried away, washed over as much as taken aback. They shout with pleasure. She has never had a man inflict love with such gentleness. It has always been a fight, a struggle for supremacy. With him she can hold herself still and he will touch her with his fingertips, she dares to close her eyes and fall into his open hands.

It takes them all weekend to get to Calgary. That first night they stay in Kelowna, find a motel with a good view, then lock the door and pull the curtain. They drive without seeing what passes the windows. He lies with his head in her lap; she steers. Vernon, Enderby, Salmon Arm, Sicamous, Revelstoke, Golden. They stay there the second night.

"It's too far to try for Calgary tonight," Thomas says. Neither wants to think of arriving.

## Destination

Field, Lake Louise, Banff, Canmore. As the mountains drop behind them and they level down, the sky fills with prairie, the immutable shape of the plain spread out like an embodied mirage. There is nothing Arachne can say, she is caught between her surprise and a sudden wrench to be part of this undulating plate of land.

"Prairie. I've never seen prairie before." She turns to him, hears herself with cautious horror. "Is Calgary like this?"

"Yes."

"I can live there."

He swallows. "I thought you were going back to Vancouver."

"Everything I own is in the trunk."

"What will you do?"

"I'll apply for a job as a bus driver."

Far away he can see the haze of Calgary. Not the lights themselves, but the band of light that rims the city. "Do you have a place to stay?"

"No. I'll stay in a motel tonight and look tomorrow."

Eyes straight ahead, he speaks in a neutral voice that he hopes will not suggest demands. "You could stay with me until you find a place. I have a big house, there's lots of room. I – " He clears his throat. "No obligation, you understand."

So Arachne is not wrong to credit Thomas with saving her. Only she knows how narrowly she has escaped, how closely the past treads on her heels, how with one stumble it can catch up with her. Arachne is willing to acknowledge the truth; but she is unwilling to face its consequences.

She has kept her fierce and private rage as cheerful vindication. The truth is that Arachne is no different than she ever was. She is amoral, selfish, dishonest. She is afraid that if the details of her amorality come to light, she will lose Thomas, her one solid connection with what she calls "the real world," certainly the respectable world, in which she is an imposter.

# Dancing

The silence after Lanie's departure is a relief. Driving home, Arachne plans her schedule tomorrow, whether she can do three or four towns and make up for lost time. She doesn't like to fall behind, her sales average dips.

She almost trips over the parcel on the front steps. It is bulky, wrapped in brown paper and tied with string, the used paper smoothed and recrumpled in the wrapping. Not delivered by the mailman on a Sunday; no address, but her first name, misspelled and penciled on the inside of a Safeway bag.

She tears the paper off what seems at first to be a metal plate, rough, blackened, the edge bent in. And turning it over, discovers a hammered copper disc ringed by chains of dancing shapes, human but without detail. Boneless arms link, electric hair jolts from one head and braids another. The faces are round, featureless but expressive in the activity of their circular dance. The chain of feet and arms and sack-like bodies is relentless as the dance they are engaged in. Relentless and comically sad.

Arachne laughs aloud. She has to. The figures, primitive, imprisoned in motion, insist on laughter. Buffoons. She turns the disc upside-down. The grotesque faces leer no differently. She turns the plate over, puts it down, shakes the brown wrapping. There is no note. She looks at the face again, the figures clowning, self-deprecating, puffing out their cheeks and turning their elbows.

It is not the kind of thing Thomas would send her; besides, he would never wrap it like that and leave it on the steps. She runs her fingers over the hammered shapes. Nothing but blobs, really, but they seem so alive. She props it against a chair and moves back to eye it from a distance. Their dance merges and continues, without hesitation, endlessly in step. On one skirt is an odd mark, what could be an initial, but she can't make it out. And doesn't try. She laughs again and leaves the beaten copper disc on a kitchen chair while she goes upstairs to pack her traveling bag, to check her sample boxes.

## And relief

Relieved to be out on the road again, Arachne discovers that the summer has turned itself around. It has rained, the fields are fuller, farmers take time to wash the gray line off their necks before they go to town, and they stop at the hotel for a beer before they go home. It is still August on the prairie, but things are moving again. Arachne pushes herself through Acme, Carbon, Twining, Linden, Swalwell, Sunnyslope and Allingham, all in one day. A record even for her. It is six-thirty when she spins her way toward highway 21 and Three Hills. She could go home to Calgary, but she's exhausted. The thought of driving another hour is too much – she needs to get out of her clothes and into a bath. In the calm between heat and the cooler night, the road is empty. People are eating supper, one farmer's car parked on the dam to his field, a row of cows swaying home to be milked. She had no image of country until she moved to Calgary. It is much closer here than in Vancouver, although Vancouver has all that deceptive vegetation, making people think they know about nature.

She can see Three Hills ahead. She begins to slow, and at the same time sees the dual flashers of a cruiser closing on her tail.

She brakes, shifts, signals, pulls over. "Shit, shit and double shit." That innocent car must have been a speed trap, and she was going seventy miles an hour down a paved but secondary Alberta highway. She pulls her registration from the glove compartment and opens her door. Might as well face him on her feet. She's tired; she won't be able to dissuade him with the way she looks. Maybe she can burst into tears. That has saved her once, but it's not a device Arachne likes.

He's a young Mountie hiding behind a pair of mirrored sunglasses. "Clocked at seventy-two miles an hour, ma'am."

Arachne looks down and scuffs her toe in its neatly strapped white sandal. It is a way of making him look at her feet, at her legs and body instead of her face, which is always wearing the wrong expression, rebellion or rage. "I know," she says in as small a voice as she can manage. "I've had a long day and my car — I kind of forgot how fast I was going." Phony, she thinks. He isn't going to buy this.

"Your car?" He glances at her hand, checking for a wedding ring.

She nods and gives him a lopsided smile. She cannot tell if he is amused or angry, the sunglasses disguise his expression.

"Where are you going?"

"Three Hills." And she thinks, what the hell, he's as attractive as any other road jockey. "To find a room for the night."

"You're on holiday?"

"No, I'm a sales representative."

He raises an eyebrow. "This is your company car?"

"No. It's mine." She puts a hand on the smooth metal. She prefers that men lust after her, not the car, although she is willing to use its attractions. She bends her knee, caresses the car with her palm, an inviting, circular motion.

He flips his ticket book shut. "Well, I was about to go for supper. Care to join me?"

Arachne makes a show of looking at her watch, knowing she has cornered herself. She should have taken the ticket. Now she'll be stuck with him. "I need to check in."

"Fine. Meet you in half an hour at the Steak House on Main."

She tries what she hopes is a convincing smile. "All right, and thank you."

Walking back to the patrol car, he lifts a shoulder, speeds away before she can put the Mercedes in gear.

Arachne thinks of turning tail and heading for Calgary, letting him wait. But he has her license number, he can always catch up with her. Her stomach feels strangely sour; she doesn't want to engage in hand to hand with a policeman. She always tries to get out of tickets. Two weeks ago she would have considered this a lark, part of a day's fun, but now she just feels gritty. She doesn't want to have supper with him, much less anything else.

Still, she got herself into it. Maybe if she acts coy and prissy, he will lose interest.

She can hear Thena clucking her tongue. "Serves you right. How are you going to get out of this one?"

"Damn you, Thena," Arachne says aloud. "What am I supposed to do?"

"Pay for your own supper, at least."

Thena relies on dry irony to keep herself going. Arachne has learned to be skeptical, but Thena is naturally so, to the point of total disillusionment. There is little that escapes her reduction, the needle of her discontent. Realism, absolute realism.

Arachne pays for her own supper. She insists. The Mountie does his best to be entertaining, regales her with stories of local lawbreakers. She should be in her element, absorbed in pursuit, the challenge of what pitch she can work him into, pushing him so that when she finally does get him flat on his back, he'll be excited more than usual, he'll be intrigued enough to perform with some imagination.

Arachne can work up no interest. He is passably good-looking, but she wants to yawn, to chew her fingernails, and instead she is forced to hack at a tough steak and mime appropriate responses. He will have a good body, well trained at least, why doesn't she feel like taking advantage? She should be downright horny.

She stabs a chunk of carrot. What is it about policemen that makes them so threateningly polite? They are used to being obeyed, deferred to. This one doesn't believe she's bored; he is convinced she is shy. Still, that's an act she doesn't do successfully. Even keeping her sullen, rebellious eyes lowered, she can never disguise her troublemaker's nature. There are clues to it in the way she moves her head, in the way she holds a fork.

As the meal ends, Arachne begins to dredge up excuses. Her fiancé expects her to call. Hell, that sounds phony even to her. Nobody has a fiancé anymore. She needs to sort her day's orders. True, but coming now, after the fact, it sounds childish. Inevitable as hours she finds him in her motel room, the same quizzical smirk without his sunglasses. She hopes he doesn't have a streak of violence.

She makes one last effort, the phone call to the mythical fiancé. Thomas is not home so she calls Thena.

"Lo," says Thena, very grouchy.

"Darling," says Arachne, watching the cop from the corner of her eye.

"What?"

"How are you?"

"Raki." Thena knows who it is. "What's up?"

"Just wanted to talk to you, say hello and wish you good night."

Thena snorts. Arachne's tone is clearly intended for someone else. "What fantasy am I helping you act out now?"

"Do you miss me?" If Arachne hopes that her saccharine act will persuade the Mountie to leave, she is being optimistic. He sits in a chair, cataloguing the room's contents, noting Arachne's open suitcase, the presence of a few sample cases. He has endless patience, he's been trained.

"Is it necessary for me to participate? I can hear the guy breathing in the background. For Chrissake, Raki, spare me."

Arachne realizes it's hopeless. He won't leave anyway. Thena will play along with her, but she is only prolonging the inevitable.

In the dark his skin feels sticky. He is sweating, he holds her as though he would like to keep his clothes on, as though he wonders what he's gotten into. Which makes Arachne feel a twinge of protectiveness; men so brash and confident until they have to reveal themselves. And he's not exactly adept, fumbling his way inside her. She has to help him, has to reassure him, but at least it puts her to sleep. She barely wakens when he gets up, pulls on his clothes without the light. He sits on the side of the bed to tie his shoes and then leans across her for a kiss.

Arachne rolls over to give him a sleepy and sisterly hug.

"Thanks," he says, "but slow down, eh?"

"Mmmmn." She is asleep again before he closes the door.

The next morning the speeding ticket is tucked under her windshield wiper. Even as she snatches it free and curses, Arachne has to resist laughing. She knows her performance last night wasn't exactly brilliant, but then, neither was his.

She scrawls a note on the back of the ticket. "Congratulations. You are incorruptible. I promise not to speed anymore," and shoves it through the mail slot of the RCMP building.

Driving again, she thinks how hard it is to feign desire, how impossible to conceal dislike. She has never learned the knack of noncommittal blandness. Years of practice, of bus driving, have made her indifference plain. And her emotion, when it is out, plain too.

# Redolence

Rumsey, Rowley, Craigmyle, Delia, Michichi, Munson, Morrin Bridge, Ghost Pine Creek, towns like their names, isolated, hopeful, doomed. Each trip, they are eroded, less proud, the settings for impossible regional fictions, their reality doubtful and confined. They are there because Arachne is selling underwear, no other reason. Their names scatter her map tentatively; their streets edge toward oblivion, their post offices lie. Arachne sometimes has the spooky feeling that they are sets. If she could dart around the corner of a false-fronted general store quickly enough, she would discover the vacancy behind and the face would be free to fall. It is an illusion that she shoves away; these places are her livelihood, they give her a reason to travel, a story to inhabit.

When she returns to Calgary, Thomas is back. She can smell him; the dead air waiting in the house has been displaced by his presence. His sleeping bag airs in the backyard, his dirty socks are in the washer, and there's juice in the fridge. Arachne never stops feeling a clench of joy that she's been allowed him. Despite life's injustices, she has Thomas. She knows she takes him for granted, she knows she betrays him, but in another sense she doesn't, he is her Apocryphal lover.

Occasionally Thomas' love hits hard enough to make

112

her wish herself different; she swears she will give up road jockeys and traveling, sell the Mercedes and buy a Ford, stop taking the pill and get pregnant, subscribe to ladies' magazines. But when she says this, Thomas laughs. "I like you the way you are. If I wanted one of those women, I'd have married one."

"But you still might."

He snorts. Thomas does not feel that he has made a bad bargain. He knows her infidelities, he can imagine her misdemeanors. But she has saved him from life with a blue-eyed and bouncy-assed fembot who would spend hours making casseroles and buying laundry soap, who would hang pink drapes. Arachne has not changed his house one jot. He likes that, the way she took on his surroundings without rearranging one chair or cupboard. He knows it's a camouflage she has pulled around herself, but she is still Arachne underneath, a stormy-faced orphan whose speech is a little coarse, who responds. When he thrusts inside of her, she moans; when she comes, she sometimes screams. Body dark, stocky, a force that seems to covet its own weight. There is nothing slender and light about Arachne; when she walks she thumps, the floorboards shudder. She knows she contradicts every ideal. Women are cherished for being soft and pliable, for their grace. Instead, Arachne displaces mass. Thomas thinks of her in scientific terms; like mercury, you are never prepared for the weight. Unthinkable that he has found a woman like this, and that she stays.

She loves him. When he gets off the bus that evening, she is waiting. She sprints down the sidewalk, buries her nose against his neck, thinking how good he smells, none of the musty sadness that she finds everywhere else, the smell of her past. When she had just come to Calgary, they went to a movie one night. After the feature started, a man sat down on Arachne's right. He was two seats away, but his smell closed around them. It was not sharply bad, like cheese, but soft and rotten, the smell of burrowed socks, windowless rooms, cat-laden carpets, a smell of such overwhelming despair that it made Arachne want to cry. Thomas said nothing, his eyes on the screen, and Arachne did not suggest they move, thinking it was her sense alone. But its proximity was terrible, seemed to intensify during the movie until Arachne wanted to retch, she'd never be rid of it. She had only one relief, and that was to bury her nose in Thomas, against his arm, in his hair, between his shoulder and his neck. He smelled so clean, so impossibly good.

So she inhales him, sucks him into her system. He has slung his suit jacket over his shoulder, and his shirt sleeves are rolled to his elbows as a concession to the heat, but even this makes him seem jaunty rather than rumpled. He puts an arm around Arachne and they walk home, trading stories. Arachne tells him about Lanie's visit, about how little she has sold. About her speeding ticket, although she omits the circumstances. All in all, she's had a bad month.

"Blame it on Lanie visiting," she says. "It's her fault. She probably jinxed me because I wouldn't let her tell my fortune."

"Why not?" says Thomas. "She knows your past. After all, she's your mother."

"Huh," says Arachne. "I don't know how that happened. I was either adopted or stolen."

## To enter the enclave

They try to relate their lives but much is left unsaid when
Arachne moves in with Thomas. Arriving at his house
that March night, in viscous darkness, Arachne is nervous.
Will she say and do the right things?

She takes only one suitcase, sets it down in the hall
while Thomas clatters to light switches, his arm cradling
map tubes. The house smells well off, the silence that hangs
in its rooms is well off. She can see the furniture in the
living room sitting prim and contemptuous. That living
room, chill and silver, terrifies her. If it reflects Thomas,
she has no business here. Actually, his mother decorated
it. After he had resanded the hardwood floors – it took
him months – she felt he needed encouragement, so she
spent a few weeks searching for a creamy-gray rug, perfect
drapes, perfect couches and chairs, their maker's name
inscribed on a discreet brass plate attached to the bottom.
It is a pleasing room, but very expensive and very cool.
The blues are so pale they resemble ice, and from the hall
Arachne can see they are the kind of chairs she does not
know how to sit on, where to put her legs. There, for
one chaotic moment, she wants to run. She does not belong
here. She will never belong here. Respectable men do not
adopt stray women who have no abilities except their
bodies. She closes one hand on the doorknob. If she goes

now, he will never find out what she is like, he will remember her with pleasure. Still, clenching that slippery brass, it occurs to her that this is the one chance she has. If she leaves now, she will never get another. She will stay Arachne Manteia, drive buses or cabs until she falls into marriage with a longshoreman or a carpenter, until she is withered and staggering under the weight of a shopping bag.

The house is filled with yellow light. Thomas puts down his map tubes, picks up her cardboard suitcase.

"The guest room is upstairs," he says. "You can stay until you find a place." She looks as though she will bolt. He wants to reassure her that this is not a trap, he has no designs on her life.

The guest room? A chastened Arachne follows him up the wide staircase. He leads her into a room that is pale and still, a white pine dresser, a single bed.

"Sorry it's so bare. I haven't fixed this room up yet."

"Thank you, it's fine."

"Would you like a drink?" If they go back downstairs, Thomas figures they might start again. He is afraid to usher her into his bedroom, does not want to appear presumptuous.

Arachne follows him, and at the bottom of the stairs, feels her stomach lurch. If he goes into the living room it will be finished, she will have no choice but to leave. She cannot handle that room.

But he doesn't. He goes into the kitchen, an ordinary place with a shabby dropleaf table and several potted plants wilting on the sill above the sink. Arachne leans against the counter and watches him pull out ice cubes, take highball glasses from a shelf. She has never seen a man move around a kitchen so easily. In her world women do these things. She wants to comment but restrains herself. And then she realizes that this man, Thomas, has a wife or a girl. Here, in this house. That's why he put her in the guest room.

Arachne is stony. "I think I should leave tomorrow."

He slides ice into each glass. "Why? There's lots of room."

She shrugs, sullen. On one wall is a framed map. The paper is creased gray, yet it is beautiful, the lines pure and sweeping, the colors poignant. It makes her want him even more, the maps, the beautiful maps. And some woman has this, probably doesn't even look at them, likes the living room best.

"Here."

Turning, she takes the drink from him.

"Do you like it?"

She nods.

"It's one of the first maps ever made of this part of the country. Dawson. A real cartographer."

Arachne stands in front of the chart, holding her glass in both hands.

"I collect old maps."

There are more. They could lead you into the past so easily, lead you through history to another frame of time. With these maps around, she would be able to transcend her own past, its rude, uneven measure, its gaps and horrors.

"Come on, I'll show you some more."

She follows him upstairs again, clutching her beaded glass. This time he pushes open a door to what is certainly the largest bedroom. It is painted pale blue, a peaceful uncompromising color. The walls are hung with maps, everywhere there are maps, rolled up, flung over chairs, coiling on the floor. Some are held open by small shot bags, others unfurl seductively. There is a rocking chair here and a big, saggy armchair, there is a tilted drafting table, another light table, India ink, colored pencils and mysterious-looking pens.

117

From one of three map stands he pulls a roll and spreads it open on the light table like a scroll. It is a map drawn on cloth, the lines tentative, an explorer's map.

Arachne touches the map, runs her fingers along its frayed edge. Thomas brings out another and another. He spreads treasures for her; she has never imagined such things exist, simple lines drawing lives, roads, places.

He never imagined a woman would be interested, would touch these maps with reverence and desire, caressing the paper between thumb and forefinger. She covets them the way he does, images that trace out hope, mapping an act of faith, a way of saying, I have been here, someone will follow, so I must leave a guide.

There, in the blue room, when her eyes lift from the map to his face, he is waiting. He wants to memorize her texture, to keep her.

He touches her face, the shadows of brow and hair, the skin of her neck. He touches and touches, a blind man and this speech. Under his hands she trembles. She bends, turns, holds herself out to him. He is more than patron, he is lover. Her lover, her Apocryphal lover, the one who will linger and stay.

Between the maps that spill the room they curl around each other, furl and unfurl like the charts. He touches her skin without the frantic urgency of their journey. Traveling, he assumed that they would lose each other when they reached Calgary, but now they have time to circle pleasure slowly, spinning it out, spinning it around themselves in a filamented mesh.

They fall asleep between the maps on the floor.

## Routes of passage

After two months Arachne gets a job with the Calgary
Transit System. They are stricter and smaller than Vancouver's; they have few women drivers. Arachne keeps quiet
and does her job without calling attention to herself. It
is perhaps the most uneventful period of her life. She is
busy being respectable, busy being loved by Thomas, although she has a sneaking suspicion that she does not
deserve his affection. Nothing has prepared her for stability,
calm, an untroubled life with a man who actually likes
her, who finds her rakish manners and her singular distrust
charming rather than malevolent. Thomas has never known
a woman quite so vivid, so high-colored. Nor does he grow
tired of Arachne, despite her awkwardness, her ignorance,
her spurts of withdrawal.

It is a measure of his protectiveness that he waits a couple
of months before he introduces Arachne to his family. He
waits until she has a job before he tells his mother that
he is having a relationship with a woman, a fairly permanent relationship. Those are the kinds of words his family
understands: relationship, lifestyle, recreation, career, situation. Arachne would say: shacked up, life, fun, job, mess.
Thomas feels he has to prepare her for his family's vocabulary. He tries to explain them to her, that his father is
a successful neurologist, that his mother devotes her time

to charitable organizations, as though their occupations will help her to understand. Thomas grew up with several television sets. He was given a compact Japanese car for his sixteenth birthday. He was fitted for braces at the age of twelve. He has always been encouraged to bring his girlfriends home. He tells Arachne these things as diagrams of his liberal and middle-class blood.

Although Thomas' brother and sisters have more conventional occupations, they are all proud of him. They know what work he does, but they are somewhat puzzled by his interest in ratty old maps. Yes, they understand that they are considered collector's items, but what can you actually *do* with them? Thomas ignores this skepticism with good humor. He knows his family feels that he is slightly off, but they are too well-bred to verbalize such doubt. Instead, they cajole him as though his eccentric interests are their pride. And, after all, he is normal enough to suit them, he has an M.Sc. in geography, he has a nine-to-five job with the Canadian Geodetic Survey, he will settle down and marry soon. They are only waiting for the proper woman to appear.

Thomas's parents are confident that they have done things right; their children have had every advantage. When Thomas asks them if he can bring a girl along to dinner, they say, of course, in reassuring tones, and tell him that Minx will be there too. Her name is really Marianne, but she has always been called Minx. Minx is married to a civil engineer who works for city planning, she is incubating their first child. Thomas' brother John is a lawyer who lives in Edmonton with his family. Thomas' sister Judy lives in Toronto. Thomas is the third child.

Thomas tells Arachne all these things, but he has not the faintest notion of how to prepare her for his family. He assumes that hers is much the same, although she has told him that her mother is a clerk and her father a night watchman. Besides, no amount of explaining will prepare her for their assumptions.

Arachne does her best. She goes out and buys a skirt and blouse, a black skirt much too long and a blouse in apoplectic pink. Arachne is herself doubtful about this combination, but she has never been interested in buying clothes. She lives mostly in her driver's uniform. And she hates to try clothes on because she doesn't wear underwear and the saleswomen sneer.

Arachne has purchased only one brassiere in her life. At fifteen the soft cotton training bra she had been wearing every day for two years was uncomfortably tight. She finally brought herself to ask Lanie for a replacement. Lanie shrugged, "Well, go and buy one then. Here's some money."

After attempting to negotiate the wilderness of lingerie in a large department store, Arachne decided that it must be easier to visit a small clothing shop and ask for assistance. She found a likely store and went inside, a hostile-looking teenager in too-tight jeans and a black leather jacket.

For ten minutes the clerks ignored her, not the kind of client they wanted. Arachne flipped through boxed bras in the rack at the back of the store. She did not understand the difference between cup sizes A, B, C and D, let alone AA. In fact, she did not actually know her size. She had not thought about using a tape measure on herself. Finally the youngest clerk, an upright and very brisk young woman in a matched sweater set and a narrow skirt, approached.

"Can I help you?"

"Yes. I want to get a bra."

"What size?"

"I don't know."

The clerk appraised her chest. "Just a minute." When

she returned she was trailing a yellow tape measure. Arachne unzipped her jacket, trying to be casual, but knowing that every clerk studiously hanging a dress, twitching a display, watched.

The clerk, wincing at Arachne's lumpy Orlon sweater, held the tape measure stiffly in front of her. That could have been the moment she decided to take a firm hand.

"It's better to measure you without the sweater. Just step into this dressing room. Are you wearing a bra now?" This said in a disdainful tone that confirmed Arachne's worst fears about herself. She knew she was hopelessly scrubby, hopelessly coarse, and she did not want this contemptuous clerk to see her round breasts constrained by the too-small, puckered child's bra.

She almost bolted but she was firmly levered into the dressing room, the wrists of her jacket snapped over her hands, her sweater, for a moment its familiar frowsy smell muffling her head. She had never in her life felt so defenseless as she did standing there, stooped, shamed, while the clerk chafed the impertinent tape on her chest, her shrinking breasts, her cold ribs.

"34B," she announced in ringing tones and ducked out of the curtained cubicle, returning to thrust a box illustrated with a petal-bra'd woman at Arachne. "Try this."

Arachne had trouble getting the box open. She had more trouble untangling herself from the bra she wore; she had not taken it off for a week. Arachne was just doing the hooks, the bra on backwards so that she could see them, when the clerk snapped the curtain open. "How are we doing?"

Frantically Arachne twisted the bra around and struggled to flail her arms through the straps.

The clerk clucked with disapproval. "Here. That's not the way you're supposed to put on a bra." She tore it from Arachne and then forced her to put it on properly, arms through the straps, bent over slightly while closing the hooks. "That way," said the clerk in the same hectoring voice, "you get full support when you stand erect."

Her arms crucified behind her back, Arachne could not get the hooks done up, and the clerk did them for her, impatient fingers cold against Arachne's sweating skin.

"There. That fits properly."

The bra was a set of horrid foam cones, already making Arachne's nipples itch. Her arms could not lift themselves, her body was straightjacketed. She stood miserably, saying nothing, and certainly did not turn to look at herself in the mirror.

"Well?"

Arachne wanted to incinerate clerk and brassiere completely, but she was at a half-naked disadvantage and she could only nod. The zealous missionary pulled the curtain shut again.

Arachne tore herself out of harness and tremblingly put on her shapeless old cotton. The straps bit into her skin, it was too small, not much more than a string. She felt safer inside her sweater and jacket, but still hesitated before opening the curtain, holding the box stuffed with the forceful bra. The clerk was waiting.

"You should have kept it on," she said. "You shouldn't be wearing that training bra." She took the box from Arachne. "Would you like to buy two?" Bitch. She knew Arachne possessed only the bra she was wearing, her underthings as meager as her life.

"Just one." Now that she had her clothes on, she was beginning to get her strength back.

A bored cash girl looked at the price, rang up the sale. "Seven dollars."

Seven dollars? Lanie had given her five dollars. Arachne

searched her pockets. No more. What could she say? That she forgot her money? Hardly. The snotty salesclerk watched her with a knowing expression.

She checked her back pocket, although she never put money there. Nothing. The clerk tapped her nails on the counter. Arachne put the five-dollar bill on the counter. The clerk picked it up. "*Seven* dollars."

"Stick 'em up," said Arachne and ran out of the store. The door swung behind her and she ran, ran. Sidewalk heaved under her feet. Around corners, down a back alley, finally stumbling aboard a bus just as it pulled away. The woman pictured on the bra box smiled coyly from between Arachne's smudgy fingers.

Home in her cupboard-sized room, she curled up on the cot. It was not possible to escape the disdainful world. She had no tools and she didn't know how to get them. She was cornered, a grubby teenager with two sweaters and four shirts and two pairs of jeans and one skirt and one bra and six pairs of cheap panties.

She stuffed the new bra in her drawer and wore nothing.

## Eat and be eaten

But nothing can prepare her for Thomas' parents, for Sunday evening dinner – Arachne says supper – with them. She has made an effort, but looking at her reflection in the mirrored closet doors of Thomas' bedroom, which is now also her bedroom, she feels like a person dressed up in another's clothes. It is already Sunday evening. She can revert to her jeans, but Thomas is wearing a suit and tie. He's waiting, wrapping a box of truffles, a bottle of wine.

She goes downstairs in bare legs and her only suitable shoes, flat leather sandals. Thomas glances up and Arachne knows that he refrains from laughing only out of kindness. She sits down on the bottom step with her head on her knees.

"I won't go."

He kneels and puts his arms around her. "I'm not used to seeing you in a skirt."

"I look terrible."

"No, you don't. You never look terrible."

"I won't go."

"I like the way you are. It will be fine."

When they leave the house, she walks toward the Mercedes, but Thomas says in a careful voice, "Let's take the Rabbit tonight."

Arachne has been hoping the Mercedes will distract attention from her, but she meekly agrees and climbs into his passenger seat. Not driving makes Arachne nervous. If she had the wheel under her hands, she would at least be calm by the time they get there. So she locks herself into a state of siege, that sullen non-expression she relied on in Vancouver.

Thomas' parents do not betray one hint of surprise at Arachne's appearance. They are affable and pleasant.

"It's so nice to meet you."

"And what an unusual name." They do not ask her how to spell it, and Arachne is grateful. She's sure she could not spell it correctly herself.

The Mount Royal house is huge and luxurious; thickly carpeted, discreetly lighted. Thomas' mother collects antiques, interior decorating is her hobby, everything is carefully placed, down to the alabaster ashtrays on the end tables. Arachne should be prepared. Thomas' mother did his living room, so chill and perfect. It is a beautiful room but a room that Thomas and Arachne seldom use, only once making outrageous love on the silvery loveseat, sliding from its precarious edge to the gray carpet to finish lying on their sides facing each other, the furniture angled and looming in disapproval. There they did not drift into sleep; they had to get up and climb the stairs to the bedroom. They have slept everywhere else in the house. The kitchen, the back bedroom, the study, even the top of the stairs. They have made love all over the house.

Arachne is sure that no one rolls across the expanse of this carpet. She sits in a tub-like chair waiting for the drink that Thomas' father is mixing. Fortunately, she has gotten used to highballs with Thomas. The only thing they drank at home was beer, although Lanie used to buy gin and pour it into her tea. Horse-killer, Toto called it.

She has chosen the chair so that she will not have to

126

sit close to anyone, the proximity of Mrs. Telfer on the couch too much. She accepts the drink and raises her glass with everyone else, although Minx and Terry have not yet arrived. "Minx is looking very well," Mrs. Telfer confides.

"But," and here both Telfers turn toward Arachne, "how nice to finally meet you. Thomas tells us you come from Vancouver. How do you like Calgary?"

Arachne responds carefully. Thomas' parents are kind, they want to put her at ease, they want her to like them. After all, they can't imagine that Thomas would make a bad choice.

There is a flurry in the hall. Minx and Terry come in, and Mr. and Mrs. Telfer rush to greet them. Thomas catches Arachne's eye and winks from across the room. "You're marvellous," he says.

But Minx is beautiful in a way that only money and years of practice can be beautiful. She wears a shimmery dress that floats around her and tiny diamond drops in her ears. Everything about her sparkles: her teeth, her hair, her polished nails. Arachne feels as though she has just emerged from a mud puddle.

Terry too shines, blond and blue-eyed, with an athlete's body. He will never get fat, he will never go bald. Their child will look like a new-minted coin; they won't have any squalling, red-faced brat.

Minx waltzes over to Thomas and kisses him. "Tom, I haven't seen you for months. Why don't you ever call? Your baby sister deserves better treatment." It is clear that they like each other, compatriots of a mutual childhood.

"And you're Arachne. What a beautiful name." Minx can afford to be generous with her praise, Arachne thinks, looking up at her, smelling expensive perfume. Arachne smiles stiffly, trying to look interested but feeling dowdy and slow. Minx is her opposite in every way. She is reminded once again of her sniveling, measly childhood. It would be easier if they treated her with contempt, pity, but they act as though she's an equal.

Arachne sinks farther and farther into her chair. It is a relief when dinner is served and they trail to the dining room; she can disguise her uneasiness in movement. But dinner proves to be worse. Instead of scattered conversation, every remark is attended and observed. She is between Mr. Telfer and Terry when all she wants to do is touch Thomas, feel his solid, muscled leg under her hand. He is sitting far away, distracted, helping his mother serve the plates.

Arachne is all right with the soup because there is only one spoon, but with the salad she hesitates. There are three forks beside her plate. Everyone else is eating, they know which utensil is required. Arachne feels again that disquieting isolation: she alone has missed the instructions, not quite heard the secret password. She is in a game where everyone knows the rules except her. She knows that she is eating her salad incorrectly, and at exactly that moment Minx asks, "What do you do, Arachne?"

Arachne gulps what is in her mouth, an odd mixture of lettuce and orange and almond. She clears her throat. "I'm a bus driver." It comes out sounding defiant, as though she has said, "I'm a terrorist."

But no one falters; they have too much grace. They chew and nod, and Minx exclaims, "That's interesting!"

It is Terry who, not having been brought up in this family, exhibits bad manners. "Not many women bus drivers, I'll bet. Do you get bothered a lot?"

This is exactly the kind of question that Arachne loathes; it is also the kind of question that no one in the Telfer family would ask, but Arachne doesn't know that.

"No." She cannot help being curt; people *want* to hear stories about her being harassed, they are titillated.

Her annoyance is clear but Terry laughs it off. "You

must have found the right approach."

Arachne is reduced to shrugging. She stabs her salad with what she now perceives is her dinner fork, an irrevocable mistake.

The conversation flags. Arachne feels that she has killed it because she does not have a more sophisticated occupation. When Thomas says her name, she almost jumps.

"Arachne is the kind of person who is unusual in a job that's always forced to relate to the public. She treats everyone as if they are special. I left some maps on her bus in Vancouver and she rescued them."

Arachne feels a rush of love for him, reminding her of the maps they both love.

Thomas' mother and father nod brightly. They are liberals, public transportation is good and public relations even better. Anyone who rescues Thomas' maps deserves appreciation.

It is Terry who finds this an amusing pursuit. "So you met on a bus in Vancouver. Tell me, Thomas, what was your line? 'Where do I transfer?'"

"Really, Terrence, it's none of your business." Minx is indulgent but rebuking. He is being vulgar.

But Terry has said aloud what none of the Telfers would have remarked; his words have spread Arachne on the set and graceful table exactly as she is, a bus driver who allows herself to be picked up. The Telfers stiffen. They do not believe in pursuing conversations of this nature, but Terry's implication is too blatant to be ignored. While they lift silver forks to their mouths, they are formulating gentle private questions to Thomas: "But, darling, what *do* you have in common?"

Arachne can hardly swallow her mouthful of salad.

Thomas is furious. Ignorant prick, he thinks. That's what happens when your sister marries a fraternity boy, a jock, an engineer. Arachne does not understand these fine distinctions, she is too innocent. Besides, he does not want her tainted by social maneuvers. She is wearing her blank, inward look; she will never come out now, never show the vividness inherent in her wide face, her strong body. He was counting on that, Arachne revealing herself. His parents are not stupid. They would see her attractiveness, her remarkable pitch. But Terry has smeared it. Now they will have trouble seeing anything. He turns to his father and deliberately changes the subject.

"Where are you going on holidays this summer, Dad?"

Minx recognizes his ploy immediately and picks it up. "You can't go off just when I'm supposed to have this baby," she cries. "You'll have to be here for July and August."

"I don't think we'll go any farther than the lake," says Mr. Telfer. "It's not hard to reach us there."

"Are you going to redo the cottage?"

And so the conversation goes, words tumbling past Arachne. She hears only scraps of words, but it is as if the language spoken is not hers. Cottage, reception, christening, association, baby, layette, namesake, godparents. They make no sense at all. To Arachne, having a kid is just that.

They begin the main course, which is lamb. Arachne has never before eaten lamb. She is surprised that it tastes like any meat. The Telfers seem to have recovered. Minx, so clearly a favorite child, spoiled, pleasured, has a way of making them all conspire, feel expansive. Arachne envies her, wishes that she could have known Thomas as a child. She is thinking this as she awkwardly tries to maneuver her knife around a lamb bone, thinking also that she will have to leave him now, she cannot wait until he leaves her, until he starts to make excuses. Something has happened and tomorrow she will take the paper and circle ads and make phone calls and find an apartment of her own. The concrete plan seems to echo aloud and, clumsily sawing at the lamb, Arachne's knife careers across her plate and jolts the thin-stemmed glass of red wine. It topples, the crystal splinters and the wine spreads itself in a malevolently large blot.

"Oh shit," says Arachne.

Thomas jumps up, thinking only of touching her, of getting her out of here, home, of holding her naked and solid in his arms, holding her on top of him like a lazy frog, her legs scissored and kicking, shudders down the flanks of her back like rippled water, her pleasure between his hands.

"It's all right," says Mrs. Telfer.

"Oh," says Minx and jumps up, returning in a moment with a cloth and salt, which she briskly sprinkles over the stain.

Arachne sits dumbly. Her hands are paws, her fingers have been removed as a special torture and she is required to eat with delicate dexterity or she will be sent to Siberia. There are critics watching, taking notes on her performance. They have taken her fingers and teeth away, the food dribbles down her chin, the cutlery flies out of her hands, she is trying to eat soup with a fork, peas with a knife. . . .

The Telfers are kind and considerate but every concession they make only emphasizes the pit between them. Arachne sees herself a swarthy peasant without stockings or shoes, dressed in cast-offs, unable to manage the simplest tools, unwashed, illiterate, unsocialized. She knows they will repress their scorn until she is gone; the aristocracy do not criticize lowlife to their faces.

# Erase

In the car on the way home she buckles her seat belt and sits tightly against the door. Thomas does not know what to do. The evening has been a disaster. He expects Arachne to cry or to rage but she is silent, becalmed in ice. He does not yet know that Arachne will not indulge in tantrums – her paroxysms are all inverted. She learned long ago how futile emotional display can be. She enacts her own performance: a very large eraser, pink and rubbery, that she scrubs across her visual memory, sweeping the edge back and forth, erase, erase, obliterate. When she begins, the image is stubborn, resistant, but if she persists, it begins to dissolve, fade, and eventually its details are effaced, leaving pink crumbs and eraser streaks, an occasional black smear. There are events in her life that are just that – heavy black pencil marks on a page, erased and erased into meaninglessness, even if the page is not completely clean.

Sitting in the Rabbit on the way back to Thomas' house, she erases and thinks about the paper tomorrow, the physical act of sitting down with the classifieds and a pencil and the telephone. She has been driving the Number 10 for two weeks now. She has a job; she can get an apartment. She will erase Thomas too, only allow herself to remember the maps, their comely ravishment. Maybe she will steal one when she leaves.

"I'm sorry," Thomas says. "Terry can be so stupid, so unconscious of what he's *saying*. It doesn't matter, my parents liked you, they want you to like them — "

She says nothing, sits rigid and forward-looking. Her profile — he has never seen it like this before — is Egyptian, inclined nose, the dark hair cut square, her long eyes houris gleaming in the half dark.

"Raki?"

She does not answer. She is erasing.

"Goddamn it, answer me."

She does not even blink.

Thomas has never felt such rage, an explosion inside his chest. He has to pull the car over and stop, the wheel slews in his hands.

"Arachne!" He is shouting. He wants to hit her.

She turns slightly and says in a voice so soft it echoes, "Don't shout at me."

He is immediately ashamed, screaming at her when the evening isn't her fault. He promises it will never happen again, but he is battering his fists against glass. Everything he says bounces back. Silently.

He rests his forehead against the steering wheel, then puts the car in gear and drives. At home he pulls her out of the car and into the house. She does not resist; she is perfectly agreeable, pliant. That is what frightens him. If she would only fight, he would know where he stood, what to do. Her calm, accepting movements are much worse. She is going to leave him. He has lost her over a dinner with his parents, a brother-in-law without the sense to power a D-cell battery.

She hangs her coat and stoops to unbuckle her sandals, then plods up the stairs. He follows her, feeling futile.

She walks into the bedroom and undresses, crawls into bed the way she always does, naked, her skin caramel against the white sheets.

Thomas does not know what to do. He can get into bed too, but he has a feeling that would be unforgivable. So he sits down on the edge of the bed, against her curled body, and smooths her hair back from her face.

His fingers are warm, but Arachne can ignore that, they are only fingers. She is concentrating on something else. He can touch her any way he wants, her body will even respond, but she is busy elsewhere, erasing.

He puts his head down against hers so that his lips are beside her ear. "Are you going to leave?"

She considers this, then says finally, "I'll look for an apartment tomorrow."

"Why?"

"I should have a place of my own."

"Why?"

"I can't stay here forever."

"I like having you here. I thought this was your house too."

She does not answer.

"Just because of tonight?"

"No. I'll have to leave anyway. Eventually."

"Because of me."

She is silent to that too. He knows her reasons. She is temporary; he may not want to admit it, but she is unsuitable, and however he may be amused with her now, he will eventually replace her. The knowledge is not so unexpected. Did she honestly believe that she could fit into his life? She can almost chuckle at her own postponed self-deception.

Under his lips the warm membrane of her ear tells him that she thinks she is temporary, a woman he will abandon. There is nothing he can say to dissuade her. She knows, just as surely as he knows he will not. He is helpless against her knowledge, against the confirmation she has had tonight.

"If you want, I'll never see my parents again. I'll move to Vancouver or Antarctica. I'll become a goddamn bus driver." He is speaking wildly. This is not the man who meets the world with urbane ease, such charming calm. "Goddamn it, Arachne, what do I have to say to convince you?"

She can feel the scene that she has almost managed to erase flooding back, clear and painful. "I can't fit into your family. I'm a freak. I can't dress right, I can't talk right, I can't eat right. Even my work is wrong. I didn't go to college, I barely got out of high school."

Arachne falls back on the pillow and stares at the ceiling. Her hands are folded across her chest, the blanket crosses her body just below her shoulders. "When I was little and growing up the way I did, I figured out that I was adopted. I knew I was adopted. It was the only possible answer. I knew I *couldn't* belong where I was, Lanie and Toto weren't really my parents, I was a baby who ended up there by accident, and someday somebody was going to find out about the mistake and fix it."

She stops and he holds himself still, almost holds his breath.

"You know," she turns her face away from him, "I kept on believing it until now. I believed it right up until tonight. And then, when your sister came in and at supper, I knew I hadn't been adopted at all. I belong where I am. It's no accident. There's no mistake. I'm nobody except an East End kid who can't do anything right, I'm Lanie and Toto's kid. Isn't that funny?" She laughs.

He can turn then and gather her into his arms, tuck the blanket around her and hold her. He has a chance, the thin wedge of a chance. "You know," he says, "it's only a game. People are just wearing costumes. Some have money to rent something elaborate and some have lots of practice dressing up. But underneath, everybody's the same."

"I don't believe it."

He looks into her face. "How can I convince you?"

"Turn me into your sister."

"You don't want to be like Minx. She's lovely, but she's a little silly. Besides, look at the hunk she married."

"That was high praise in my neighbourhood."

"Well, it's not in mine." He licks her nose, an eyebrow. "Do you really think that stuff is so important?"

She shrugs.

"It's nothing. You can pick it up in a week. I'll show you. From now on it'll be knives and forks and how to make useless conversation." He nuzzles her neck, kisses her ear. "Just don't tell me you want to change your name to Jane Smith, and don't you dare turn into a proper Waspish lady in bed, or you're out, I'll put all your possessions on the sidewalk."

She bites her lip. "You can dress a monkey up but you can't teach him to talk."

"You're no monkey."

## Disguise

Arachne agrees to let Thomas turn her into a respectable woman, or at least the appearance of one. He promises not to make her wear deodorant or shave her legs.

They go to a dress shop, Woman's Move. Arachne is nervous. They look through the racks, Thomas making suggestions and Arachne shaking her head. She finally agrees to try on two rather gypsyish dresses. They are odd and frumpy enough to emphasize Arachne's outlandishness. She recognizes this immediately and is ready to give up. There's nothing that will make her look normal except blue jeans.

But Thomas is outside the dressing-room door. "Here," he says, handing her a soft red dress, "try this on."

Arachne looks at it doubtfully. It is one of the things she rejected.

"Come on, just try it."

To her surprise, the dress settles on her body with friendliness. When she turns to the mirror, she sees a serious and decorous young woman who does not call attention to herself. She will never look elegant, but she can look grave. The color of the dress is good with her hair; for once her eyes are not so markedly strange.

When Arachne steps out to present herself to Thomas, she does not need to ask how she looks. She turns in front of a bank of mirrors and confronts this quiet transformation. Oh, she hasn't been turned into any princess, but she looks respectable.

A salesclerk has brought Thomas a chair and is showing him different articles of clothing.

"I like this one," says Arachne, looking with dismay at the growing number of things on the hook outside the door.

"All right, we'll take that one. But while we're here, you might as well try on some other things."

Arachne opens her mouth to protest but he holds up his hand. "A game," he says. "Remember?"

If Thomas is costuming Arachne, he does so with a skill that leaves an indelible mark on his uneasy protégée. In one afternoon he gives her trappings, the trick of illusion. It is not a question of glorious plumage but of imposing spare lines on that sullen body, of drawing the eye away from her rebellious face.

The clerks in the shop are fascinated. The man has impeccable taste; he knows exactly what is right. Even if the girl wants something, rubs the cloth pensively between two fingers, he shakes his head, overrules her. He adds accessories, belts, scarves, shoes, even stockings. The clerks watch and comment, throw themselves into this transformation, so different from those hopeful, hopeless women, caught between teenage children and faithless husbands, who sort through their racks looking for bargains.

They show Thomas everything in the shop, make suggestions that range from the most conservative to the most exotic. Between the two extremes they put together a person with style and definition, whose clothes seem part of her face and body. Arachne is dressed.

"Would you like to work here?" one of the owners asks Thomas, almost serious. "You have excellent taste."

He smiles and looks at Arachne. He is doing this for love, to provide her with camouflage, a disguise.

"Wait," one of the clerks says, "remember that green outfit that we could never sell? No one knew how to wear it, it was so strange. Where is that?"

"It's in the back," says the owner. "I had to rescue it. It's made of such fragile material and all those thick women were trying it on."

When the clerk shows it to Thomas, he frowns, then nods. And when Arachne emerges from the dressing room, they are all silent. This is not a disguise, this is Arachne, disturbingly so. It is silk, a fine, watered silk, two pieces, a tunic and narrow pants slit at the ankle, the green of Arachne's eyes. It catches green lights in her hair, makes her sloe-eyed, remote. She is more than beautiful, she has stepped from a carved wall, her mutinous face, the glaring question of her eyes, her wide bones. The costume makes her almost frightening; certainly Arachne is frightened. The clothes are supposed to cover her nature, not blare it out.

"Do you like it?"

Arachne looks down at herself. The silk whispers on her skin, a gossamer web through which her body shines. She shakes her head. "I could never wear this."

The clerks sigh. "It was made with you in mind."

"Take it," says Thomas. "It's good to have something in reserve."

The price of the afternoon is high, the women almost apologetic when they add the total.

"I can't afford it," says Arachne, "and I can't let you pay for this."

"We'll split it. I'll pay for it now and you can pay half back. And," he gives his card to the owner, "if anything comes in that looks like it's suitable, call me."

"Don't forget, you've always got a job."

He laughs. "I only costume her."

They have cut off the tags and Arachne is wearing the red shirtwaist, carrying her jeans with all the other parcels. On the sidewalk he hugs her. "Was that so bad?"

Arachne shakes her head.

"Now, first lesson in knives and forks. We might as well celebrate and go out for lunch."

"Please," says Arachne. "All in one day?"

"I promised you could learn it in a week. A game."

"All right. Just remember, you can dress a monkey up, but you can't take it for lunch."

## And difference

She can pass now, you would never know the girl who spilled her wine. She is sometimes unsure, but if she moves slowly and watches how everyone else does things, she can cover her tracks. Arachne's natural inclination to dissemble helps a great deal. She is not so much an actress as a double agent, an escaped criminal who has survived by relying on what slender veneers are available. She wonders, though, if she should have let Thomas manage her, even, by God, dress her up and fix her manners. She is disgusted by women who need men to rescue them.

Still, alone with him, she is herself, as angry and abrupt as she wants. There are rooms she can withdraw to, no dubious eyebrows, no questions asked. Her luck is changing; her lust too. He does not interfere but he comforts her, he strokes her body.

They inhabit a peculiar refuge in the Sunnyside house, Arachne working at her orders on the kitchen table, Thomas tracing a line on a map, their bodies in the bed hungrily familiar. Thomas cannot imagine wanting more.

Like Thomas, Thena can only imagine the chisels that worked Arachne before she came to Calgary, but she knows Arachne's present, her life now. Indeed, they tell each other everything, they are brutally honest. Thena is privy to all Arachne's current indiscretions, the road jockeys and travels, her thefts and dishonesty. It does not make her like Arachne less, although she is blatantly skeptical, disapproving. She thinks Arachne is crazy and she tells her so, but they are friends. Equally disillusioned with the world, they suit each other.

Although Thena's anger has to do with men, their control over the world. To her, even the kindest man is a dictator.

"Men. *Men*. Always get their own way. And women, letting themselves be led by the nose." She flings her cup into the sink and breaks it, the pieces grating against the stainless steel as she gathers them. "Just to make sure he lets you, you ask. 'Can I buy a new coat? Can I take a course? Can I go to the bathroom?' " She throws the broken china into the garbage and makes a face. "It's all those asking women, they're the ones who keep repeating how happy they are. They're the ones insisting that we don't have any problems."

Arachne is accustomed to Thena's tirades against men, against the women raising their sons to emulate their husbands. Thena's rages are predictable but Arachne is sometimes shocked by them. She does not understand Thena's deliberate hatred. Arachne has always hammered against the impossible: fate, birth, life. She hates wider, more general things, has never focused on something specific. But then, Thena has good reason. And she has arrived at anger late in life. Arachne, Thena argues, has never been subject to the same hell she emerged from, has somehow missed being taken over, owned, married, sucked in. Thena uses these terms with a bitter emphasis, a self-satisfied fury. And she is trying to instill the same emotion in her daughters.

"Motherrr," groans Theresa, "puuleese."

Thena's bitter pill is that although she has enrolled her daughters in self-defense courses, although she insists on

142

soccer and assertiveness training, they still want ballet lessons and miniskirts, bras and high heels.

"They're trying to kill me," moans Thena.

"They've got to find out for themselves." Arachne knows this is small comfort.

"And make the same mistakes I did? Waste all that time?"

"There's not much you can do."

"Oh yes, there is," says Thena. "I'll send them to live with their goddamn father and his new wife for a while, see how they like that. A good dose of him will cure them."

"I wouldn't. They'll probably think he's charming and enjoy every minute of it."

Which makes Thena dig out another cigarette and sigh. "You may be right."

Thena's daughters are teenagers, fourteen and sixteen. They are normal teenagers; they do not want their mother's bitterness. They want to be like everyone else. Arachne remembers that desire. She had it too but she learned very quickly its impossibility, that she was not the same, would never be the same. There was nothing she could do about her difference, nothing to do but exploit it, call attention to the fact that she was crossing every boundary. It was a way of declaring herself, of drawing a line. She knew where she stood. Outside.

Arachne tries to explain this to Thena, but Thena does not understand. She expects her daughters to be courageous. They refuse. They mince to school, they experiment with makeup, they are themselves.

They regard their mother's friend with suspicion, even though they like her. She is "weird," stated in a half-admiring way. They are glad she's not their mother. Then they'd really have a problem.

But for someone who is so virulent about men, Thena is extremely solicitous about Arachne and Thomas. When Arachne teases her about this, Thena defends herself. "He's

143

not like all the rest. Hang onto him, Arachne." Thena's real concern is that her friend will stay happy; she wants to protect her from having to face the nasty altercations she has undergone. She is convinced that Thomas will not fail Arachne. Of course, she fails to take Arachne herself into account.

## *An incursion between tomes*

Viking, Jarrow, Irma, Fabyan, Wainwright. Viking mutters to itself under its breath, Jarrow hides its face behind its sleeve. Irma Co-op takes five dozen cotton briefs; it must be the heat. In Fabyan Arachne sees a Dutch immigrant family weeding potatoes, dust rising from their hoes, feet in wooden shoes. She stays in Wainwright, and the bar grumbles below her room until three in the morning, the floor so thin she can hear the thud of glasses on terrycloth-covered tables, the snap of the pool cues, the spin of the shuffleboard, the chink of the waiter's change slots. She is ready to go downstairs and join the noise, but getting dressed would be too much trouble, so she contents herself with drumming her heels on the floorboards.

She is grumpy all the way through Czar, Amisk, Hardisty and Lougheed, which affects her sales. She's not persuasive when she's tired, can't sell underwear with bags under her eyes. No matter how she flashes peppermint colors or thrusts silky crotches into their hands, they won't place orders if *she* doesn't look right. She has complained of this to Thena, the product's tyranny, as if she's supposed to be its best advocate.

"What do you expect, selling underwear?"

"It's perfectly respectable. Everybody wears it."

"Except you."

"They don't know that."

"You are a hussy," says Thena.

Which she still believes, will believe forever, given what she knows about her friend. And she knows a good deal. Not to mention what she surmises. Arachne returns from the road with a store of chronicles for Thena: tales, descriptions, narrations, expositions. She is explorer for Thena's determined enclosetment, a messenger from the world. And needs her too. For what is a traveler without a confidante? Every adventuress requires a teller of her tale, an armchair companion to complete the eventualities.

Which are the same as ever, the Mercedes dusting into a one-string main street with an art deco gas station, some false-fronted stores and a post office in the local gossip's front room. The train stations have all been torn down, the hardware stores sag. Arachne swings into another Co-op or Redbird or Market with her clipboard, her order pad, her sample box. Bullies and cajoles, threatens and teases, entertains or coerces them into ordering, their cautious future making them hedge. The only good thing about panties is that they are not perishable.

In Sedgewick she can hear the man in the next room snoring. Killam, Strome, Daysland. Difficult towns — they are all too close to Camrose, too close for confidence. Arachne hates Camrose; it feels like an overloaded village without the innocence that makes villages endearing. She gets there early, so she walks down main street. The Chevys rev past, between half-tons and heat. Here is the bakery, the theater, the five and dime, the music store. But the library, three blocks down, is new brick, and on impulse, Arachne turns in. It will be cool there; she can sit for a while. She should have gone on to Heisler instead of staying here tonight.

The library is cool, but disconcertingly, there is a lecture going on, and Arachne is trapped by a virtuous librarian who says, "There's a chair on the right-hand side second from the back. He's just started."

What can she do but lean on her spine and yawn? The man is in full flight, his voice nasal. The audience is bent forward. The woman next to Arachne scribbles notes.

"What's he talking about?"

"Shhh."

"The trick is to get down to it. Sit down at your typewriter and let your imagination flow, let your mind capture all the possibilities of the situation. Imagine having your name in *Playboy*. Imagine agents from all over the world selling your rights. All you have to do is start right now."

Arachne looks around. The women are middle-aged, in sensible shoes and glasses. "What's he talking about?"

The scribbling woman gives her a dirty look. "Getting published."

"Oh." Arachne slides one foot out of its sandal and raises her leg. She surveys her chunky foot and wonders if it would do to paint her toenails, since she refuses to shave her legs.

"The trick is to throw yourself into it body and soul. Why, look at Marcia Grist. She signed a contract for fifty thousand dollars. Of course, that was Mannikin, but who's to say you couldn't do the same? All you have to do is try."

"What did you say he was talking about?"

The woman glares.

"So remember, follow your instinct and don't be dissuaded. Who's to say that you won't be chosen? All you need is dedication and inspiration and you could be the next success story!"

Arachne giggles, and the woman beside her slams her palm down on her notebook and turns. "Can't you shut up? This is important."

"Is he going to tell you how to model too? I've got some really nice underwear I can show you."

The woman stiffens, then gets up and whispers to the solicitous librarian before moving to another seat. The librarian taps Arachne on the shoulder. "You're disturbing the lecture," she says. "You'll have to leave."

"But I'm not doing anything," Arachne says aloud. "I'm just trying to figure out what he's talking about."

"Please leave."

"Why?"

"Do I have to call security?"

Arachne shrugs and scrapes back her chair loudly. "You'd think this was a church," she says. They do not even turn to watch her, so absorbed are they in their evangelist. Arachne gives the library the finger. "Camrose," she says, scuffing down the sidewalk.

## Memento mori

Heisler is better, cheerful because it has a ball diamond and a café. Everyone in this town is from the same family. The signs outside the houses have only first names: Albert and Rose, Louise and Denny, Marvin and Bim, Tommy and Sal. A prolific family, barn-raisers and beer-swillers. And the man at the general store loves panties; he stocks far more than he ever sells. Arachne suspects he has a fetish, that he caresses them when he's alone, that he buries his nose in their film, imagining the young girls who will wiggle into them. He favors fruit colors, cherry and lemon, lime and plum. He does not need persuasion, although he takes every opportunity he can to fondle Arachne's knees, will crouch for brown bags or string or a can on a bottom shelf. She's used to him, his hand cupping her kneecap, his quick slide up her thigh; used to clenching her legs together to stop his fingers.

Forestburg, Galahad, Alliance. She is going to strike south on 36 and take 9 into Calgary, home, so she rushes the last two. Alliance is strangely deserted; even the town dogs hide under porches. She turns the Mercedes hood south and leaves main street in a cloud of dust. Ahead of her is a slow-moving Ford and ahead of it another slow-moving half-ton. They crawl stubbornly down the middle of the road. The dust is thick, choleric. Arachne pulls out to try and pass, and sees, stretching ahead for two miles, a line of low-throated, headlit cars, the funeral procession as decorous as any mule would be. Behind Arachne the headlights stretch back to town. She turns hers on and stays in place, prowing into the haze of cortege that accompanies death, a good death, a family and community death that clears the streets and locks up the dogs.

They grind their way up the hill to the cemetery, and by the time the last one parks along the ditch the burial has begun, the preacher's hair plastered across his skull and his face raised to yellow, suitably doleful. The flowers are mostly glads, their spiked faces cheerful upstarts against the rub of black cloth elbows and the cracking of joints, a few thin sniffles that Arachne has to strain to hear. She herself picks a buffalo bean and adds it to the heap on the coffin. Funerals are good for sales. They make people clear up affairs, clean out their old underwear and buy new.

Once the coffin is in the hole, neighbors begin to call to each other, to dare to scratch a leg. There will be a good wake, Canadian rye and a local fiddler. Arachne climbs into the Mercedes and gets away ahead of the pack.

But when she pulls up in front of her house, the white-haired old man is sitting on the front steps. Patience is carved in his immobility; he has been there a long time. His clothes seem sifted with dust but his white hair and beard blare light. Arachne goes up the walk and stands in front of him. He looks at her and opens his hands, palm up, in a gesture of submission.

"What are you doing here?"

"I wait for you." He blinks heavily. "You are away long."

"How did you find where I live?"

He shrugs.

Arachne cannot shake her sense that he has been there all week, although she knows Thomas is home.

"I see your husband."

She nods.

"You have my dance?"

"Dance? Oh, *you* left that! It's beautiful. Where did you – "

He picks up his cane. "Come." He takes her hand, the way a child takes the hand of an adult, and she is led.

"Is it close enough to walk? We can drive."

His face bunches into a webbed smile. "I am tired."

So she puts him in the passenger seat, throwing her clipboard and maps into the back, then drives as he directs her. He does not seem quite sure of where he is or where they are going, but they pull up in front of a white-siding bungalow on the city's northeast side. He stumps away from the car to a detached garage behind the house, pushes the door open and gestures Arachne inside. The light is cobweb-hung and green. When her eyes adjust, she sees a jumble of tools and tables, sheets of reddish copper, yellow woodshavings, a line of wooden mallets, everywhere hammers. In the middle of the cement floor stands a solid block table and on it a copper oval with the beginning of a shape.

"You carve the figures?"

"No, hammer."

He sits down on a low stool and pulls what looks like a stump between his raised knees. With a small metal hammer he begins to tap at a triangle of the shimmering metal, the solid chink molding the surface into laps, scales of indentation giving the copper texture and surface. His face falls into serene concentration, hand turning, turning the piece while the other lifts and falls. He holds it up to her. "You hammer thin but it makes harder."

Arachne holds the nubbed and glossy scrap, a dedication she cannot fathom, hammering metal to life hour after endless hour. The comic figures dancing circular and

151

linked hang on the wall of the bedroom. She stares at the copper disc when she wakes, lying next to Thomas' flexed leg, his arm flung across her. It catches the morning light in greenish-gold, the grotesque figures tripping their circumference in shambling ecstasy.

The garage door is flung open and the woman from Crowfoot's grave stands, arms akimbo, in its framed light. "Papa. Are you picking up people on the street again?"

Arachne looks at her in amazement. She is rough and taunting, almost castigating, as if the man were a child.

He shakes his head, mute.

Arachne steps forward. "We've met. We're friends."

The woman ignores her. "Now, Papa, you know you're not to give those plates away. They're worth too much money."

"Anna — "

"Reuban'll have to start keeping track of your stuff. It's too expensive."

"He's just showing me," says Arachne.

"He's getting old, he doesn't understand. And it's almost time for supper, so you come in, Papa. You were off wandering around all afternoon, I almost got in the car and went looking for you." She turns. "Come in the house."

The man shuffles to his feet. "My daughter. I am a burden . . ."

Arachne holds out the mulled scrap of copper.

"You keep."

He closes the garage door regretfully, and Arachne frowns at his slowness. He didn't seem so old that day at Crowfoot's grave.

But he touches her arm. "Your name Arachne."

"Yes," she says. "Yours is Josef."

# *Confidante*

Arachne drives straight to Thena's place and, over a pitcher of martinis, recounts her old man, graveyard, motel room, copper plate, garage and all. "I wonder how he found out where I live."

"Doesn't surprise me," mutters Thena. "You pick up the damnedest people. Sounds like he's crazy."

"I think he's just desperate to touch somebody."

Thena grimaces. "Before you know it, you'll be saving his immortal soul by screwing him. Christ, Raki."

"Oh no. He's too old."

"They're never too old," says Thena darkly.

"Come on."

"I'm warning you. You live with the only nice man in Calgary and you're always inviting disaster. Aren't your road jockeys enough, you've got to start picking up old strays? Can't trust one of them between the age of one and a hundred."

Kate, her oldest daughter, comes in and wrinkles her nose at the martini pitcher. "You've been *drinking*," she says.

"Yeah," says Thena. "Call Alcoholics Anonymous. Call the social welfare department. Call your father and tell him to come over quick, so he can catch me drunk and lower my support payments."

Kate giggles. "Oh, Mother."

"Huh. The moral majority strikes again. My kids monitor my alcohol consumption. Take my advice, Arachne, never have a kid. I've learned the hard way."

"Is Thomas coming over?" asks Kate sweetly.

"Yes," says Thena. "Go curl your hair and put on high heels. You need the practice."

Only Thena gets the whole truth. For what is a traveler without a confidante? It is impossible to fictionalize a life without someone to oversee the journey. And Thena is the perfect confidante, discreet if opinionated. She is trustworthy, reliable. She has always watched with a clear eye and a bitter disregard for tender feelings, even her own.

Thena is a coincidence. If they had known, they might have looked each other over more carefully, hesitated. Almost certainly they would have hesitated. Arachne found Thena stridently aggressive; she found Arachne unformed and raw. Although they confess that they seized upon each other the day they met.

Arachne sits on the grimy, oil-smelling couch in the corner of the garage, pretending to read the newspaper while she waits for Angelo to lower the hood, to rub his hands on his ubiquitous rag, to shake his head as he walks to the cluttered table that serves as his office. And he scrawls indecipherable items down on his work order, shakes his head all the while he explains what he has done and why. Arachne trusts Angelo but she distrusts his world, territory forbidden to her. So she sits like a supplicant on the edge of the vile green couch, smelling rubber and oil and metal and hearing the perforated hiss of air. She surveys the scuffed toes of her sneakers, bends her head over a smudged newspaper. She is tolerated but not welcome, not like the briefcase-carrying men who come at five, who clap the mechanics on the back and shout questions above the roar and clang. They are led to their cars like conquerors.

Arachne scowls and crosses her legs. Angelo is still

working on the Mercedes; she can see a determined elbow. She will have to wait. She was lucky to find him here in Calgary, although he's not as good as George.

But she senses the undertow when the woman slams the rickety door and stands belligerently two steps inside the garage. The men see her but continue to clank wrenches, protected by the cars they are working on.

She waits for acknowledgement. Arachne skims her, then rattles her newspaper. At least she knows the ritual. If you're a woman, you wait until they notice you.

The woman shifts her feet and shouts, "Hey!" but no one moves and she waits, holding her purse against her side and looking more and more uncomfortable. Finally she taps her way across the oil-stained concrete floor to the couch, a journey which all the mechanics watch from over fenders and under lifted hoods.

She sinks down beside Arachne, stretching her legs straight out as if her feet hurt. Then she unstraps her shoes and drops them with a clatter to the floor, folds her hands over her small, rotund belly and wriggles her toes.

"Well," she says, "how long does it take before they deign to notice you?"

"Depends. Just when you think you're one of the boys, they figure they should put you in your place."

The woman grimaces. "They better be good. A man I know told me to come here, but he's kinda stupid."

Arachne looks around nervously. Mechanics, she has discovered, have remarkably sharp hearing. If you criticize them, they take quiet revenge, make you wait months for an appointment, scratch your paint, sit on your car seats without covering them. Angelo intimidates her, but she has learned that he loves the Mercedes, that's how she gets what she wants.

"This is a good shop."

The woman sighs. "I'm trying to be hopeful but I know

what they're going to tell me. 'Forget it.' "

"Forget it?"

"The car. Finished. Kaput. Heap of junk." She slides open a package of cigarettes and reaches for the tin ashtray. "The last legacy of my dear departed husband." She snaps a lighter at the end of the cigarette as if she were finalizing him. "My ex-husband," she corrects herself. "Two houses and two cars and two kids. I get the house that needs a new roof, he gets the house that has double-glazed windows. I get the old 'reliable' car and he kindly takes the gas-eater – it's only two years old. I get the kids, he gets a new wife. It's a classic."

Arachne is not astonished. She has heard perhaps a dozen variations on this lament, some of them from people who have included the particulars of a sex life in extremis.

But the woman laughs and wrinkles her nose. "Well," she says with some relish, "I'm glad to be rid of *him*. Even if I'm stuck with the blue monster. I'll probably have to buy a new car."

A survivor, thinks Arachne. Mousy hair, fine nets at the corners of her eyes, but enough wit to look forward to a new car, enough confidence to take off her shoes in a garage.

"Which one is yours?"

Arachne points.

The woman raises her eyebrows and turns to look at her. "You drive that?" She takes in Arachne's jeans, her aging jacket.

"No, it drives me."

The woman squints at the car. "What is it?"

"A 1959 Mercedes."

"Where did you find it?"

"Someone gave it to me."

"Whew. Some present."

Arachne sees the Mercedes as she must, a pompous car

that is old but still awesome in its fatness. Even now there are times she is convinced that when she tries the door, it won't open, when she turns the key in the ignition, it won't start, she will be hauled off by the police as a car thief.

Gabriel's car, parked in front of the house when she came home from school. It always made the boys hesitate and edge by slowly, so that Arachne learned early the car was magic, it had its own protection. Gabriel would be inside, talking to Lanie. Arachne never caught them at anything else. Not that she even thought about it. What could he want with Lanie, sad as he was, with his crumpled face and brush-like moustache, the nervous way he sat on the edge of his chair?

Arachne did not take part in the worshipful homage paid to the car. It was just a car. She would never have one, she would always have to rely on public transport. She thought the way the boys eyed it was dangerous. To be so openly longing was to ask for disappointment. And when the gang hooted approval, she scowled. "Cut it," she said, so that they looked at her sidelong. Only later did it occur to her that the car consolidated her command. It impressed them. And her disregard for it impressed them even more.

She liked Gabriel. He paid attention to her. When she slouched in, he sat up. Always dressed in dark blue with a dazzling shirt and a narrow tie. Of course, Arachne did not know the significance of the way his clothes were cut, but she knew that against the background of the house, Gabriel looked as alien as any orchid in the Arctic. He came from somewhere else.

She knew he loved her, loved her the way that no one had ever loved her. He never brought her a present, he never gave her money. He did not touch her or kiss her, give her advice or ask her what she was doing. He was grave and courteous, even distant. But he loved her. When she banged the door and scuffed into the house, she could feel his love. But they kept it a secret.

Arachne flung a torn textbook to the couch and stomped through to her bedroom. "Hi, Gabriel."

"Hello, Arachne." She appreciated his reserve.

When Gabriel was there, Lanie made a point of showing motherly concern. "Hang up your coat. Gabriel, can't you persuade her that it's not lady-like for a girl to wear a leather motorcycle jacket?"

Gabriel didn't care if she was lady-like or not. Gabriel didn't ask what grade she was in now, whether she would pass or fail. Gabriel didn't ask her what she was planning to do with her life. Yet she knew that his silent presence protected her.

When he died, suddenly, stepping out of the car one sunny May morning into a heart attack, curled with death on the sidewalk, she was bereft. Gabriel could not die, he had no right to abandon her.

"He's left *you* the car," said Lanie, leaking blue eye shadow. "All those years I put up with him mooning around, coming to me for advice, and what do I get out of it? Nothing. Zippo. His wife won't even tell me he's dead."

"You filthy sleaze. You were nice to him all this time because you wanted his money."

"I did not," said Lanie hotly. "Just a token would of been nice, just a remembrance for all the afternoons I wasted listenin' to him."

Arachne was nineteen and strong and angry. She kicked over a chair and while it was still bouncing, swept a lamp off the table with her arm. She screamed at Toto. "Why don't you kill her? Don't you know why he hung around? He used to come before I was born! Are you sure he's not my father? She was probably screwing him."

Toto broke her arm, a crunch Arachne did not even feel. He threw her onto the sidewalk, slammed the door and locked it. Arachne was only repeating a story she had always heard, how Gabriel would come over and talk about her before she was born, how he would watch Lanie. Gloat over her, she said. But Arachne had given it a different slant.

When she hit the sidewalk, Arachne knew she had left home. She would not live with Toto and Lanie again. She limped to a phone booth and called her probation officer.

## Legacy

Arachne got a job as a night cashier at a gas station. The probation officer helped her find an apartment.

The lawyer told her that she could pick up the car at Gabriel's home; his wife wanted to meet her. Arachne couldn't drive. She asked Mitch, the least raucous member of the gang, to come along.

It took them an hour to get there on the bus, and when they found the number of the gate on Southwest Marine Drive, Mitch looked up at it doubtfully. "Geez, looks like this is the place."

Arachne was not dressed up; she had nothing to dress up in, but even if she had, she would have felt it was against her principles. Gabriel liked her the way she was.

They walked up the curved gravel drive to the front door and pushed a button which rang faint chimes inside. The door was opened by a young woman, a maid, but Arachne had never seen a maid in her life and so she stuck out her hand. "Hello, I'm Arachne Manteia. You must be Gabriel's wife."

The maid stared at her. "You want to speak with Mrs. Greenberg?"

Arachne nodded.

Mrs. Greenberg was a pinched woman who looked as though she dieted too much. She did not seem surprised at Arachne, but she was overtly contemptuous. In a very formal sitting room she informed Arachne that according to her late husband's wishes as expressed in his will, Arachne Manteia was to have his 1959 Mercedes Type 300. The registration had been officially changed and the insurance canceled. Arachne would have to get plates and insure it herself. If she had any questions she could contact the lawyer.

Arachne did not know then why he left it to her, a monolithic black boat with a high front grill, this six-cylinder, overhead cam, inline, water-cooled, fuel-injected, four-speed ticket to flight, but now she does.

The woman has fired another cigarette and is staring at her discarded shoes. A wrench clanks against the floor, a tire bounces, the hydraulic lift squeals.

Arachne turns and says, "When I got this car, I didn't know what to do with it. Imagine, I didn't even know how to drive. A friend of mine took me to a parking lot and taught me everything in one afternoon. The next day I got my license."

She stops abruptly, feeling she has said too much, but Angelo rescues her, scuffs over, rubbing his palms on his oil-darkened overalls.

"It's ready," he says to Arachne. And turns to the woman. "Yours'll go for a while, but it's just about had it. Next winter..." He shrugs, refusing to be responsible for Alberta temperatures.

The woman looks up at him. Then she straps on her shoes and stands up. "How much will you give me for it?"

Angelo steps back. "I don't want it."

"Come on, what's it worth?"

He shrugs. "Three, four hundred dollars."

"You give me two hundred and we'll call it even."

"But I don't want that old wreck."

"You can use it for parts," says the woman.

As Arachne drives away, she sees the woman walking stiffly down the street. She thinks of offering her a ride, but remembers Thomas making supper and decides not to stop. Under her hands the wheel is a comfort. She weaves through congested evening traffic, thinking of Gabriel.

And she has found Thena, although a garage named Venice Imports is an unlikely place for confidantes to meet. But Arachne only likes women who care about cars as much as she does anyway.

## *Traveling to travel*

In that first year with Thomas, Arachne is happy. She drives the Number 10 bus, alternating shifts, working overtime if Thomas is out of town, going home impatiently if he's in. She never imagined happiness as normal. Thomas has polished her rough edges; she has learned how to dress and eat, how to talk and walk. Her street swagger is gone. The only time she lets the old self out is naked in bed with Thomas, but they are both satisfied, have adapted to each other as well as their differences allow. They have become best friends.

Even driving a bus is more agreeable here. The passengers are quieter, less anarchic, less likely to shout or throw up. Perhaps the cold interferes with human contact, a relief for her, even though the first few months icy drafts penetrate her feet and she can hardly feel the pedals by the end of her shift. But she's lasted the winter, survived. It isn't nearly as bad as the legends. She has even survived the Telfers, won their cautious liking. For the first time in her life, Arachne dares to feel secure.

From Calgary roads spider over the prairie. Arachne pores over Thomas' maps, the lines enticing her to quest beyond the city's radius. She gets into the car and sets the bonnet toward the sun. She is learning travel, the pace and progression of journey, the multifarious seduction of

163

movement. She returns to Thomas vibrating at a pitch that he can take into his hands and drink. He is the author of those maps but he has never known their ultimate affirmation, the consummation of the pact between traveler and traveled. He only draws them; she traces them for him, leaving the pen-line of her passing.

Arachne travels to travel. Her only paradox is arriving somewhere, her only solution is to leave for somewhere else. Still, she returns to Thomas. The maps he draws and colors that year are unimaginably beautiful, while Arachne travels a smorgasbord of roads, turning corners at a whim, seeding the car's stately body with prairie dust.

The day that Arachne takes highway 21 north to Three Hills and Trochu, Delbourne and Alix is so precisely June that she is drawn into a canvas; now the road curves this way, now that. She debates going east toward Stettler and Coronation, but chooses to continue to Bashaw, and then turns off on a twisting gravel road that follows the north side of Buffalo Lake. When she hits a railroad track, she turns again, north. She has never been so deep in country, the parkland patched with poplar and willow, rounded by sloughs, divided by barbed wire. This world to her eyes seems mournfully gothic. The towns are one-street false-fronts with a few adjunctive houses crouching under water towers, but between their self-abuse she can pace the railway and the river north. Donalda makes Arachne think of vanilla, Meeting Creek is picturesque and abashed at the bottom of its valley, and Edberg appears with jackrabbit alertness after a low rise. Some prosperity here, one street is oiled. Arachne parks in front of the hotel. She would like a beer to bead the dust in her throat. But the red-painted hotel bar door is locked, the explanation, "Closed today for school picnic." The store too is closed, its windows opaque.

Arachne drives east past the graveyard, a tattered graveyard full of weeds and unexpected deaths, and sees far beyond a patch of water. School picnics are always at the lake. She swings the car onto the clefted road that leads down to the Battle River valley.

She never had a school picnic. Raki celebrated the end of school by stealing hubcaps that she sold to a slightly older fence. Her summers were spent delivering fliers, collecting bottles, handing out Lanie's leaflets:

LANIE:
READER AND ADVISOR
TEACUP – CARD – PALM
Lanie can and will help all who come with
love – marriage – health – business.
Lanie will make no promise she cannot keep.
All readings private and confidential in her own home.
324-1053

Raki could not compare notes on longing, could not match what she wanted with what she was able to get hold of. How did she celebrate the end of school, not having to sit within the prison of blind-drawn windows, while outside the city hummed green? Arachne cannot remember. What she chooses to remember are not the ends of things, inevitable disappointment, but the beginnings, while they still contained anticipation.

School proved to be bigger but more restrictive than home. The desk cramped her knees and the seat was hard. She could not stand up and walk about, could not leave the room when she felt like it. This was prison, hemmed in by a teacher's voice more insistent than Lanie's, a smudged and blue-lined page, a thick red pencil. She was not even allowed to look out of the window, and in the morning the teacher inspected her fingernails. That was when Arachne learned to lie. Did you brush your teeth this morning? Did you eat breakfast? Did you do your arithmetic? The only things she could be caught on were those which exacted evidence, like the arithmetic. It was then she decided that the only reliable things in the world are tangible.

School's compensation was that Arachne met other kids, and snotface Mitch became a derisive but useful companion. His vocabulary of abuse was larger than hers, and his knowledge of the neighborhood more intricate. He revealed possibilities that Arachne was unaware of – the garbage behind the Children's Hospital that sometimes yielded syringes and needles, how to get pennies for pop bottles collected door to door. If there was any knowledge to be gained, Arachne got it from him.

## At the Battle River

So why, given the fact that she remembers school as relentless captivity, does she follow the Edberg school picnic, turn the car down the winding road that leads to the Battle River? The barbed-wire gate of the pasture beside the river road sags, a hand-lettered sign stuck to a post — "picnic" — and an arrow. Arachne drives through, leaves the gate open behind her and follows the track over the rough grassland to the trees that she sees doubled into a fold of the valley. Has living with Thomas made her sentimental, lecherous for scenery that until now she has abjured, turned a black leather shoulder to? A school picnic implies teachers and children, baseball and sack races, mothers who compare their potluck contributions, fathers who sidle behind a bus for a drink. Is it just Arachne's perverse curiosity, does she want to see that particular bend in the river as it is drawn on her map?

Children finger her windows, bounce on the leather upholstery, test the car's knobs. Even before she pulls up, they have taken over. Arachne has some difficulty getting them out, rolling up the windows and locking the doors. Even then they hang over it. "Iz this yer car?"

She wonders what she's doing here, what can she want with a picnic of rural Albertans, but when one of them pipes, "Are you Johnny's aunt?" she says, "Yes, where's Johnny?"

167

"He's hunting cactuses to put on the bus-driver's seat." Even though he gives them gum at Christmas and Easter, they'll put cactuses on the bus-driver's seat just to see the look on his face, to hear him say, "*Jesus*," when he jumps up.

Arachne joins the line of people heaping food onto paper plates. This is a community picnic, everyone is welcome. Someone will yell to Johnny, "Hey, your aunt's here," and he will continue wading in the muddy river, he will feel the pricking cactuses in his pocket, ready for their subversion, and he will say, "Yeah?" Later he will ask someone, "You seen my aunt?" because he will want to show her the cactuses, what fine ones he's found, and a kid will wave his hand and say, "Yeah, she's over there," and Johnny never will find her.

Arachne eats her picnic lunch with the bus drivers, who are discussing the new buses they expect to get next year if the damn county comes through with its promises, then she wanders off to look at the river, brown water waving its path to join the North Saskatchewan. Up the bank the softball game is starting; she hears cheers and scattered clapping. The sentiment is always that the teachers, those tyrants, must lose, and so they do their best to win.

She swishes through the long grass, the drone of heat there beside the bronze water, its silent movement. She imagines the way it looks on Thomas' map, a crinkle and then a bend curving in on itself, the oxbows so deceptive, curls cutting their own path shorter. She comes upon a clump of willows and beating through them, finds a heap of abandoned clothes.

Her first impulse is to hide them, but she knows that would be unforgivable, some naked person searching these willows, swatting mosquitoes. Ducking back into the trees, she sees a sleek head emerge from the water, a white body, back, bum, legs somersaulting. A woman is swimming alone and seal-like, singing, caroling over the brown surface of the water, stolen away from the picnic and her children's whining demands, splashing in her own afternoon.

Repelled by the squelchy bottom, she wrinkles her nose as she wades out of the water, her big-breasted body streaming. Arachne begins to retreat, but the woman waves cheerfully. "The water's fine. Coming in?" She walks toward Arachne, turning her face into the sun, lifting her arms and shoulders to its heat, her short strong legs and rotund belly making her look jolly and sensual, a woman who loves food. She picks up the T-shirt that lies on top but makes no move to put it on. Instead, she towels at her hair. "You show up everywhere," she says.

Arachne looks at her, startled.

The woman laughs. "You're the one with the big fat car."

Arachne remembers – Angelo's, the woman who badgered him into buying her old heap. "What are you doing here?"

"I could say the same to you. But at least I know how you got here."

"How did you get here?"

"Train," says the woman, stepping into her underpants. "Brought the kids up to spend a few weeks with their cousins, get them out of the city, away from all this boy and clothes stuff. They can kiss horses for a while." She zips her slacks and looks up at Arachne. "You got any kids?"

"No."

"Huh, lucky. Little buggers drive me nuts. Glad to get rid of them." She dresses as though she goes skinny-dipping every day, as though she and Arachne are friends. Arachne is wary. She's not sure whether to join or abandon this woman.

The woman carries her sneakers, trying to avoid stones

as she walks. "Hey, are you going back to Calgary tonight? I'd really like a ride home. I wouldn't have to wait for the train in the morning and I could say good-bye to the little buggers right now."

Arachne doesn't want her. She was looking forward to a long sweet drive, the car humming, and she is not sure why she agrees to take the woman. She will have to listen to her all the way, two and a half hours at least.

They plod back to the sporadic yammer of the softball game, the children fighting behind the backstop, the teachers trying to quell their authority this last day before they slide their drawers shut on lesson plans and report cards. Everyone is jubilant, full of picnic food, of softball, of rye whiskey, of the smell of the brown river, the thought of cactuses and bus drivers. The softball game is in full swing. The batter (the new high school teacher whom all the girls are trying to seduce, the one who gets pregnant first will marry him; they wrestle him to the ground behind the curling rink, they attack him in the back seats of cars, they sneak up behind him in the post office) has just hit a high fly which the outfielder catches, so that those cheering for the teachers groan and most of the kids hanging on the backstop wire (a backstop and bleachers here, in a cow pasture beside the Battle River?) scream with wild and ecstatic glee. It is that kind of day, passionate and dirty. Fathers and mothers call each other names, kids call each other names, kids call their teachers names. Behind the backstop two fathers are slugging each other while their wives tug at them from behind. "Stop it, stop it." But the men are enjoying themselves and they punch cheerfully, licking blood from their upper lips. Far up the river's opposite side a group of teenagers is smoking dope, secure in their distance. In a fold of the hoodoo'd valley Johnny and his friends have found a bed of cactuses, he takes them all, he can put them on *all* the bus-drivers' seats, his father's car seat, he will have his revenge. He stuffs his pockets full, sticking himself; he needs something to carry them with, so he takes off his shirt and puts the cactuses in, ties it like a bundle. They will be back in time for ice cream, Loretta from the Creamery, and they hurry back along the river, only stopping to chase a garter snake, and once more when they stumble on a couple necking in a light-dappled poplar clearing. They sneak behind the trees until they can see. It's Tom and — hey, they can see her tits — it's Enid, she's fast, she'll do anything. They shiver with delight, maybe they will see them doing it, but Enid isn't having any of that, so they burst out of the trees and run through the clearing whooping while Enid clutches her blouse. They race toward the ball game yelling, "Ice cream, ice cream," and the game dissolves, everyone runs for the picnic tables, Loretta with the brown tubs of ice cream in her van and the silver of her dipper flashing. The only ones left are a clump of serious-faced Mennonites off to one side, who are not supposed to run for ice cream, although they may watch the violence of the ball game, and the woman, who yells at Arachne, "Let's go!"

The car is grubbied, mirrors crooked and a dent on the hood where a heavy child sat; the aerial is hung with a garland of dandelions, the grill is spattered with bugs. But deserted. Everyone is licking ice cream, gathering dishes, waiting for the bus driver to sit on a cactus, trying to lose their report card so they won't be whipped for failing, trying to find Johnny's report card to see if he passed or failed. Arachne and Thena drive away quietly, ahead of the pack, ahead of the village of Edberg.

"You haven't told me what *you're* doing up here," says Thena.

"I just drive around the country. I ran into that carnival."

How can she explain her inordinate lust to drive, to cover road miles, to use up gas? There is no map for longing.

## Advice

She may never be able to explain her lust for driving to
Thena, but on that first journey back through the Lacombe
parkland and south, they become friends, relating their
lives while they eye each other and circle each other and
sniff each other.

Thena makes the cautious advances. Arachne has never
had a woman friend, never liked women or trusted them.
Arachne's companions, confreres, have always been males.
Women stay away from her. She is too tough, too dangerous.

No wonder she hesitates at Thena's ubiquity. Yet she
likes the chubby little woman, her mousy hair, her sardonic
tongue. When she drops her off in front of a house in
north Calgary, she hears her own voice saying, "If you
want help looking for a new car, I could . . ." Thena
wants to replace the clunker.

Arachne finds Thomas in his blue room. She wraps
her dirty arms around his neck and lets him swing her
onto his lap, and while he kisses her, she recounts her
day at the Edberg school picnic. And lying under his
propped elbows on the floor, after he has made her sweaty
body sweatier, she says, "I met a strange woman."

"Stranger than you?"

"At least as bad."

172

It is no surprise that a week later they are tooling down Crowchild Trail in a new Firebird, Thena perched behind the wheel and Arachne strapped into the passenger seat. Thena drives like a nut, whipping in and out of traffic, cutting off signaling buses. She is every bus-driver's nightmare, which Arachne points out to her. Thena whoops with pleasure.

"Well," she says to Arachne as they spin back to the dealer, "what do you think?"

"Don't you think this is a little gauche for you?"

"All the better. I need something like this. Make my ex drop his eyeballs."

The car seals their kinship, their reciprocity. They disparage each other, they scream at each other, they are brutally honest with each other. And so it is that Thena can tell Arachne she is crazy. She is right, oh yes, she is always right. She is right about the road jockeys becoming addictive, she is right about Arachne's job selling underwear, she is right about Thomas, and she is determined to be right about all men, those bastards. Her anger, her determination to oust them from her life, have confined her to voyeurism. And so she watches Arachne, meddles.

And, after all, Thomas encouraged Arachne to apply for the job with Ladies' Comfort, suggested that it would give her a reason to drive to all those small towns she's so interested in, enable her to follow the webbed maps she's so fascinated by. That did it. Arachne is fine as long as she drives the bus. She behaves herself. Thomas has reformed her, turned her from street urchin into a passably respectable – not lady, Arachne will never be a lady – but person. He has polished her, turned her between his hands like an alabaster bowl. He's no fool. He isn't deceived. He knows about the road jockeys, Arachne's indiscretions. He is not stupid but patient. He is going to stay her Apocryphal lover, provide her with an ultimate map. He is willing to bide his time, to put up with infidelity, and he will win in the end, through sheer tolerance. When she is unfaithful, he loves her harder, with persistent tenderness.

Thena's advice to him would be to lock Arachne up. She knew all along that traveling around the country selling underwear was asking for trouble. She knows Arachne's proclivities. Oh, she would never betray Arachne, run to Thomas and tell him, but she worries. She knows that Arachne is not likely to find another man who loves her the way that Thomas does, and having gone without that love herself, she knows how much it's worth.

When Arachne first experiments with road jockeys about a year after she begins working for Ladies' Comfort, Thena is aghast, "Just tell me," she demands, "why this is necessary. Is Thomas a bad lover?"

"No, he's a wonderful lover."

"Then why?"

"It's a game, something to do."

"That's immoral."

Arachne makes a face. "My behavior has some bearing on the greater good of mankind?"

"No, but at least you could try."

"Why? The whole world is full of lies. Lies are the world. If everyone were pure and truthful, society would collapse."

"That's no excuse."

"Look, Thena, I can't help it, I just get this itch. It's something for me to do on the road."

"What about Thomas?"

"Thomas knows I'm no saint. Besides, I always come back. And those guys make him look good by comparison."

"You're a slut," says Thena.

Arachne's face twists a little. "The fact is, I was raised as one. Try growing up the way I did and you'd be thankful just to survive. I'm happy with Thomas but I'm not used to things coming to me so easily. If I gamble a little, maybe I'll deserve him more."

"That's the stupidest rationalization I've ever heard. You'll lose him."

"He's not mine to lose."

So Thena puts up with Arachne's bad behavior, saying only, "Don't come to me if you get knocked up or if you get a dose."

Arachne grins. "You'd think that was justice. Don't worry, I'm careful."

But is she careful enough?

## Constellations

Arachne traverses the prairie and parkland with a persistence that should make her ache with lust, would usually have her combing the streets for potential relief, a cowboy, a barber, a veterinarian. But she goes home to Calgary every night, seems to take refuge in Thomas, who is working on an elaborate topographic map of the Rocky Mountain trench, who lives in a conglomeration of India ink and iridescent colors. He is taking an astronomy course; he wants to do celestial maps.

Arachne sits in the big chair listing her orders while his hand under the circle of light draws the sweep of a hill, the tortuosity of a river. When it is truly dark, they study the sky, and he names the constellations for her: Cassiopeia, Orion, Andromeda, Corvus, Perseus, Ursa Major, Monoceros, Gemini, Cygnus, Caela, Lyra, Ophiuchus. She tilts her head back and follows the path of his litany with sleepy peace.

She had always wanted a telescope, knew she could divine a world different from the one she was stuck in, the key on a string around her neck, the itchy woolen socks inside her rubber boots, her chapped knuckles and runny nose. The stars were far beyond the sodden, bleary streets she scuffed through.

She sometimes woke to look up at the faint gray cobwebs

swaying in the ceiling's corners and imagined what it would be like if she could have everything she wanted. But she knew, the only way to get anything was to go after it herself.

The day that she saw an ad in the paper for newspaper routes was the day she thought she had found a solution. She begged bus fare from Lanie, and rode downtown to the office to stand in line with a bunch of knowing little boys. When she got up to the desk, the man behind it looked at her.

"How old are you?"

"Eleven." She was lying.

"You're a girl."

Arachne nodded.

"Sorry, you have to be a boy and at least twelve years old." He waved her away. "Next."

Arachne scowled. What difference did it make? She could deliver papers as good as any of them.

At supper Toto looked at her closed face, her rebellious lower lip. "What's the matter?"

For the first time in years, Arachne began to cry.

"Jesus, what's the matter?"

She told him, between sniffles, how if she had a paper route she could save up for a telescope.

"Hell," said Toto. "You can get a paper route. Don't tell 'em you're ten, say you're twelve."

"They won't believe me."

"I'll come with you. They'll believe me."

Arachne sniffed. "I still look like a girl."

"We can fix that."

"Oh no, you don't," said Lanie. "She looks horrible enough already. What are you gonna do, give her a brushcut?"

Arachne giggled.

"What does she need a paper route for anyway? She'll

just spend the money on comics and junk."

"Everyone will tease you," said Toto solemnly, ignoring Lanie.

"I don't care."

He got an afternoon off work and took her to his barber, who cut her hair short at the sides with a cowlick in front. When the barber showed her the mirror, Arachne laughed with pleasure. She could not stop looking at herself, turning her head this way and that.

"All right," Toto said on the way downtown. "You're a boy and you're twelve years old, got it?"

"What's my name?"

"Raki. Who the hell knows the difference?"

They went up to the same man behind the same desk and ten minutes later Arachne had a paper route six blocks away from home.

Every night after school Arachne picked up her papers, put them in the canvas sack slung over her shoulder and, staggering under the weight, distributed them door to door.

She saved the money, counting and re-counting it when she made her collections. She kept it knotted in a woolen sock stuffed down the front of her pants or in her pocket. She had a system, trading her change for dollar bills, her dollar bills for fives, her fives for tens, her tens for a twenty. She could reach into her pocket, feel the rough wool of the sock and know what it held.

By December she had almost forty dollars. On the last day of school before the holidays, she ran home to do her route. It was drizzling, some of the papers were wet, heavier than ever, but she finished and trudged home thinking about the stars wheeling above the overhung clouds.

"Hey, kid, where you going?"

Another kid, skinny but bigger than her, not someone from her school.

"Leggo, I'm goin' home."

"Let's see you try."

"What d'ya want?" Arachne tried to shake herself loose, but he was tenacious, dirty, he twisted her arm behind her back.

"What d'ya got?"

"Nothing," said Arachne, fighting to get away.

"What's your rush?" He slapped her lightly, meaningfully, on the ear. "Just show me your pockets."

The money was stuffed inside her pants, so Arachne showed him her pockets, empty except for a bit of string and a bubblegum jawbreaker, which he popped in his mouth. She almost broke away from him then, but he grabbed her again.

"Wait a minute, wait a minute, where d'ya think you're going? That's not all. Let's see what else you got."

"Nothing," said Arachne. "Lemme go, I'll scream."

"Go ahead, nobody cares."

He tore at the string around her neck but when he discovered it was a key, he flung it back against her chest. "Street rat," he said scornfully. "There ain't anybody at home."

He might have let her go then if Arachne had been less frantic, but her urgency betrayed her. He held her the way a dog holds a large rat, twisting her arm, poking at her back and her coat and her stomach.

"Hey, what's this?" His fingers found the lump of sock under her clothes.

Arachne bit, kicked, scratched, almost tore her arm out of its socket. They went down, rolling in the alley, a scramble of teeth and knees. But he was too big. She wound up flat on her back in the wet gravel with him sitting on her stomach.

"You little creep," he said, dribbling spit on her. And he bounced on her chest so she gasped. "What d'ya got in your pants?"

"Lemme alone."

It was hard work but he was enjoying himself. "After

I see . . ." and he reached for her waistband again.

Once more she exploded, a ball of animal, willing to claw his eyes out, bite his hand off. Surprised, he did the only thing possible to overwhelm her. He banged her head against the cement of the alley, banged it hard, cracked her skull against the stone and knocked her cold.

When Arachne came to, she was lying in the alley. Her pants were half undone. Her sock was gone. She lay there for a moment, looking up into the viscous darkness, the rain thinning the blood that seeped from her head. Clouds hid the stars. This then was life. It would never change.

Now she remembers her life before Thomas as one long night full of rain. Here, in the high, clear air of Calgary, the stars seem closer, hot with light. And as his voice counts worlds they cannot see, as his hand reshapes her skin, Arachne wants for nothing but does not dare believe that this will last.

*Notebook on a missing person*

You see, it is easy to find out about Arachne's past, only too easy. She has a record, after all. And if there's anything missing, Lanie will fill in the spaces. She likes nothing better.

It's the present you're after, maybe even the future. With a past like that, what chance does she have? For here you are, taking stock of her life, and if eternity is comprised of all moments gathered into one, where can you put Arachne now, at what point in that momentum will she stop?

## Swath

When Arachne discovers the old man sitting on the front seat of the Mercedes one morning, she does feel a quick touch of guilt. She has forgotten him, although she wakes to the copper dancers every day.

He sits facing forward, erect and unblinking, as though waiting for a driver. She opens the passenger door, leans in toward him.

"Josef, what are you doing here? How did you get into the car?"

"You do not come."

"I'm sorry . . . It's the busiest time of year."

"You forget me." His mouth is stern but his hands tremble.

She touches his shoulder. "I'm sorry. Look would you like to come with me today? I'm only doing one town."

His bright head nods.

"We can stop by your house and ask your daughter."

"No ask. I come."

"Won't she be worried?"

He shrugs. "If I ask, she say no."

When Arachne gets behind the wheel, he pokes his cane into the back, stretches his shanks wide on the black leather seat. The car turns south.

It is the end of November, a fall tortured by its own

brilliance, the great plain unrolling itself in an orgy of gold. The sky's bowl, the diagramed fields, even the Rockies shimmer gold. Arachne is dizzy with it, the sun that should have been chilled by November swamping her with warmth, a steady drone of combines undertoning the days with the sweet dust of grain chaff hanging over all, a smell so extravagantly heavy it seems dispersed by another deity, drifted down from an era when bare-legged women tossed baskets of wheat against the sky to winnow grain from chaff. The busied combines, heat and heaviness swarm the car; it seems to take forever to reach Nanton. When the Lancaster Bomber monument finally appears, they are both drowsy. Arachne pulls up in front of the Red and White. "Want to come in?"

"I wait."

She sells two dozen Modesty and a dozen bikini prints after a haggle over Ladies' bulk markdown. When she comes out, his silver head is stretched back against the seat; breath whistles through his open mouth. She considers, then goes back into the store and buys some apples, cheese, juice and crackers. When she opens the car door, he sits erect, blinking, his eyes hooded and narrow, an evil magician's.

They drive east then, the combines circling with them until the gold sinks into indigo and vermilion and they stop to chew apples beside a grassy slough.

"We should find a skull," he says.

"Here? There is no graveyard."

"No need."

"We'd have to fight over it."

"You fight."

"I've given up."

The sky darkens and overhead appears a sliver of moon so thin it seems glass. "Fight, angry, good for people. Makes change."

186

She feels his fingers on the sleeve of her blouse.

She stands, takes his hand. "Come."

They walk through a wide, fragrant field, the thick rows of winnowed straw circling themselves inward. In the last light Arachne runs ahead jumping the swath, her legs flash pale below the lift and flare of her skirt.

She heads toward the field's far corner and he follows, stumping his cane through the stubble that pricks his ankles. When he reaches her, it is suddenly dark; they are mere shapes against darkness. His cane drops and they stand holding each other, her arms against his back and her head tilted up to his. They stand leg-braced together in the perfumed field and the cooling night with time to hold a hand against a circle of skin, to curious shape and texture. His skin is worn, rough. He is unused to touch, almost recoils when her hand reaches under his shirt, when she brushes across the hair on his chest, his nipples. But when they lie down and he presses himself against her, the straw is thick and warm, a sky-arched bed that holds them close to the ground. They lie side by side, only the shapes of their faces clear, although they recognize each other in their finger-stumbling bodies. She would like to stare into his eyes, know him, but he turns his head with a groan against her shoulder.

Arachne has had countless men, men tender and gentle, brutal and careless. With her good body she has taken them all, sucked pleasure from them despite their haste or ineptitude. And she has Thomas, who knows what she wants before she wants it. But this man is strangely wild; he calls her from her body despite the cane flung down in the stubble, his slack skin. They are thieves locked in the same cell, a man with too little and a woman with too much.

They have their hands on each other; their mouths too. She has never felt a mouth as hot and wide as his, the bones of a face against hers so insistent. Arachne is unprepared. When his suspenders are untangled and he slides into her, she arcs herself upward, digging him inside, animal and burrow. "Wait," he whispers against her ear, but she is already screaming, a hoarse long cry that he can feel columned from where he enters her all the way up her throat. He plunges his arms under her buttocks, but that only rushes them closer together.

Riding under his weight, the straw a cushion and above his head the moon spiked against the sky, Arachne is lifted beyond herself. They have not shed their clothes but they are searingly naked, shorn of all costume, all disguise, a man who has fled half the world and four score years, and a woman who wants more, more, always more, the broken halves of rebel and assassin whole. They reach beyond the touch of skin, beyond longing and desire. Disorder and dissent make order whole, give it reason. He's completed the act begun so long ago, passed on his insurgence with his hands, the two of them one piece of the universe observing itself.

Their bodies raw, cooling despite the warm straw, she brings her hand up to his face. It is wet. Arachne turns her head, the field drawn with poplars black lace against the feathered sky. "Look," she says, "the trees."

He raises his head from her shoulder. It is what you see at the edge of your eye before dying, black trees etching an autumn wind.

They stumble out of the field supporting each other. Inside the Mercedes they straighten, pull at their clothes, wipe a hand across their mouths, pick straw from their hair, his beard. And drive silently home, to the city's flaring light crouched on the horizon.

When they pull up in front of his house, the door is flung back immediately and his daughter pummels down the steps. She wrenches the car door open and hauls at

Josef's arm. "Where have you been? I've been frantic, I almost called the police." She glares at Arachne. "What do you think you're doing, taking him away? He's not well, you'll upset him for weeks."

Josef pokes his cane out the car door, thrusts it at her. "Anna, stop. Only a drive in the country."

"A drive in the country! While I'm sitting here chewing my knuckles and worrying, thinking you've fallen, you've had an accident!" She grips his arm as he steps from the car, then sticks her head inside and hisses, "I don't know who you are, but I don't want to see you around here again. Upsetting an old man. Leave him alone, you hear me!" She thumps the car door shut and with both hands clamped to his arm, leads Josef up the front walk.

Arachne looks after them. In the field he walked upright, uneven but quick. Now he shambles, bent and subdued under her iron love. She puts the car in gear and drives home to Thomas.

## Accidents of birth

It is a lush, heavy fall. Arachne circles out from Calgary, collecting her winter orders. Madden, Dogpound, Bottrell; Water Valley, Cremona, Elkon, Bergen, Harmattan, Westward Ho; Sundre, Bearberry, Garrington, Eagle Hill. Dozens and dozens of pastel pinks; boxes of white cotton briefs; hundreds of flavorful bikinis, hued and tinted and blushing, riotous and gaudy, their abbreviation suggestive. And the Midnight line, the solid black, the black lace, the black inset, see-through and opaque, demure and come hither.

Despite their profusion and number — it is a prosperous fall even with the dry summer — Arachne's orders are as neatly listed, as calm and systematic as ever. She does two or three towns a day, she jollies a store owner into ordering an extra half dozen of Modesty, she leaves behind a wash of satisfaction. When she has gone, with her samples and her order book, disappeared under the yellow leaves, the storekeeper rubs his hands in anticipation of a good winter, a generous Christmas. Strange that she is so good at this job. She has hardly demonstrated an aptitude for public relations.

She is herself puzzled at the persona who steps in, takes over, the mask that falls into place when she pushes open the myriad general-store doors. Is it the challenge of a role? Is it her love for disguise? Or a reversion to some innate gene that she does not know she has inherited, that of a bourgeois shopkeeper eager to do business, unctiously willing to bargain? There are moments, standing in a plain dress with black pumps, her hair combed, her nails clean, jotting down an order, when she does not believe that the body she inhabits is hers.

She remembers herself as a crude fifteen-year-old, the one girl in the gang, the leader, a position she kept only by being more daring than any of them, more obnoxious, reckless enough to make them uneasy, not sure if she wouldn't turn on them too. The boys she gathered around her were the misfits and discards of the other gangs, fat and squeaky, cross-eyed and retarded.

They did not know they were a gang. Arachne did not tell them, although she named them the Black Widows. And it did not take long before they looked to her for approval, ideas, before they fell in with her suggestions. After school Arachne threw her dog-eared books inside the door and strolled off for the Dutch café, knowing that the gang would be there, drinking coke, smoking.

Until one spring dusk, cutting across the park after an expedition to the dump to try and find stuff to sell, they met a gang that was the terror of the neighborhood, the Chinese gang, kids whose fathers owned grocery stores and laundries. It was exactly that time of night when boys are taunting and belligerent, they ache for a good fight before they have to go home.

The gang singled out Lee, their Chinese friend.

"Lee Wong. Wong Lee," the leader sang out. "What are you doing hanging around with a bunch of whiteys like this? Perverts and retards. Lee Wong, don't you have no sense?"

Lee shuffled his feet and scowled. The Chinese kids would not let him join their gang. His family were poor, recent immigrants from Hong Kong.

"Don't you got nothing to say?"

They faced each other, the Chinese kids graceful and superior, enjoying their game.

"Hey." The leader shoved Lee. "What kind of gang is this? Dumbbells, retards, cripples." He looked at them one by one, then he came to Arachne. "Girls."

In their humiliation they had forgotten Arachne. They only had time to see her streak forward, knock the leader to his knees. She held his head back by his hair, a double-bladed throwing knife she had stolen from an Army surplus store at his throat.

"Take it back," she said.

"What?" whined the boy.

"All of it. Then beat it, assholes," she said.

They muttered and scowled but finally turned and trailed across the field.

Then everyone wanted to join. New kids showed up at the Dutch café, bought them cigarettes, played the jukebox for them. They began to realize they belonged to the most feared gang in the neighborhood.

The gang deflected Arachne from the humiliations of growing up, from Lanie and Toto and a world that was not her oyster. It remained a clutch of swaggering city rats, too young to get a job, too old for childhood, all of them pimply-faced and squeaky voiced East-enders. But it provided her with a cover, an excuse. She was a chunky girl with greasy hair and sullen, wide-spaced green eyes, wearing a battered leather jacket, alert, watching. She would forget nothing. If she waited she would find her thief. She roamed the streets with her surly friends, gathering shards of knowledge like broken glass. And she looked for him, certain that she would recognize his crest of hair, his wall-eyed skinniness.

She was not surprised when she saw him; she knew he frequented the same failed future she did. It was in a poolroom on Granville. Arachne stood at the side and watched, recognized him without bothering to confirm if he belonged to his history. He didn't remember her. He'd robbed or beaten plenty of kids in the four years since.

She shucked the gang and waited outside, tailed him when he left. The next day she waited again, in the alley behind his walk-up, quietly patient. When six o'clock had gone and she knew he would be heading uptown again, she weighed the knotted woolen sock, its blunt heft, in her hand. There is no weapon so lethal as a sock full of pennies. It can kill a man if he's hit right.

When he came out of the apartment's back door, oblivious, cupping a match to his cigarette, she stationed herself behind the fence he had to pass. She had only one chance to hit him; and with all the windup of David's sling, she did, squarely behind the ear. The surprise on his face as he stumbled to the ground felt even sweeter to her than the thump of the sock.

She did not wait to see if he was alive or dead, did not even deign to take his wallet. She stepped over the smoldering cigarette that had rolled from his fingers and walked away, flushed and clear-eyed.

It is no wonder then that she stands in shoes she can hardly recognize, that she sometimes steps back, expecting disaster, her real self to emerge, bow, recapture her. She may have given up sneakers and leather jackets, cigarettes and street fights, but she is still Arachne, underneath it all she is still herself.

# Calling

Arachne goes to visit Josef. She parks down the street and walks to the house quickly, hoping she can duck around the back without his daughter spotting her. But she is there at the window, tight-mouthed and watching. The garage door stands open and through it she sees Josef bent above the block table, his back broad but shrunken, his legs thin within the loose trousers, blue suspenders over his shirt. She hesitates. There is something so powdery in his stance, so shaky that she cannot believe what they did in the field. He must have been powerful once; his frame juts through age. Now he seems immensely old, laborious and balanced attention evident in his shrunken buttocks, revealing lost strength and muscle.

"Hello."

He does not turn, does not hear, inhabiting that world of fierce aloneness the old seem to desire, almost pleasure in. The hammer follows its beat and he moves with the rise and fall of the steady mallet undulating through his posture.

She knocks on the open door.

He turns, seems confused, his face hooded in thought.

"It's me."

The deep creases in his forehead and cheeks do not change. He nods.

Arachne steps inside. Does he even remember her?

But he seems to. "Come, come." He bends again to his work. He is embellishing a large, thick sheet and the design that emerges is more repetitive and stylized than on her plaque. It is arabesque, a complicated chain of curlicues and triangles, ring within ring within ring to a center that pulls all together.

"Is a *demirlija*," he says.

"What's that?"

"Tray for table. Can be a table."

It is large, almost three feet across, with the inflexible revolution of a mantra.

"Is complicated, but so long, so dull. You repeat and repeat." His intricate chink does not stop; the twisting circle emerges from the chisel-like tool in his unerring hand.

"Do you make your living like this?"

"My daughter. I am a burden."

"She doesn't like you to have visitors."

"I have no visitors. Only you."

Arachne sits on his low stool. "Well, she sure gave me the evil eye through the window."

He chuckles. "I am trouble. Give things away. Copper, tools, expensive."

"You shouldn't have to work now."

"I am old. I should sit and think? It is for pleasure."

"The one you gave me — it's beautiful."

"You like?"

"Yes."

"Where did you put?"

Arachne cannot tell why she hesitates. "In the bedroom. . . . When I wake up, I can see it."

He nods.

"Why did you leave it for me?"

"You are like me. Stubborn. Black. At the grave you refuse to go."

He stops hammering, holds his hands out. Arachne's

body surges. She wants to wrap her arms around his frame, touch his knobbed and flaccid skin again. She bends to him, cradles his head against her belly.

"No," he says. "No kill."

"How old are you?"

His voice is muffled into her clothing. "Almost ninety."

"That's old."

"Yes. I should be dead." He puts his arms around her, tightly, holding her through flesh, into bone.

But when the woman bustles into the garage, they spring apart, guilty children.

"For shame, you hussy," she says. "You've upset him. He's not used to people. What do you want here anyway?"

"Anna, stop. She is my friend."

"Well, she didn't even come to the door."

"I'm sorry," Arachne says shamefacedly.

The woman ignores her. "You come in now, Papa. It's getting late." She puts a hand under his arm, raises him, turns him toward the door.

"You come again," he says to Arachne.

She shakes her head.

"Yes, you come."

Arachne follows them out of the door. The woman grips his arm as though he will topple without her, and Arachne remembers how he moved inside her. Now he seems helpless, diminished.

Outside, the woman releases him with a little shake as though to ensure he stay fixed, and turns to lock the garage door. His smile at Arachne is conspiring; he makes the motion of a man holding a woman in his arms.

Arachne's story makes Thena fierce with disapproval. "Road jockeys," she says, "are one thing, but planning to kidnap an old man?"

"I'm not planning to kidnap him."

"It sounds like it. I can hear it in your voice. Just

196

remember, old men are big babies. They whine, they slobber, they're incontinent. It's a natural outcome of the way they live their lives. Bastards."

"He's just an old guy who's attached to me."

"Huh. I wonder why. Have you screwed him yet?"

Arachne grins.

"I figured as much. Listen, all men are dangerous if you give them a chance, even old ones."

"What chance can I give him?"

"Humphh. You'll come up with something. I know you."

Truly, it is not the wanton in Arachne that attracts her to the old man. She saves that aspect of herself for ditches and granaries, motel rooms and bars. Josef's shabby frame has hooked her sympathy the same way Thomas hooked her trust. Sympathy, trust: Thena puts them all in the same garbage bag. To Arachne the difference is plain. She can lay herself in Thomas' arms with complete faith, while her sympathy for Josef is more like recognition, an indication of what she might become, a reminder of the ragged child that Raki was. What makes her feel his surrogate, his deputy? One genuflection over an unburied skull, a resurfaced bone? One quick tumble in a field? The dead are dead. Arachne is alive. And, for that matter, so is he.

## Another incursion between tomes

The fall holds its breath so long that when it lets go, winter is virulent. The roads are filthy and Arachne's trips are drawn-out expeditions. A sudden blizzard forces her to stay at a farm one night and another afternoon the Mercedes dies and she walks two miles in 30-below temperature. She swears to Thena that she will give up this hopeless occupation.

"I thought you loved that job," says Thena.

"When I took it you told me I was crazy."

"You are. But it suits you. You'll never get another job like it."

"I'm tired, I'm tired of grotty motel rooms and greasy restaurants and dangerous roads. I want a rest."

"Well, take a few weeks off. It's almost Christmas."

"What," mused Arachne, "if I had a baby?"

Thena rolls her eyes. "I'd report you to the child welfare authorities."

When she comes home from snow and ice and ditches, Thomas is there, plotting his maps in the room with the blue walls, measuring, checking the contours, the coordinates. To him everything is tactile. When Arachne returns from a trip, she does not have to tell him where she's been, he can read it in her body, in her expression. He waits for her. The blue walls do not press in on him, they are as good as sky. And he loves her. Arachne wakes

198

to find him looking down at her, his hand hovering above her face as if in blessing.

Her body waits for him. There's no mistaking that. He only has to put his hands on her to make her swim. Arachne tells him he could be just a pair of hands, he's so good with them. He maps her body with the same intricate detail he uses on geography. His hands and darkness, their most logical link the body.

The winter makes the stray cats in Sunnyside yowl. "Listen," says Arachne. "Listen."

Beyond the window a long vociferous cry that holds itself in violin.

Thomas stops moving under Arachne, turns his head. "What do you think they're doing?"

"Imitating us."

If so, it is a requiem of no small satisfaction.

Arachne finishes her circuit two weeks before Christmas. In January she'll begin gathering orders for spring stock, the flowered bikini season. She sleeps for two days out of sheer exhaustion, and says to Thena again, "God, I'm glad that's over. The storekeepers were vicious, they expect stuff delivered in two days. And they don't want to order enough in September, they're so damn cautious. It's only when they start running out that they've got to have a gross of black lacies for last-minute Christmas shopping. I can't stand another season like this one."

"You love it," says Thena. "Selling men the instruments of repression for women."

"What? Now underwear is repressive?"

"Well, you don't wear it. I think I'll stop too. Come the revolution we'll line all the black panties up against the wall and shoot them." She giggles; they are drinking rum and egg nog.

Arachne shakes her finger. "That's definitely a violent image. It won't do."

"Christmas makes me violent. What am I going to get

the little buggers that won't encourage every perversity they already have?"

"Books," says Arachne. "Let's go shopping. I need to buy Thomas a book of maps and I don't know how to read. You can help me find it."

So they take the Mercedes and end up on Seventeenth buying bagels. "There's a bookstore down the street," says Thena. "Let's try that."

Through its glass windows the store looks crowded, but they push the door open. A hushed and shifting crowd stands listening to a man read.

"Oh no," says Arachne, "not again. This happened the last time I got near books."

"Wait," hisses Thena, "isn't he that famous poet, the one who writes all those filthy poems about women?"

"I don't care," says Arachne. "Let's go."

But Thena has already wedged her way between attentive backs and Arachne can only say "Shit" under her breath. She settles her rear on a ledge of coffee-table books where she can stare out the window while she waits. The poet is reading poems all right. His voice rises into passion and desperation, descends to gloom and cynicism. Arachne squints at the shoppers passing on the sidewalk, their necks pulled into their collars, their breath hostile. She twitches, she digs the wax out of her ears, she looks through a book of antique cars and is almost ready to leave Thena there when the poet's voice stops and the standing audience applauds.

She finds Thena with a glass of wine in one hand and an oyster impaled on a toothpick in the other. "Let's go."

"Not yet. We showed up just in time. Have some wine."

"How come the wine?"

"Oh, they're launching this guy's new book of poetry. Got to spill some wine on it."

Arachne helps herself to a liberal glass and a chunk

of cheese. The poet is autographing his book for people, tossing back hair and witticisms while he scrawls his name on the flyleaf. He is approached with coyness, mostly by women, who ask him, "Would you mind, just say to . . ."

"He shouldn't mind," says Arachne to Thena. "They're all buying his book."

"That's the idea." She sniggers. "He was every bit as bad as I thought he was."

"How come?"

"Couldn't you hear? Women are nothing but – "

"Fauns, angels, gold, waterfalls, rice, birds, windows, daydreams, trumpets, jewels, knives, caves, fortresses, bridges, accordions, cookies, chalk, teeth, can openers, grasshoppers, hourglasses, idols, bread, lagoons, magnets, lightning, meadows, mountains, motorcycles, oracles, ninnies, songs, umbrellas, volumes, tomes, they are the penultimate muse." The poet has run out of breath. "How did you like my poetry?" he says to Arachne.

"I couldn't hear."

"Humphh," says Thena. "It's typical. Masculine view of the world."

He grins at Arachne. "Do you think so?"

She shrugs, takes a swig of wine.

"Women are *muses*. Our whole life is spent trying to understand them, praise them, capture them, worship them, win them, overwhelm them, love them – "

"Destroy them." Thena is not deflected by the poet's concentration on Arachne. "You're no different."

"And you love it," says the poet.

"Humphh. That's what you think, that's what you want to believe."

"What do *you* think?" he says to Arachne again.

She shrugs. "I dunno."

"Raki," says Thena. "You know what happens. Huh. Either we're rocking them on our laps or keeping the world a holy place or dressing up in black underwear" – here she jabs Arachne with her elbow – "to get them excited. It's all a hoax, muses."

The poet throws back his head and laughs. He has good teeth, he's proud of them, it's his vanity over his teeth that prevents him from smoking a pipe. "I see. You're the straight man and she's the executioner. Here, let me give you a copy of my book. You can use my poems as examples."

He scribbles his name and holds the book out; neither Thena nor Arachne reach for it and he finally thrusts it toward Thena. "You'll get lots of use out of it, so take it. Enjoy."

He moves away and Arachne says, "You've made a conquest."

"Not me, *you*, with your deliberate refusal to listen. He loves women that play hard to get."

The poet is back with a bottle. "May I?"

Thena holds out her glass. "Sure. It will make the conversation go down better."

Arachne laughs and joins her. "Why not? Didn't think drinking had anything to do with books."

"Oh, it does," says the poet seriously, "very much indeed. Where would we be without the grape to inspire us? Are you a poet?"

"Me? No, I'm a sales rep."

"An underwear salesman," says Thena viciously.

"You're making it up."

"Oh no."

"And you?"

"I'm a housewife par excellence. First-class, neurotic, valium-motivated, divorced, tied to two bratty kids and mad as hell. And it's all *your* fault."

"I didn't do anything."

"That's what they all say. Come the revolution every

one of the men on trial is going to say, 'Me? I didn't do anything. I'm a nice guy.'"

"And you're going to be Madame Defarge with your needles and your black wool keeping track."

"Right. Off with his head."

"Who's Madame Defarge?" asks Arachne.

"Oh, innocence. You should stay away from your friend here, she'll corrupt you."

"I've already tried," says Thena gloomily. "It doesn't work. She won't cooperate."

All three drain their glasses and Thena says, "Well, Raki, let's go. I need to buy a clock. All my clocks are out of joint."

"I'm in town for a few days," says the poet. "Can I take you for dinner?"

Thena looks at him in disbelief. "Not on your life."

He looks at Arachne. "What about you?"

Arachne shakes her head. "I don't know anything about poetry."

"I don't care."

"But she does," says Thena, taking Arachne's arm. "Come on, Arachne, let's get out of here before he really turns on the charm. Thanks for the book. See you at the guillotine."

## With monologue

Which should be the end of it. Except that the next morning
when Arachne is driving down the street after taking
Thomas to work she sees him flailing against the gale-
force winds with his arms pumping and his teeth as fixed
and perfect as the day before. There is a howling blizzard
tunneling between the downtown high rises, the snow
spumes and falls in deceptive waves and the temperature
is 30 below. She stops the car and reaches across to open
the passenger door. The poet peers in at her, puzzled.

"Oh, it's you."

"Get in. Don't you know you could freeze to death out
there?"

He shakes wet snow over the seat.

"Where are you going?"

"Trying to find some decent breakfast. Hotels have awful
food. Trying to capture the flavor of Calgary."

"But you can't even see."

"Might be part of the flavor."

"Huh. Only fools go out in this."

"Fools and poets. Have you had breakfast?"

"As much as I usually have. Do you like omelettes?"

"If they're good omelettes."

Arachne turns the car down toward Eau Claire. "Okay,
this is it."

"This is a lumberyard."

"It makes great omelettes."

Arachne is mostly interested in the food, although the poet is a curiosity, an added exponent. She hardly pays attention to his monologue, his dissection of the restaurant; the food, the reading last night, the bookstore, the people he was drinking with, the reviews his book has been getting, the interviews he did yesterday. He's an egotist; he watches Arachne but does not want to know about her. Impeccably preoccupied, he devours his omelette without paying attention to its taste or beauty. Arachne does not believe she deserves his contempt. She enjoys her omelette and watches the poet's performance from a distance, as though he were an orchestra hired to accompany a meal. He's putting his back into it, she can tell. For what? She isn't going to applaud, wait trembling for him to include her. Poets aren't her type, she's certain they're always looking for women to put into their poems. Not that she reads poetry. Who does? Her eyes are inscrutable, but behind them she finds him amusing, pulling all his strings.

She can tell that he would be an uneven lover, erratic, would jump from point to point on a woman's body, like one of those join-the-dots pictures, hasty and irregular, urgency motivated by his subsiding reputation, the fact that he has not been included in the latest anthology. Arachne cares nothing about reputations and anthologies. She eats her omelette and drinks her coffee and even has to squelch a yawn.

When he puts his hand on her knee under the table, she does yawn, even though she's polite enough to aim away from him.

"Let's go back to my room. I'm dying to fuck you."

"I'll drive you to the hotel anyway." Arachne puts on her coat, trying to decide if he'll be worth the effort. If her guess is right, his technique will not outweigh his

205

egotism, but she wonders if he can stop talking about himself long enough to seduce anything. She puts him into her car with a motherly solicitude that does not stop his monologue. He continues talking even though she's outside scraping the windshield, brushing snow off the hood. Perhaps he is trying to convince himself.

But when she stops in front of the hotel entrance, he grabs her wrist. "Come on, straight man. Aren't you curious to see if your executioner friend is right? You'll have the pleasure of reporting back to her."

Arachne runs her fingers around the steering wheel, nods. "I will."

A doorman in a fur coat taps her window. She rolls it down. "Do you mind if I leave the car here for a few minutes?"

"Not at all, ma'am. Just leave the keys in case I have to move it."

"A few minutes," says the poet as they walk across the lobby to the elevators. "What do you think I am, a three-minute wonder?"

Arachne shrugs. "I don't know, do I?" He is the most boring man she has ever met, and yet she's curious. How does a man like this make love to a woman? With his eyes tightly closed? Now he's talking about how fortunate she is. Does she know how many women chase him, are dying to go to bed with him?

Arachne says no, she doesn't know, and they step out of the elevator.

His room has not been made up; the sheets and blankets are balled in the middle of the mattress, as if the poet has slept badly. A copy of his book is on the bed table — he reads himself before he goes to sleep. That could be the reason for the bad night, thinks Arachne uncharitably. A pair of striped pajamas lie limp-legged across the bed. She turns to him with a grin.

"You wear pajamas?"

"Why not?" he says defensively. "They're warm, I sleep better." He grabs her. It is not a lunge but a definite grab, as though if he doesn't get his hands on her right away, he'll never have the chance. She's still in her coat, his arms are vised around her and he chews at her lips insistently. Arachne wants to laugh. She has had countless men but none so close to adolescence. She pushes him away gently and takes off her coat. Poised on the balls of his feet, he watches her with foxy brightness, trying to decide how to rush her next.

A key turns in the door. The maid's Indian face is dark and unclaimed. She makes up beds with razors between the sheets, puts out poisoned soap. While the hotel guests are out, she tries on jewelry, perfume, clothes, parades herself in front of the full-length mirrors. "Oh, sorry."

"Come back later," says the poet.

The maid slams the door.

"She's more your type."

"You are inscrutable."

"What's that?"

"What's that, she says." He addresses the television. "Have you ever seen a woman who pretends to know so little? I suppose you're going to say you don't know why I asked you up here."

"Oh," says Arachne, sitting on the bed and unlacing her high snow boots. "I have a pretty good idea." She unbuttons her shirt, stands up to unzip her jeans and shove them off.

Thena has always said that if men could imagine the way we watch them making love to us, they'd think twice about doing it. She takes a bitter delight in their ridiculous vulnerability. "The ones with cocks have power," she says, "but having a cock does not necessarily make them powerful. For one thing, they look stupid."

"Oh, come on," says Arachne.

"Take a good look sometime. You see enough to take a few minutes out."

Arachne has never been so distanced that she could stand outside herself and watch, but with this poet she finds herself doing exactly that, an odd position where she floats above the two of them, craning her neck to catch the nuances of their movement. The expression on her face is droll, not disgusted or disparaging, but a quizzical, eyebrows-raised expression. Arachne has a hard time preventing herself from laughing, she has to bite her lip and close her eyes, pretend that her smile is one of pleasure. Her body responds as well as ever, it is irrepressible, but her mind refuses to relax, insists on observing every twitch and sigh. The poor poet, she cannot prevent herself from thinking, even with her legs wrapped around him. When he terminates the exercise, she strokes his back. "That was lovely," she says and rolls over and falls asleep.

## And occasional verse

When she wakes, after-storm sunlight waters the room. It is still, only the sound of a pencil rasping paper. So, she thinks, he stops talking when he writes.

She muffles a yawn. Better keep still. The minute he knows she's awake, he'll start talking again. She lies quietly, enjoying her body's calm and the tepid light, then pantomimes waking, stretching, yawning, sitting up. She swings her legs to the floor and reaches for her socks.

"You're awake." He advances around the bed, both hands behind his back. "Do you know what I've been doing?"

Arachne pulls up her jeans. "Hmmm?"

"I've written a poem. I've written you a poem." He holds out a sheet of paper but Arachne shrugs on her shirt before she takes it. She looks at the sheet, turns it over.

"Read it."

She turns it upside down, cranes her neck. "Where does it start?"

He snatches it away from her, holds the paper in front of him and adjusts his face before he begins to read.

### Rose Kissing

Then I said, We will always have
this as a memory. And you said,

209

To imagine this is truer
delight than any remembering.

Your mouth is for words, your mouths
for kissing.

To kiss is no soft push of face
toward face, no longing skin.
The quintessence of kiss is the push in
side, that rose beyond the skin.

Where we kiss there is no skin
or memory.

Arachne does up the last button on her shirt and tucks it into her pants. "What does it mean?" She looks up at his face, disheveled, silent. He's standing there with a half smile, almost tender, and she suddenly likes him, likes his poem. She holds out her hand. "Can I keep it?"

He folds the paper in half and gives it to her without a word. So that she kisses him properly before she leaves, holds his trembling wish to control words in both her hands and then goes quickly.

The maid is slouched against her cart outside the door, smoking. "You done then?"

Arachne smiles serenely and gives her the finger before she clumps her boots down the carpeted hall. Although she has to give the doorman a five-dollar tip, she feels marvelous.

She does not tell Thena about the poet but she keeps the poem in the glove compartment of the car.

## From a distance

Arachne's greatest consistency has always been her faithlessness. Thomas knows but does not reproach her. He watches, waits, knowing it's fear of love that gnaws at the roots of her sleep. He is more than a benefactor, he is her rock. In life she betrays him a hundred times, but in secret never. Arachne wakes to find him looking down at her, his hand hovering above her face. It's then she hates her undisciplined conscience, thinks of giving up on Ladies' and settling into Sunnyside for good. She smiles at him and thinks of it but continues to travel, still follows roads as endless as skyline.

That spring is a good one for Ladies'; they have several new lines. Even Arachne likes them, feels that they are decent panties, the colors palatable, the thread not that awful plastic stuff that wears holes in your skin. They are made of a new material silkier than nylon, a cotton blend, they feel light and seductive. And the colors – lilac, pearl, apricot, champagne and smoke – are suffused with romance. There is only one slogan-printed panty: *A woman without a man is like a fish without a bicycle.*

Arachne gives the first sample to Thena, who sniffs and says, "Never thought underwear manufacturers would get sensible." As if the slogan had inspired the designers, there is a bikini printed with old-fashioned bicycles along with the whimsical flowers and unicorns and owls and elves and toads. Arachne feels that the patterns are for children rather than grown women. Still, it is an improvement. Ladies' has hired several women in management.

And this year Arachne goes to the spring sales conference. Usually she does not go, even though it means a free trip to Winnipeg. Ladies' Comfort sales conferences are designed to make their employees feel part of the gang, a feeling that no longer appeals to Arachne. She avoids the group outings to St. Boniface cathedral, Louis Riel's grave, Lake Winnipeg, Portage and Main. Her fellow sales representatives are what one expects panty salesmen to be like – not crude, but crass. Middle-aged men who look like drummers, who carry Ladies' Comfort panties along with other saleable items: Scotch tape and candy bars. Because they do not dedicate themselves to underwear, they don't sell much; Ladies' is trying to figure out a way to stop this itinerant moonlighting, but is ultimately benevolent.

It is not an easy thing to attract underwear salesmen. Although the men joke and make crafty innuendos, they are diffident and a little embarrassed. Selling underwear is faintly ridiculous. They do it quickly, get it over with, slide it between the other items that they gather orders for.

It is no wonder then that Arachne is Ladies' most successful sales representative. She has dedicated her life to underwear with a zeal that Ladies' has never before prompted. Their large distributors, the ones who take care of city department stores, usually surpass all the individual salesmen. They provide the biggest orders, huge standing orders that keep Ladies' prosperous. But this year Arachne has single-handedly sold more than anyone. It is an unprecedented occurrence and Ladies' is going to give Arachne Manteia a special award at their annual banquet;

she will get an engraved plaque and a cash bonus.

Arachne has spent the winter selling with a flat-out determination that she is herself unaware of. She covered her territory and beyond, circled her way through derelict towns gathering orders that reverberate for years afterward, a profusion of panties spilling down from the dusty shelves of stores. The owners and managers are not quite sure why they ordered twelve dozen polka-dotted bikini prints; it must have been a mistake, no one will take the blame. But when they take inventory, when they go back and check the books, there is the order signed by their own hand, below the neat lists of Arachne Manteia. So they blame her, witchery, and for years afterward no one can sell anything, not one pair of panties. The demand has died.

Arachne does not take the brunt of this. Confronting her own achievement, she realizes that she has glutted the market, and after the banquet she demands a new territory.

In Winnipeg Arachne stays at the Fort Garry Hotel, which is where the sales conference is always held, and while everyone is out surveying the flooding Red River, she explores Winnipeg her own way. She does some shopping, finds a beautiful old map for Thomas, stops for a beer. She feels adventurous. She has almost forgotten what it's like to be alone, the deep-breathing freedom of it. She rummages through a sex shop, gives a coughing Indian a five-dollar bill, wanders into a Ladies' Auxiliary bake sale (where she buys a dozen brownies) and checks out a used-car dealership.

She buys a plastic-tasting cup of coffee and sits on a park bench beside the dirty, swollen river. Watching the water sway, she thinks of what has happened to her. Arachne Manteia, maintaining a steady relationship with a respectable man, has lost her old self. She's relegated the leader of the Black Widows to a broom closet, the gas station cashier to oblivion, the paper route to childhood, the bus driver to experience. She is not Raki at all but a tied and tagged creation of a world she doesn't belong to.

So she should be grateful when a young man in a raincoat sits down beside her on the bench.

"Are you Arachne Manteia?"

She looks at him. Can't she even be anonymous anymore? "Why?" she asks belligerently.

"I'm sorry, let me explain. Someone pointed you out at the breakfast meeting the other morning. I'm one of the accountants who goes over your orders. John Dumont." He extends his hand.

Arachne stares at him for a moment. Then she realizes he's with Ladies' Comfort. "Oh yes. What are you doing here?"

"I could ask you the same thing. Didn't you want to see Gimli?"

"Not in a bus with forty-nine other sales reps."

"Good point." He chuckles self-consciously. Arachne Manteia has become an obsession of his. He checks all her orders, tries to find in them her life and reason, endows her with a mystique nothing short of romantic. You can hardly blame him, an industrious young man who spends his days over figures, who should be working for a large tax company but is thankful to have a job. It's true that Arachne is one of a dying breed, a rep who makes traveling her life, not like the new ones who want to work six or seven hours and return home at night to suburban houses and spouses. Arachne travels with passion, sells with the tenacity of the converted. He has ached to meet her, he waits eagerly for each sales conference, but this is the first she has attended, although she's been with Ladies' for four years. "I've always wanted to talk to you. You're one of the best sales reps we have . . ." He is stumbling all over himself.

Arachne looks at him darkly. "Thanks," she mutters.

"You're going to win the award for sales," he blurts. This is supposed to be a secret but he doesn't know what else to say.

"Me? I just do small towns."

"You've topped them all."

"The distributors?"

"Yes."

"Jesus, people in cities must be giving up underwear," says Arachne.

"Maybe we all should." He's trying to make a joke, get closer to her, but she takes it literally.

"Yes, maybe we should." And then she laughs. "Imagine. Old ladies and respectable wives without underwear. Kids without underwear, teenage girls without underwear. It's not really necessary, but everyone would be uncomfortable, you'd see it on their faces."

He laughs too, and they like each other. Arachne does not tell him that she has given up underwear, but it's one of the reasons she laughs. At least she has that to silence her cynical conscience; she hasn't stooped so low as to put on underpants or wear a bra.

He suspects that anyway. He imagines what she's like under that severe navy dress, and he aches. He shifts and hopes she cannot see his discomfort, then stands and ties the belt of his raincoat and asks if she's walking back to the hotel.

On the way he gossips about Ladies' Comfort, the wars that management has, the new designs, the changes that are planned. He does not tell her that her lists and her Mercedes are legend, or that she's an exception, the only rep whose car expenses are paid completely. He does tell her that they are sometimes shocked at the amount of her repair bills, but management always approves them.

"Huh," says Arachne. "If they didn't, I'd quit. I've put thousands of miles on that Mercedes for them."

She finds herself liking John Dumont. He's attractive, easy-going, a perfect candidate. Still, she has to consider Ladies'. She wonders if he has the sense to refrain from bragging.

## Conference fever

She plays with him for two days, even kisses him outside her room the second night. Arachne concludes he is safe, she can indulge without the whole company sniggering.

They dissect Ladies' with a vicious and unrestrained humour, spend much of the conference in each other's company, unobtrusively but anticipating. He knows she is checking his discretion. She needn't worry, he wants her to himself, wants to savor knowledge of her body when he goes over her orders, wants to have a private view that he can turn to on interminable days when the figures begin to jumble and the Manitoba winter closes into dark at three o'clock in the afternoon.

Arachne has brought along the green silk costume that makes her look so brilliantly dangerous. She wears it the night of the concluding banquet, lets it mouth her body and her movements so that the men in the room have trouble breathing when they look at her. Even the President, a respectable, gray-haired family man, finds his hand reaching out to touch her, has difficulty stopping it, has to fill it with items from the buffet. Jellies and pickles and roast beef, salads and sauces and small sweet cakes, it is a western buffet with every kind of meat and relish: roast beef and ham and pork and corned beef and cabbage rolls and turkey and chicken and lamb, all sacrificed for Ladies'

Comfort. There's wine, sweet wine and dry wine, red wine and white wine, dessert wine, sherry, and the bar is open for two hours beforehand, rye and gin and vodka and scotch, even rum.

"What'll you have?" booms the bartender to the bald and speckled, the fat and constipated, the thin and ulcerous salesmen. "What'll you have?"

Arachne leans over the bar and says softly, "Soda water."

He looks at her, the nipple he can see under the green silk, the curve of breast, of shoulder, of flank. "Right," he says, winking, pressing the button on his spout. "Sensible young lady. Don't want to get too carried away in this crowd." But as she takes the glass from his hand, he finds himself unable to resist. "I'm through at twelve."

She smiles and turns away. By twelve they'll be singing hymns with drunken abandon, they'll be waltzing to the fiddle orchestra, vomiting in the washrooms. By twelve Arachne intends to be between the sheets.

She is besieged until the leading evangelist of Winnipeg, who is the Vice-President's brother-in-law, stands to recite a long and passionate blessing. Then there's a rush for the buffet. They surround her, jostle against her, they breathe on her, crack jokes, make faces, all in an effort to get her attention. It is the President who rescues her, makes them fall back, although they still cannot tear their eyes away, they fill their plates without looking at the food that falls from the spoons. The President himself brushes a hand down her naked back, a pin-striped leg against her green thigh. He succeeds in getting down the length of the table only by gripping his plate with both hands. At the end he realizes he has put hardly any food on it, and Arachne has slipped away, returned to her seat beside John Dumont.

After they have all eaten and eaten, drunk and drunk, the President stands and begins the yearly after-banquet ritual: citations and retirements and promotions, and last but not least, the award for the best sales. Everyone is used to one of the distributor's people winning, so when Arachne's name is called, there's pandemonium. They stamp their feet and bang their glasses, whistle and shout, "Speech! Speech!"

Arachne clutches the brass plaque and the envelope with the bonus cheque against her green silk chest and bends toward the microphone so that the whole assembly can see a flash of white breast. "I thank you and my Mercedes thanks you. If it weren't for the Midnight line, I wouldn't have this. Hurrah for Ladies' Comfort!" The assembly erupts with shouts of delight, screams of laughter, cries of "More, more!" "Take it off!" They are giddy with lust, with their own importance as sales reps for Ladies' Comfort, and when the President stands to make his concluding remarks, to announce that the bar will be open and the band will be playing, they are still drunk with that one flash of Arachne's breast.

"We want Arachne, we want Arachne, we want Arachne, more, more, more."

The lights on the ceiling begin to sway and the floor begins to buckle, and one fat, red-haired salesman from Charlottetown yells, "Bun him." The Quebec delegates, who always sit together and who think that Ladies' head office should be in Montreal, take this opportunity for civil insurrection and cry, *"Merde, Merde."* And the buns (hard as rocks and left over from a conference the week before) begin to fly, along with a few forks and glasses, a few balled-up napkins. The head table retaliates and some joker who has brought sample panties begins to fling those so that the air is full of rose and canary and turquoise falling like flowers upon the round tables and the delegates.

Arachne and John dash for the door, Arachne clutching her plaque and her purse, in which nestles the white envelope with the cheque, in which also nestles her hotel-room key. Safely inside her door they collapse into each other's arms, wild with three days of restrained lust. Arachne shucks off the green silk while John tears at his tie, fumbles with shoelaces, buttons, zippers. Arachne stands naked, watching him. "Why do men wear such elaborate clothes?"

"You — " he grabs her, still wearing his shorts, his socks, "should be ashamed. You don't wear any underwear."

"I refuse," she says, pushing his sky-blue shorts down his legs. "I refuse."

"It's a principle, eh?"

"Right." She wraps both legs around him.

They have forgotten the socks.

What is it about making love to a stranger? When the circumstances are clean and you don't have to ask about consequences, is it love, is it real? There is something square and direct about fucking for its own sake, no other considerations: wifely or husbandly duty, buying, selling, pay-off, gratitude. The thought of having to sleep with a man under a marriage certificate, having eaten and clothed with his money, conceiving his children to justify existence as his sweet and lovely parasite, makes Arachne cold. She can think of no faster way to achieve frigidity. To her the true exchange of hearts within the bonds of holy matrimony speaks death to the life of the body. This shock of pleasure that she gets from this strange man's stubby penis and gentle hands is pure. She can dig her fingers into his muscled back and feel herself unfaithful as always, faithful to only her body, her reliable, well-tuned body.

Above their parallel breaths in the depths of the hotel below them they hear shouts and merriment, sirens and splintering wood. The annual sales conference has hit its peak.

Flat on his back beside her, in the still-lit ravaged room,

he expels a long whoosh of air. "Is it because we waited or because I wanted you so badly?"

Arachne curls beside him. "It's the noise downstairs. Can you hear that?" There is the sound of raining glass, shouts, screams.

He groans. "We've learned to budget for it right from the start."

"A bad sign for underwear salesmen to be so violent."

"Year-long repression."

Arachne rubs her leg down his. Her adventure resumes.

*From above*

The sales award gives Arachne a sense of achievement. She attacks her new areas to the east with renewed enthusiasm. Thena is right. She will never find a job that suits her better. The spring days spin themselves into a thread of driving, driving, inveigling suspicious prairie stores into ordering mushroom and tangerine, blush and Egyptian panties.

On her birthday Thomas wakes her early in the morning and drives her north of the city to an open field. She is almost too tired to ask where they are going, imagines herself asleep and dreaming.

Two men are mouthing a fan into a huge raw scar of silken color. All the colors of her panties melded together, a soft glister of royal blue and purple, flame red and sun yellow. The silken cone swings up slowly, like a man lifting himself on his elbows, then, as the propane jets pump heat into its heart, struggles to lift free. Arachne and Thomas climb into the swaying basket with the grumpy balloonist and feel themselves lifted, caught by a windless stillness. The balloon floats up, beyond the earth's curve into a morning of distant mountain teeth and blue fields. And then drifts above that map of road and land and slough and fence. In the south the towers of the city catch rising light, gold and spinning. They are suspended there, at the center of currents, swaying under the shimmer of a silken web that stretches its filament arms to cradle their cocoon. Beneath them the prairie unfolds in wedges of yellow and black, with small monopoly houses perched on their periphery, roads spidering together into the clusters of towns.

Arachne laughs. "Thena's dog is afraid of balloons, did you know that? Before he goes outside he scans the sky, and if he sees one, he runs and hides. It's as if he's convinced that they're unnatural, doesn't believe they should be in the air."

"I wanted to find you a map," says Thomas, "but I thought this aerial would be better."

Arachne looks down at the slow ground and thinks of traveling, spidering her own map over the intricate roads of the world.

## The disinterred

Balloon creature, like the grotesque dancers on Josef's plate, she is reminded of him and drives past his house. She hasn't seen him since fall. The garage door is padlocked and the windows, covered from the inside, look blindly into the yard. She rings the doorbell but no one answers, the house menacingly still. Which bothers her and the next day she drives by again, knocks loudly on the door. The scowling teenager opens it.

"Is Josef there?"

"No."

"Where is he?"

"Had to go into the home. Mom couldn't keep track of him anymore. If she turned her back he'd be gone, wandering down the street."

"I'm his friend, Arachne. He. . ."

"Oh yeah, he talked about you. He wanted to see you."

"Did he want to go into the home?"

The teenager laughs. "We just about had to tie him down. But he's senile."

"Where is he?"

"Mountain Shadows. He'd probably like company."

Arachne walks into the foyer, looking around to see if he's with the old men watching the door. They look at her milkily, their eyes filmed with a tired futility. One of them stretches out a skinny paw, begins to speak, but she hurries past.

He's not in the dayroom or the sunroom or the games room. Arachne even checks the smoking room, but there's only an old lady sitting in a corner, hunched over an elegant extra-long.

She finds an abstracted nurse. "Oh, he's in his room. He stays there mostly. Sulking. He'll get over it."

Arachne walks down an endless white corridor that seems like the entrance to a dream where walls are terrifying and forever. She stops at 212, his number. Should she knock? It seems unnecessary, a mockery. She pushes the half-open door and it swings inward.

He's looking out the window. His back is toward the door and his shoulders are winged against the world. She hesitates.

"Josef?"

He seems not to hear, nodding meditatively over the stretch of brown grass outside the window.

"Josef?"

Before he swivels the chair around to face her, his back, broad as she remembers it, fills her with longing, a jolt of lust. He turns. He is the same. His old magician eyes hooded and sullen, the awkward jut of his nose and chin. But his face lifts to hers in a proud grief. It is naked, stripped, shaven clean. His hair has been trimmed back into silver control, tight, short.

"Josef!"

He stares at her, eyes burning above the deep creases carved into his face.

"Eh, Arachne. They shave my beard off." He feels at his face with fingers thickened and frail. "They come at me every morning with cold water and razor." His voice trembles. "They say I am dirty, must be cleaned."

Arachne stands helpless while he weeps. She takes a step

toward him and abruptly he swings his chair around, his back to her.

"Josef." She kneels beside his chair. "Do you have to be in here?"

"Anna, she . . . can't . . ." He hovers on the edge of the ugly, raisin-colored chair with tears falling onto his stilled hands.

Arachne puts her arms around him and they are grappled together in a fierce hook of rage and lust. Under his shirt, her hands search the tendons in his arms, and for a breath the bones they discover are merged, the grain of each other's skull their own. His legs are hers, his arms grow from her, her mouth tastes what he feels. He is with her, grafted into her, the rough carpet under her knees, and her arms pulled from their sockets. They stumble to the bed, the high and austere hospital bed, and against its lowered railing they fight to zipper themselves together, to find under their dying skin a bone, arrowing themselves into an element deeper and deeper, tearing at clothing, age, distance, breathing enormous until he slides inside her. Then they are both still, hold their breath. In the hall the squeak of a rubber-wheeled trolley. And gently he moves, his face buried against her neck, one hand under her right buttock, one against her hair. She curls around him, strokes the sad, loose skin of his back and pushes one foot against the steel rail at the end of the bed into his rhythm. They refuse time.

They might have slept. Arachne jostles him. "Hey, get dressed."

He fumbles into his clothes, muttering, "They tie me at night. Like a baby's crib, the sides."

Arachne goes through his drawers, takes a clean shirt, clean socks, clean underwear. "Have you got a warm coat, gloves?"

He points to the closet.

"I'm just taking you for a ride, got it?"

He nods. "We hide?"

"Well, let's just say I think you need a holiday."

The disapproving bed watches them leave.

When she gets him into the car and starts driving, she knows she doesn't want him along. How can she take care of him? He's old, and she'll be responsible if he dies on her. She looks over at him. He's sitting poised and anticipatory, as if the moving car prows them into escape. What will she do with him?

"Just don't wander off on me, okay?"

"I not wander off." He is indignant. "I walk sometimes. Anna get so hot about me lost. I'm not lost."

They stay that night on the edge of Medicine Hat, sleep together as if deprived of sleep for months.

Arachne does Piapot and Carmichael, Simmie and Scotsguard and Admiral and Cadillac. He naps in the car or wanders the wind-wiped streets, investigates abandoned houses and railway stations, brings back scraps that he has found: wooden peg nails from a window frame, an antique baking soda can, a filigreed metal stovepipe cover.

At night they cradle each other without desire or intention. Arachne wonders if the nursing home is searching for him, if his daughter has notified the police. She feels his bones press against her side. She sleeps. And in the darkness they talk. Words, a language where they do not have to dissemble because the speaker cannot see the other's eyes, words disembodied, no layering to voices without face or body. It is the narration of captives who lie awake between their sleeping guards relating experience, why they are both prisoner, their private acts of revolution. She tells him some of hers: Lanie, Toto, east Vancouver, buses, Gabriel, the car. She has no idea if he understands or even hears. The words fall from her mouth into the stillness between them, small stones.

And his.

"Krajina, Grahovo, Gornji Oblajaj, Belgrade, Sarajevo. No return. Korana river, the mountains, the fields up the mountains, all colors. Slatted fence around the yard. Mud, dust. Water from the river, in the yoke with tin buckets. My mother white apron shadow by the door. Always she wore a kerchief pulled over her face. My father big moustache. His eyes so black, he shout at my mother that my eyes pale. They beat him with sticks once, the Austrians."

Arachne is stupefied, the words soak through her skin to her bones.

"The Austrians. Big men, big boots, feathers. Serbs nothing but slaves. We live in Bosnia, but we are Serbs. Except that we are nothing, not Serbs, not Bosnian, not Austrian. They made the young men fight, the ones who do not run away and hide. Made us fight the Serbs, ourselves, big men with sabers. I remember the sabers."

The names bewilder Arachne, their litany confuses. She knows nothing of what he speaks, but she recognizes a chord of the same bitter displacement that she remembers tasting. East-ender Raki shredded by her own time and place.

"Did you fight?"

"Yah. *Crna ruka*. Only I am left to tell. We won. But not before death. How did I come here, I do not know. I alone escaped."

She cradles him against her. *Ujedinienje ili Smrt*. Union or Death. She drifts, restless, thinking of tomorrow's sales, of Thomas at home, of this old man, of Gabriel's Mercedes.

Her dreams are the maps of convoluted journeys.

## Wild Woman

They sink farther and farther into prairie that mirrors the landscape of their confusion, and the wind echoes their exchange. Arachne works in slowly advancing circles, a movement determined by coulees and bluffs, the winding rivers they cross again and again. From Cadillac to Pambrun, Neidpath, Wymark, Chortitz, Blumenhof, back to Pontex, on to Kincaid, Lafleche, Gravelbourg, Kelstern, Vanguard, back to Gravelbourg, then Mossbank, Assiniboia, Rockglen, Willow Bunch (where he disappears and she finds him in the basement of the local museum, asleep on the Willow Bunch giant's bed), Bengough, Ogema, Ceylon, Minton. The Mercedes spins a froth of dust and gravel, the prairie folds itself around them, the sky blazes.

In Minton Arachne has to wait while Jack Ross serves customers.

"Wife's gone to Weyburn for the day," he grumbles. "Got a bad hip, and standing on this floor all day don't help."

"Isn't the clinic in Estevan better?" Arachne is mentally reducing the size of his order. Without Jess, Jack settles for a dozen of everything. He doesn't like lengthy discussions of "wimmin's stuff" and he always brightens when Arachne's samples are stowed in her car and he can tell her about the town's latest accident, death or fire.

"She goes to the chiropractor. Seems to help. But she's gone a whole day and I've got to manage."

Arachne checks his old stock while he rings up a customer's order. She's making a notation when Josef pushes open the screen door and stumps inside. She left him sleeping in the car. She goes to him. "Are you all right?" Jack is sure to notice, will say, She's done for now, taking her grandpa on the road with her. Ladies' will have to find another rep. She almost giggles. But the screen slams again and the pair who come in are as curious as she and Josef.

"What'll we get?" says the man.

The girl fairly spins in his radius. The man, sixty at least, holding a cane even, white-haired, a scarred face, laughs down at her with indulgent delight. She swirls around him, filling her arms.

"Bread. Cheese. Eggs. Coffee. Steak. Have you got matches?"

"Yes," says the man, openly caressing her buttocks.

Josef and Arachne watch across a pyramid of cans, their mirror image free and pleasured, no inheritances, no legacies.

"Juice," says the girl. "I'm so thirsty in the middle of the night."

"Chocolate," says the man, and the girl throws her arms around him and kisses his cheek.

"And butter — "

"Yes, of course, don't forget the butter."

They deposit everything in front of Jack's cash register.

"Oh, bacon! Where's the bacon?"

"I'll slice it right up," says Jack drily. "Side or back? Side's $2.29 a pound and back's $2.99."

"Back," says the girl, rubbing one leg against the man. "Half a pound."

"Do you know," asks the man, "where we can find a

huge hill that's supposed to have some effigy on it?" He fingers the girl's arm.

"What hill?" Jack moves the slicer back and forth.

"Some high bluff. Saskatchewan archives said it was around here. Supposed to have a human shape on it."

"Don't know," says Jack. "I think you're better off going over Big Muddy way to Bengough."

The girl is suddenly serious. "Aren't there any high hills around here?"

"Could be," Jack mumbles. "They say there are but I've never seen any."

The girl lifts a serious face to the man. "Maybe we're looking in the wrong place."

"We'll find it. We know it's there." He gives Jack some bills and they bang out, each holding a bag in one hand, the other busy touching skin.

Arachne takes Josef's arm. "Jack, what are they looking for?"

"A motel. There's one close to Bengough."

"Come on."

"There's miles of prairie to fool around in. They don't need to do it up there."

"Where?"

"Wild Woman. Why are you so interested?" He looks from Arachne to Josef and back again. "If you want to know, you go over to Big Beaver and ask old Dunc. You can find him in that Drop-in Centre. He knows."

"All right. Now, what's your order?"

"Dozen of everything."

On the oiled street Arachne opens the trunk and throws her sample boxes inside. The movie set seems to blink and then hunch itself lower on its props, bizarre lumber against the April sky.

They find him, old Dunc, sitting on a rungless wooden chair outside the door of a cinder-block hall watching two men pour the town's new sidewalks. "You gotta go east, then south. Highest hill for miles around. Line rider used to sit up there, watch the border." He chuckles. "No Yanks in those days." His eyelids, loose and sagged, cannot hold themselves open. Each lid is carefully anchored to his eyebrows with white bandage tape, as though he wants to prevent the narrowed, diminished vision of age, stay watchful. "You can see everything. Up there." He spits carefully onto the new cement. "That other pair was going up there too."

They are unprepared for the cone that springs over the last gravel rise. It looks a worn volcano planted there, looming into sky. Arachne searches for a road, finally finds a barbed-wire gate to a gravel pit. She cuts her hand forcing it open, then skirts the pit until the Mercedes is hidden behind the cliff. They pull on their coats, lock the car and climb. Arachne slowing herself to Josef's caned pace, silent, scrambling, they climb. Disappear, vanish into another element.

On the ridge the fierce wind thrusts at them. Arachne looks at the sky, at the circle of world below them, and begins to dance. Old Dunc was right; up here she can see everything, everything. It is a long way east she has circled and circled, finally come to this nipple of land on the breast of the world, immensely high and windswept. She spins, then stops and looks at Josef crouched over his cane, his spun hair torn, his face papery in the dust-flinging wind. She takes his hand and pulls him with her, down to one of the hill's folds, flanked against the nose of the cone.

And there they find the Wild Woman, her stone outline spread to infinite sky, to a prairie grassland's suggestion of paradise, a woman open-armed on the highest hill in that world. They trace her outline: arms, amulet, hair, teeth, skirt, breasts, feet. Arachne stands between her legs.

Her face speaks, the welcome gesture of arms, the amulet's adornment, the breasts soft curves, immensely eloquent. Arachne's small shadow falls within the woman's shape, the stone-shaped woman. She stretches out inside the woman, lies within the stones on her back beneath that wheeling sky, arms outflung like the woman's, her head cushioned on a circle of breast. Josef stands between her legs, watching, then he stumps away.

The ridge is sheltered from the gusting wind; it is almost warm here. Arachne will never get tired of looking at the sky from within the woman's arms, but she finally rises and stares beyond the outline of rock to the horizon that wheels four dimensions around her. What secret burial she makes before she walks down the steep ridge to the car and the waiting old man is buried there.

## Apprehended

When Arachne answers the door, it's the shoes she sees, highly polished black shoes that mirror her, distant and oblated. Her eyes travel from the cruel toes up the black pants and uniform coat to the square, clean-shaven face.

"Miss Manteia?"

"Yes."

"You're under arrest. The charges are kidnapping, transportation out of the province and intent to extort. Come with us, please."

*Notebook on a missing person*

*You try to get the next part of Arachne's adventures from Thena, the one person who should know what happened after Arachne returned from that disastrous trip with Josef. At first she's reluctant to talk. When you approach her, she sucks in her lower lip and scowls. "Let the dead bury the dead," she mutters. "It's nobody's business."*

*But you are persistent, you want to know how the whole business ended, what happened to Arachne. You hang about, bring over the occasional bottle of Scotch. You try to persuade Thena that she's the keeper of history, the perfect mirror. She never could resist an audience.*

*"I told her so," she says. "I told her what would happen. I told her a hundred times if I told her once. Did she listen? Not on your life. Just did what she felt like and to hell with the consequences. She never paid attention to me anyway. She told me everything, but she never listened to me."*

*You ask Thena whether she ever met Josef and if she knows what happened to him.*

*"How am I supposed to know? Probably back in the old folks' home. Road jockeys are one thing, but kidnapping an old man is quite another. Besides, all men are the same, whether they're ninety or twenty-nine. Should be lined up against the wall. I told her, but she wouldn't*

listen. Oh no, not Arachne. She always knew better."

You try to interrupt, but Thena is off and running. One of her daughters is planning to get married, of all the stupid things to do. "She'll end up a slave for the rest of her life. And what is he but a law student who'll sponge off her until he finishes school and then decide she isn't good enough for him."

You want to deflect her back to Arachne, and you ask if Arachne was ever married.

"No, although she could have, Thomas would have married her. Now there's a man. Arachne never appreciated him. He did everything for her and he never asked for a thing, just loved her. There aren't many like him around. There aren't any like him around. I don't know what happened to him. And he knew what she was like. It didn't make any difference to him." She is silent for a few minutes, pursing her lips. "He loved her. I told her a hundred times, 'Take it easy, don't lose him, Arachne,' but she didn't listen. Got that stubborn look on her face that meant she wasn't going to hear."

You want to know if it was the incident with the old man, the alleged kidnapping, that ended the relationship.

Thena peers at you as though you're crazy and laughs.

She is cagey. You can't persuade her to say anything else for a long time. "Did the police send you?" she demands.

You explain that you're only interested in finding out the real story, but she persists in denying all knowledge of what happened. Until one mid-winter afternoon when you arrive late, after five, 40 below in Calgary, and Thena has been drinking. She's not drunk but she smells unmistakably of Scotch. Surprisingly, she seems glad for your company and even brings Arachne up herself.

"Afternoons like this I miss her. She'd come over and we'd talk until late, drink together. Sometimes we'd get so silly Thomas would have to come and pick her up, take her home. She was a great one to drink with. We could talk, we could. We lied to the rest of the world but together we were brutally honest. I still miss that. I keep thinking she'll be back, show up some winter afternoon and just walk in as though she'd never left."

You look at her with shock. You thought she was dead.

"Dead?" Thena screeches. "Where'd you get that idea? She's as alive as I am."

You read in the paper she was dead.

"The paper." Thena sniffs. "Pack of lies. Between the press and the police, all a pack of lies."

You want to know where she is now.

"How the hell am I supposed to know? Have another drink."

You narrow your eyes and try to detect the truth, but Thena hums as she cracks ice from a tray and douses the ice with Scotch.

You insist that Thomas must have aided and abetted her escape.

"All he did was post her bail."

How much of what Thena says is true? You know that Arachne felt she had found a home with Thomas. Why would she leave? Maybe he threw her out, the kidnapping charge the last straw, sick of her infidelities, of putting up with her blatant indiscretions. Maybe he would rather have one of those blue-eyed bland young women who are part of his past. Maybe he would like to get married and have babies and it's unlikely Arachne would agree to that. After all, Thomas too must come to the end of his patience. You think he deserves better than Arachne, so faithless, so ungrateful.

Thena hoots with laughter. "You're crazy. Thomas is not typical. Besides, he could afford to wait. He knew that Arachne would always come back."

*Then where is she now?*

*Thena looks smug. "The story's not over yet."*

*And that's all you get out of her. She stops right there. No matter how many bottles you bring, no matter how you cajole her, she will say no more. She treats you to political lectures, to long rantings about equality and choice, but she pretends Arachne doesn't exist.*

*So be it.*

## Bail skippers and bacchants

Thomas bails her out and she vanishes. She gets into the Mercedes and drives west along the Trans-Canada highway. Over the rise that Calgary shrugs against, haughty phalanxes sucked into the roll of prairie. She takes French leave. Drives the spill of highway west past the Kananaskis and into the Rockies. Within their flanks Arachne begins to flex her fingers, to crane her neck to see to the top of those blue settles of granite. At the park gate she rolls down the window.

"Staying in the park?"

By the time she gets away from the gum-cracking girl in the booth, she has one of the famous yellow stickers with the miniature beaver looking at its tail stuck inside her windshield, distracting her vision; she has to stay, she has the sticker.

She tries to drive on, through to Lake Louise, but she can't get out of the traffic circle until the third exit and then she's driving into Banff, past tourists in Cowichan sweaters and bellboys off duty. There are boys, dozens of them, a Boy Scout jamboree. Arachne keeps one eye on the sidewalk and one on the traffic lights all the way up Banff Avenue and over the bridge. There she has to turn either right or left. She veers, wavers, then swings left, eyes on the flash of a furry leg pushing a bicycle pedal up the hill. And following that road, finds nowhere to go but into the phalanx of cars nosing the portico of the castle-like hotel at the top of the hill. A red-haired parking attendant opens the car door, flourishes a bow.

"Leave the keys in the car, please. Indoor or outdoor parking?"

"Indoor." She sits until he extends his hand, takes her elbow.

"Help with your luggage?"

"No." She lets him close her car door, lets him escort her to the foot of the slabbed steps. She's wearing the blue jeans that are worn thin at her inner thighs. She's wearing a cherry-red sweater knit with large loose stitches. She has no luggage. She had not planned to run away.

In the lobby are five hundred women dressed in blue jeans and sweaters and five hundred women in polyester dresses. The women in dresses are standing in demure knots, nodding their permed heads and keeping their eyes fixed on each other's faces. The women in blue jeans are swinging from the banisters and luggage racks. One is doing leg raises off the horns of the buffalo head over the door. Women are balancing luggage on their heads, pinching the bums of bellhops; they are sprawled over the Gothic chairs, the courting chairs, the stately Queen Anne wing chairs, the demure Princess Mary chairs, they are whistling at their friends on the mezzanine, dropping their suitcases and flinging coats and waving keys. They are booking massages and whipping out their business cards and demanding suites with jacuzzis and the location of the swimming pool. Arachne is hemmed into a line and can only escape after writing her name and business address on a registration form.

The clerk behind the desk presses a key into her hand. "We're sorry the room has green carpet but we're overbooked and we can't change it."

Arachne starts to object but is shoved along to the bank of elevators and a set of open doors. All fifteen women inside are bumping against each other with designer brief-cases. All the floors are punched. Arachne does not look at her key. "I need a drink," she says.

"Mezzanine," says the woman behind her and the elevator light flashes M and stops with a ting. "Here we are."

Arachne is marshaled by their briefcases, black and navy and burgundy and brown leather, bumped into the lounge to a table overlooking what must surely be a backdrop — there is no real scenery like that in the world. The women turn their backs to it and begin to trade business cards while they order double dry martinis from the tartan-skirted waitress.

"An olive."

"A twist."

"With ice."

"Without."

One woman in Lena Wertmuller glasses leans toward Arachne. "What are you in?" she asks. Behind her green glasses her eyes are yellow.

"Sales." Arachne reaches for the closest martini.

"Law," a sonorous brunette. "The international law of the sea."

"Computers."

"Chainsaws."

"Landscape architecture."

"Publishing."

"Temples."

"Erotic art."

"Dictionaries."

"Eyelashes."

"Warehouses."

"Bones."

"Martinis."

Someone giggles. Someone pats Arachne's knee.

"Dykes."

It is getting dark. The mountains are hazy cones through the glass.

"Where's the banquet?"

"The ballroom."

"No, the Alhambra."

Arachne tries to get up. She can't. She tries to put some money on the table, a two-dollar bill to be exact.

"Don't bother," says a woman with buck teeth. "It's on me." She signs the bill with a gold pen.

Arachne seems able to move only in the middle of them, their bodies at her back and shoulders, their briefcases bumping her knees. But at the elevator they disperse, vanish in crowds of women all dressed in blue — navy blue and baby blue and pale blue and turquoise blue — faces scrubbed and shining.

"Wait," says Arachne, but the women are gone and she gets into an elevator alone. She pushes seven. The elevator goes down and the doors slide open at Arcade. They stay open. Arachne steps cautiously into recessed darkness, a bank of winking video machines.

"Bam," says a throaty female voice. "Bam, bam. Gotcha." Her briefcase leans against the machine and her head is thrust inside the screen shield.

Arachne tiptoes past, finds a staircase that spirals down, that arrives at the swimming pool.

"Sign this," says the attendant.

Arachne signs and he tosses her a towel, turning back to watch a woman flipping somersaults in the deep end under his desk. She climbs a staircase, another staircase, not sure if she's going up or down, finds herself in a corner, a sweaty Japanese masseuse just coming out of a cubbyhole.

"You next?"

Arachne looks at the masseuse's huge-knuckled hands and shakes her head.

"The sauna's in there. Take a shower first."

"Thanks," Arachne mumbles. She takes off her jeans and sweater, hangs them on a hook. She thrusts one foot under the shower. She opens the sauna door. The women inside are silent. She pulls the door shut behind her.

One woman is lying stretched out on the top bench. She is naked, staring at the ceiling, her hands linked behind her head, bored and contemptuous. Two women are crouched on the lowest bench in the corner, huddled close together. They wear bathing suits, flowered bathing suits that bulge over their chubby flesh. One wears her glasses, which are fogged up. The other has her eyes shut. A fourth woman, small-boned and cheerful, is the only one who looks at Arachne. She smiles. She moves over, pats the hot cedar boards beside her. She pulls up her legs. She is naked too. Arachne avoids looking at her crotch. She sits beside the woman and tries to keep her legs together.

The one lying down turns her head toward the two in bathing suits, and Arachne sees, with shock, that her whole face is distorted. One side is completely different from the other, unmatched, two halves of two different faces put together.

She addresses the two flowered swimsuits. "Are you ministers?"

"Oh no," they say in unison.

"But your name tags say you're with the Women's Ministry."

Arachne looks. Name tags are pinned to their bathing suits.

They giggle. "We're not ministers. We're members of the fundamentalist churches of the West. We're here for a retreat."

The woman keeps staring at them. Sweat drips slowly down her face. She does not wipe it away. "Then why is it called the Women's Ministry?"

"Because we *share*," says the blond one. "We're here to

talk about women's ministry in the world. We have – "
she hesitates, "meetings where we discuss our role in life
and our relationship to our families and to God."

Sweat is running into the halved woman's eyes. She
does not blink.

"You know," says the brunette, "where we evaluate
things. A chance for a closer walk with Jesus. We come
here to refresh ourselves, contemplate."

"What do you *do*?"

"Oh, we have three or four prayer meetings a day."

The small woman beside Arachne giggles. "We can hear
you singing."

The halved woman suddenly sits up, swings her feet
down to the second bench. She stares at the bathing suits.
"Who leads your meetings? Men?" She sounds like Thena.

"No, women," says one.

"Well, mostly men," says the other.

"Ministers' wives," says the first. "They have a special
calling."

The little one giggles again. Arachne, facing the ques-
tioner, sees that she is completely halved. Her eyes are
different colors. One is bright blue, the other dark brown.
One half of her hair seems blond, the other dark. One
leg is tanned, one pale. Even her pubic hair; one half is
curly and one straight.

"Do you have any female ministers?" The interlocutor
is relentless.

"No," says the first.

"Yes," says the second.

Two halves snorts. "Make up your mind."

"It's sometimes easier to talk when your husband's not
around," volunteers the first. "That's why we come here."

Two halves jabs a vicious kick at the air. "Why have
a husband at all?"

"That's not all," says the second. "We learn." She takes

246

off her glasses and looks directly at the halved woman. "What do you do?"

"She's a painter," says the little one beside Arachne.

"Are you here for a conference?" asks the blond bathing suit.

"Yes," says the little one. "Women First."

"What's it about?"

The woman shrugs and her breasts bounce happily. "What do you think? Women first."

But the second bathing suit is still holding her glasses in her hand and staring up at halves. "What do you paint?"

The woman scowls. She lies down on the top bench again. She addresses the cedar ceiling. "The world. The fucking male-dominated, ministry-oriented world. Revolution. Kitchens." She punches an arm up into the air. "Railway tracks."

"Pictures?"

"Ten-foot canvases. Twelve-foot fences. I'm painting Nellie McClung on a granite rock face fourteen miles from here. I'm going to take up sculpture and chisel a statue of Isis out of Mount Lougheed."

The bathing suits look at each other. They are as red as lobsters but hardly manage a drop of sweat. "It's getting hot in here. We have to go now." The door thuds shut behind them.

The little one giggles. "Avee, you drove them away."

The halved woman drops an arm over her face. "Fembots."

But one sticks her head back in as though conscience prompts her. "You could come to one of our meetings. You're welcome."

Halves growls. "No, thank you."

"You could come to ours too," the little one chirps. "You'd find them interesting."

The head vanishes.

"They're going to pray for you," snorts halves.

"I need it."

"Are you really a painter?" It's the first thing Arachne has said and both women look at her and begin to laugh. They refuse to tell her. When she has sweated and sweated, she showers and gets back into her clothes. The women are still in the sauna; they seem able to withstand infinite heat.

She drops her limp towel in the attendant's basket and threads her way back to the elevator, past an old-fashioned ice-cream parlor, past the video arcade again, the woman still shooting spaceships. "Bam. Bam. Bam. Bambambam-bambam. Gotcha." Her hand is on the lever, her knee is braced against the console. Arachne cannot help herself; she picks up the alligator briefcase and walks into the open elevator doors. She looks at the number on her key. Room 426. She steps off at four into a mirrored wall, a hiss of tropical plants. Her room is huge, a triple-sized bed and a football-stadium bathroom. The carpet is blue. She cocks her head at herself in the mirror and snaps open the briefcase. Inside are pamphlets, brochures, paper, a somewhat crumpled silk blouse and a name tag. *Women First*. Arachne puts on the silk blouse, pins the name tag to it and goes down to dinner.

In the elevator she asks another briefcase, "Where's the banquet?"

"The Alhambra. Time for a drink first?"

"Why not."

In the middle of a long diatribe on investment, the woman buys Arachne two more double martinis. By the time the silk and leather, the cashmere and denim and velvet, the tweed and suede and tartan and mohair and linen and batik and camel's hair and flannel and corduroy are crowding into the banquet room, Arachne is buzzed, her ears are singing with gin.

They meet Women's Ministry head on and there is a scuffle with the polyester and worsted and wash and wear and rayon and tricot and lamé and jersey and acetate and calico and chiffon and gingham. They elbow each other for direction, surging back and forth, until the briefcases, wielded as weapons, win, and Women First stampede the other group, crushing corsages and trampling open toes, tearing a lacy sleeve, unbuttoning a high collar. Ministry hold their purses against their well-supported chests and try not to brush the bouncing breasts, the unstockinged thighs that flash from slit skirts, try to pull themselves back from contamination. Several have Bibles under their arms, they are going to a meeting, they have had a decent early supper, none of this standing around drinking and eating crab dip for two hours. They avert their faces, their chins tremble with righteousness. Women's libbers, all the trouble in the world comes from women's libbers. They have heard in the elevator that a big one is going to address this conference tonight, a really famous one, one of those who started it all, who's responsible.

Arachne is swept into the ballroom with the briefcases and shoved to a table which has ordered its evening's supply of wine in advance. The table seats ten and there are twelve bottles of dry white on guard in the middle. Arachne plops into the one empty chair, and the introductions begin again.

"I'm in deep-sea diving."

"Fur coats."

"Management consulting."

"English as a second language."

"Nuclear medicine."

"Electrical engineering."

"South American refugees."

"Real estate."

"Tea kettles."

Silence, and they look at Arachne expectantly.

"Oh." She looks down at the napkin she has unfluted in her lap. Should she say she's in underwear? She makes a quick decision. She may be asked to produce evidence. "Cars. Old Mercedes."

The woman who said she was in fur coats leans toward her with breathy excitement. "Really? I'm trying to buy an old Mercedes. Do you know where I can get one?"

"Sure. At the moment I'm driving a 1959 Type 300."

The woman catches her lower lip with her teeth. "How much?"

Arachne bounces her fish knife on the edge of her bread-and-butter plate. "Twenty-five thousand." No one could want to pay that much for the old hearse.

"Done." The woman pulls out an eelskin checkbook and proceeds to scrawl the amount with a fountain pen. She rips the check out and waves it in the air to dry the ink. "Let's celebrate. I can't believe my luck."

The check is handed around the table to Arachne, who folds it neatly and slips it into the thin billfold she carries in her hip pocket.

They drink to the woman's purchase. They drink to the car. They eat salmon mousse. They drink to the conference. They nibble green salad. The bracketed lights on the wall swim, the ballroom grows dimmer, warm and soupy, perfume and unshaven underarms and white wine and all the heads of shampooed, shiny, blown-dry hair. A night breeze drifts through the high, leaded windows. The women bounce in their chairs, a few cha-cha between tables, a few more begin to smoke cigars, baked Alaska yet to come and thick black coffee and liqueurs and the guest speaker. They are waiting for her, she is going to get them going, set them up, they will be ready to drink all night, argue all night, wander around the building, break into the pool and skinny-dip. The attendant will come down in the morning to discover his towels used and the pool full of debris, floating a few champagne bottles, a soggy sock, a negligee.

Right behind Arachne is a table with two men. The men sit beside each other, but on either side of them is an empty chair. They are diffident but assertive; they belong here as much as anyone, they have paid their fee and come to hear the women's libber, to hear if she is really as great as their wives say she is. Their wives are at home taking care of the children, making sure no one breaks into the house. They'll want an objective report.

The guest speaker is seated at the head table, picking at her food. She looks tired, as if she's been breathing life into banquets for months, years. She helped to start everything, she is supposed to be brilliant. She has no choice.

The baked Alaska arrives and the woman of ceremonies stands to introduce the speaker. She begins a long recital of words and deeds, assets and effects that the guest has wrought. It's unnecessary. She is an icon, a figurehead, a priestess. When the introduction is over, the room's throat roars open. Then she stands, tall, a golden Amazon. In the expectant silence before she begins to speak, the woman with the checkbook grabs the tail of a busboy's coat and demands in a stage whisper, "Quick. A bottle of cognac."

The titan speaks. Her voice low, hoarse, reaches into the farthest corners of the room. No one can escape its gravelly, tongue-licking power. Under her words the women in the room melt, they flower, they lift their expectant faces toward her podium, they sigh, they nod, they shout with laughter, they clap, they pound the tables with their fists. They love her, oh, they love her. She talks for them, all their mute and tongue-clipped mouths one wordless inarticulate cry for her bright shining, for her laughing anger.

She runs fingers over their skin, touches the faces held up to her, she gives them everything she can. She is moving that banqueting ballroom forward step by step, putting the stones of words in their mouths.

"Equal rights."

They chant the line back to her. And in the pause after their shout, they hear beyond the partition behind the guest speaker the strains of a hymn, the polyester women in their meeting. They still. Perched on the edges of seats, arms across chair backs, elbows propped on tables, they listen to the quavering voices of the Women's Ministry. "Jesus loves me . . ."

The guest speaker grins and goes on, her rough unsteady throat carries the room forward while the thin plaint of the hymn drifts quiet and stops. When she reaches the next point, they tense, ready, and when she cries, "Pro choice," the ballroom sings back. *"Choice, choice, choice."* After the shouts have died and the toppled glasses stopped splintering, they hear the voices of the Ministry rise again, this time struggling valiantly with "Amazing Grace." But they can't keep it up, they don't have the wind or the training, they haven't been drinking since five this afternoon.

*"Husbands in the home."*

The men at the table behind Arachne are shifting and looking at their watches. The women are half on their feet, they are hot, they can storm battlements. The leader's words are tensile, they lift worlds, she has shaped these thousand bodies into one concerted effort.

*"Equal,* equal, equal." They will not let her go, they chant her name, they surge toward her, they stand, they toast her. The two men slip out the door.

Arachne escapes to the bathroom, washes her face in a marble basin. There are a few spots on the borrowed silk blouse, the name tag is askew. She tries to read it upside down, looks at it in the mirror, but cannot make out the name. She heads for the elevator and punches four. The elevator goes down, stops at Arcade. Ting. Arachne sticks her head out. The green shield of the video machine seems brighter, almost eerily hot in the dimly lit hall. She sees a shapely ass, an elbow.

"*Bammm*. Gotcha. Forty-three free games."

The elevator doors begin to close and Arachne ducks back inside, pushes four again.

In her room she takes off the blouse and pulls on her cherry-red sweater, folds the blouse neatly and tucks it back into the alligator briefcase. She takes the stone staircase down and sneaks up on Arcade from the other direction.

"Uh-huhu-ugh – hu. *Bam*. Bambambam. Gotcha. Forty-five."

She sets the briefcase down beside the vibrating machine.

# Getaway

The riotous night has its effect. At seven o'clock the next morning the hotel is dead. Arachne goes downstairs with her key and turns it in at the desk, tells the clerk to send the bill to Ladies' Comfort. When the attendant brings the Mercedes up to the steps, she tips him five dollars and says, "You didn't see this car."

He looks down at the bill in his hand.

Arachne holds out another five.

"Right, ma'am."

Arachne heads down the hill and drives through Banff trying to figure out how to get back onto the Trans-Canada going west. Banff is asleep on its feet except for one black bear rolling garbage cans down an alley.

She keeps going until she hits the circle and damn if she doesn't get stuck again. She goes all the way around twice before she manages to escape. But then she is going east, back the way she came. She thinks of spinning a U in the middle of the slow Sunday traffic, and then decides that at the first main road she'll turn south, get off this highway. Back roads are always better. Besides, the fur-coat woman might get the word out looking for her. She reaches into her rear pocket and looks at the slightly crumpled check. Twenty-five thousand dollars. Enough to keep her going for a long time. The way that woman was slinging her checkbook around, she didn't look as if she'd miss an odd thousand here or there. Arachne owes it to herself to be independent.

At a sign that says Kananaskis, Arachne turns south. For a while there is pavement, but after an hour the road becomes gravel, a forestry trunk road. It is dusty but deserted, exactly the road she wants; it will take her all the way south to the Crowsnest Pass, and she can cross the Rockies there. Mountains and waterfalls blur her drive but Arachne has no time for scenery. She needs to get to Pincher Creek, check the oil, gas up the car, get some money.

## Signatory

Monday morning the bank is empty. Arachne endorses
the check with a flourish, presents her driver's license and
other identification to a sleepy teller. The teller verifies
the signature, yawns and reaches for her cash drawer, turns
the check over. She blinks, opens both eyes. "I can't give
you this."

"Why not?"

"It's too much money. You need a co-signer."

"Come on," says Arachne. "You can phone my bank
in Calgary."

The teller shakes her head.

Arachne slams her hand on the counter. "Do I have
to go all the way back to Calgary to cash this?"

"What's the trouble?"

Arachne turns to a puckish, black-bearded face above
a body type that she recognizes, powerful chest and belly
dwindling to almost insignificant legs.

"Oh, hi, McKay. She needs a co-signer, somebody who
knows her."

"I'll sign. I know her."

"You do not," says Arachne.

"Like hell. Here, Arlene, gimme that."

"Okay, long as you stand behind it, McKay." She counts
out two hundred and fifty one-hundred-dollar bills as if

she does this every day. Arachne sticks the bulky pile in her jacket pocket and buttons it up.

"I'd put that in my bra if I were you." The teller cannot resist advice.

"Don't wear one."

When Arachne swings out the door, he's leaning against the hood of the Mercedes. "You gonna buy a ranch or a mine?" He looks like he belongs in the Klondike gold rush, a solid, meaty body and dreamer's face.

"What are you selling?"

"Me? Nothing. Just bumming around. Nice out here. Going to the Pass today."

"What's it worth?"

"The mine? Couple of thou. Hang onto it and it'll increase."

"What would I do with a mine?"

"Investment."

"Is it a gold mine?"

He kicks one toe of his cowboy boot with the other and looks sheepish. "It's a coal mine."

"What would I want with a coal mine? What would anybody want with a coal mine?"

"Real pretty location. Historic site."

"I'm too busy taking care of myself to worry about history. You better go talk to the government."

"I'd feel lots better if you had it." He grins crookedly. "We could be partners."

Arachne gets into the car and slams the door.

He shrugs and strolls away, barrel-chested and bow-legged. Arachne watches him go, then swings into the street. The bundle of bills feels heavy. When he doesn't turn, she drives onto the sidewalk right beside him, reaches over and opens the passenger door. "Well, make up your goddamn mind. Are you coming or not?"

He unfolds his legs under her dashboard. "Go west."

He is, he tells her, Dougall McKay, miner, entrepreneur, self-styled historian, archivist and rescuer of the Crowsnest Pass, heavy drinker, big talker, drifter, gambler, high-rigger, helicopter pilot. "Ever been in the Crowsnest?"

Arachne shakes her head.

"Well, ma'am, you have yourself the most knowledgeable guide in the West. I know it like the back of my hand. Born there, grew up there, worked in the mines, the Maple Leaf, the Bellevue, the Hillcrest. Half Wop, half Scotch." He laughs and pulls a flask out of his hip pocket. "Literally. Want a snort? I've drug half the Crowsnest back to Calgary trying to save it from being broken or rusted or buried or thrown away. This used to be a booming place."

The string of scattered buildings they pass look like sunken and decayed stumps of teeth.

"The whole Pass is poetry."

Arachne groans.

"No, I tell you. Listen. Lundbreck, Maple Leaf, Passburg, Burmis, Hillcrest, Frank, Blairmore, Coleman, Sentinal, Crowsnest, Summit, Michel, Natal, Sparwood, Mosmer, Fernie. Gone now. Yep. Remember growing up, driving the pass, count the towns like you'd tell the rosary. Oh, don't raise your eyebrows. I was raised a good Catholic boy, first communion and everything. The Mohawk tipple, the Leitsch Colleries. Want to see the Hillcrest graveyard?"

"No," says Arachne. "I'm sick of the dead. Overdosed."

"Squaw's nipple." He points. "Want to stop for a drink?"

They drive off the highway into Blairmore, trace the few streets like a crossword puzzle while he rambles on about prohibition. He can't be much more than forty, yet he talks as if he's been alive since the beginning of the century.

The miners' houses are crouched boxes spilling down the mountain flank and the streets weave between them drunkenly. They are saddened, aged, no one goes down the mines anymore, comes up black and grinning to sluice dust from the throat with pitchers of beer; singing in the streets on Friday nights, dancing once a week to the fiddles of the Whiskeyjacks, all to the eerie call of the whistle that leads them in and out of the black mouth in the side of the mountain.

"Behind each house is a smaller house, a bachelor shack," says Dougall. "Single guys used to rent the garage, the workshed, live there. They weren't really bachelors – immigrants who'd left their wives and kids in the old country and were working to get them over here. Worked their whole lives some of them, and the families never came. And then, some of them came and *whoooeee*, they didn't get along anymore. Booze and whorehouses and coal mining don't sit too well with old-fashioned European girls. Used to be able to hear some real drag-'em-out fights. Women always won too. Some guys still live in them shacks, going to die there surrounded by rusty tin cans and antique whiskey bottles. Want to meet one, a real miner?"

Arachne is trying to decide what she wants. "Why not?"

He directs her to a battered gray shed with a crooked stovepipe smoking above it. He pounds on the door with his fist and hollers, "Hey, Frank, *Frank. You home?*"

"Coming."

When the low door is hauled open, the man standing hunched there blinks in the light. He is oversize, tremblingly heavy. It does not seem possible that he fits within this structure. "Dougall?"

"Right, old boy. How you doing?"

"Bring me a bottle?"

"Sure did. Here you go." And he hauls another bottle of Scotch from an inside pocket of the jacket. "Friend of mine wants to meet you."

"Well, come in, come in then. Find yourself a place

to sit. Clear some of that stuff off the cot there."

The shack is dark and musky, like an animal's cave, junk leaning precariously, long underwear cast in its drying. A savage orange tom leaps from the bed and streaks out the open door. Arachne sits on what seems like a nest of feathers and fur, coats and shoes. This burrow is enticing. She thinks that she too would like to live like this, live herself into a profound and breathing darkness. She sinks into the miasma of the room pleasurably, feeling its rancid corruption soak into a tissue of herself that she recognizes, slovenly, happily rank. She watches the obese miner and Dougall McKay drinking, their kitchen chairs tipped back, their legs hoisting their bellies. They are reminding each other of a past that Arachne has no interest in, but their web of stories arouses in her a nostalgia for disorder and unwholesomeness, the satisfaction of a tattered life with no obligations or rewards. She is lusting after tawdriness again, as if it might be a refuge. And she realizes, listening to the two men chip away at the past, that she is escaping again. No, running toward anonymity, absorption, relief from expectation. If only she could take Thomas with her, but he is drawn by his maps, outlined by the lines that shape landscape. Arachne wants to sink into it.

She struggles up. "Dougall."

He flaps his hand. "Take it easy. We just got here."

"I'm late."

"For what? Your own funeral? Have a drink."

. He rummages on the table and peers inside a beer glass. "Jesus, Frank, don't you ever wash anything? Here, Scotch will sterilize it."

Arachne takes the glass warily. The scum around its edges doesn't bother her but her willingness to drink herself into a stupor with these two buried men does.

Dougall grins and nods. "Drink up." Under his black moustache his mouth is red and wet. "Then we'll go look at my coal mine. Black gold, right, Frank?"

"No goddamn gold down there." The bulging miner has shoved aside the litter on the table and is resting his head on his arms. "You're imagining it, Dougall."

"Hey. This lady's going partners with me. What do you know about it?"

Arachne feels her pocket. The roll of bills is bulky. She drains her glass. She sits down on the nest of bed again. She waits, swings her feet. She has another drink. And another, the Scotch gone now, colorless liquid from a Mason jar. She does not listen, she soaks. They are talking underground, the daily descent into a place where, when the lights go out, your own hand is alien, unconnected to you. You can strike yourself and not know where the blow comes from, you can fumble forward but even with caution cannot prevent the darkness from laying its smooth hot hands on your shoulders and forcing you to your knees.

They have entered darkness, lived in it, eaten it. No social callers intent on vicarious experience, but tenants, owners of darkness, bound by a lease to carry it wrapped around their legs, gloved on their hands. They do not translate their coal-dust living but wear it undulant and vampire until they accomplish death. Arachne drinks and warms her hands on their lightless life. They have what she has always wanted.

## Buried alive

It is pitch black when she wakens and the first thing she notices is the smell, as fetid as if she has been moldering in a shared grave. She is lying on her back; her own snoring has woken her and now her quiet breath forces her eyes wide. She can feel her pupils dilating, to no avail. There is not one crack of gray light for them to fix on, nothing but the smell. Cautiously, she flexes her leg. And feels herself wedged between two sodden bodies, covered by them, held by their arms and legs in a grotesque parody of post-coital tenderness. The fat man's knee across her upper thigh is a log; Dougall McKay's muscular arm imprisons her breasts. She shifts again, a secret effort to throw them off, but they sleep without the slightest adjustment to her movement, the rank pungence of their weight.

She licks her lips. Her throat is dry; she wants water. It is so thickly dark that she cannot be sure if she's really awake or only imagining sleeplessness; still, the smell persuades her that she must be conscious. She moves again, tries to shift the leaden bodies that are holding her close to their sleeping flesh. It is no use; she might as well be bound hand and foot. Arachne cannot breathe. She begins to struggle, to twist arms and legs and trunk against their indifferent bondage, a long, muffled struggle where

262

she fights desperately to release herself from their inflexible hold. Constricted more and more, she feels herself rising into a scream, a cry both beyond darkness and death, rising. She makes one final Herculean effort and the weight lifts.

"Aaaahh."

Her limbs are her own again. The bodies beside her are shapeless sacks. She has been sleeping between the two men, but what else, what else? Her coat has been taken off, but her clothes are still on, and her shoes. To her right is the moist obesity of the miner; to her left is McKay.

"Dougall, Dougall McKay."

"Ughhh." He fends her off with a foggy elbow and Arachne thinks of his dark knowledge lying beside her for how long: hours, days?

"What time is it?"

"Fuck off. How'm I supposed to know?"

"McKay, goddamn it, I can't breathe in here."

"Then go outside."

"Let go of me."

"I'm not touching you. Shut up, eh?"

Arachne pushes her way over the mute bulk of the man's flesh and crawls along the floor, hitting chair legs, knocking over bottles, brushing aside the ankles of long underwear. She finds a wall, crawls until she reaches what must be a door. She fumbles with the latch, a wooden bar laid across a metal hook. "Damn." She flails against the door as if it too is alive and inert, slams her fist against wood and it releases her, swings open to cool streaked dawn, the air so unsullied that she enters it with something like pain. She holds herself against a scrawny poplar with one hand while she clutches her other arm across her chest. And then, retching, stumbles to her knees. Her stomach revolts.

She stays on her knees, both palms flat on the ground,

heaving. Beside her there's a rustle and then the sound of urine sizzling against a tree. "That bad, eh?" McKay asks calmly.

"Christ. What was that stuff?"

"Frank's number one moonshine. Whooee – you sure did drink a lot."

"I'll die."

"No, just feel a little tilted for a week."

"You bastard."

"I didn't make you drink the Christly stuff."

"You could've told me."

"You're a big girl." He tucks himself back in his pants and steps beside her. "Here. Want a hand?"

"Don't touch me."

"Okay, sweetie." He fingers his belt reflectively and looks down the stumbling hill of the town. "What do you do for a living?"

"What?"

"Sorry. Wrong question."

Arachne sits back on her heels and looks up at him. "What the hell do you care?"

He shrugs. "Just interested."

Arachne reaches for the pocket with the stack of bills. It is flat, vacant. "All right, McKay."

He spreads his palms, looks away. "I'll give it back. Just say I'm holding it until you see my mine. I'd really like a partner."

"You motherfucker."

He swings around then. "Lady, you'd never have gotten that money at all if it hadn't been for me. Right."

Arachne manages to stand. "That's what you were doing in the bank? Looking for a sucker. Take what you want and give the rest back."

"Oh no, I'm an honest man. I'll show you the mine. We'll write up an agreement."

"I don't give a flying fuck about your mine."

"But you've got to see it." He is genuinely puzzled.

"I just want to get the hell out of here." She wipes her hands down her jeans.

"Let me say good-bye to Frank."

"I'm leaving."

He shouts something inside the door of the shack and comes back with Arachne's coat. "Don't you even want this?"

"I'll have to air it for two weeks to get the stink out."

"No smell on you?"

Arachne glares at him and gets into the car. He grins across the seat. "Too good for it. What are you, some kind of rich little runaway?"

"No! I'm an underwear sales rep."

He guffaws. "Sure."

"It's true." She gestures at the back seat. "There's my samples."

He reaches back, lifts the lid from a box. "Hey, aren't they sweet?" He picks out a pink pair, fits it over his face. "You don't really sell underwear."

"Damn right I do."

He whistles. "Well, I don't object to that. You're a qualified investor."

"I wish you would stop pretending. You're just taking my money."

"Your money, oh ho, *your* money. Where the hell'd you get that check? You didn't look so comfortable about it."

Arachne veers over to the side of the road. "Take the fucking money and get out."

"Hey, don't get so touchy. All right, I won't ask." He settles back and tips his chin down on his chest. "An underwear salesman. You meet the damnedest people in the Pass."

Arachne can only snarl.

Down the road he sits up. "Hey, hey, pull over here, off the road. Now we've got to walk a little."

"Why don't you get out. This is just a dumb game."

"No game, sweetie. Come on."

They climb until they reach an open portal, a wound blasted into the side of the mountain. A wire mesh gate covers the opening, padlocked, grate against darkness.

McKay steps back, points. "There it is."

"It's closed."

"Hell, yes. Don't want adventurous kids getting lost underground."

"Can't we get in?"

"You want to go down there?"

"Sure."

He laughs. "No, sweetie. I brought you here to see it. You can't say I've cheated you, but there's no way I'd take you down there or go down again myself."

"But I thought you liked it."

"I did. Once."

Arachne goes up to the entrance and peers through the barrier. She sniffs the darkness, its dank chill seeps thinly past her skin. It is the dead air of complete lightlessness, raw and undiminished. Arachne shivers, steps back.

McKay grins. "Yeah. Underground. Real nice place. Let's go."

They return to the car and he says nothing, brooding over his tipped-down face.

At the sign for Fernie he says, "Okay, this is where I leave you." He pulls out the roll of bills, separates approximately one half and tosses the rest on the seat. Before he slams the door, he leans into the car and gives her a wide satyr's grin. "Thanks, sweetie. Stay away from moonshine and don't sleep in any strange beds."

## Ambush

Arachne continues down the highway for a mile or two, then spins a U-turn and drives back the way she has come. She returns to the mine, the foul reticent portal mouthing earth. She hooks her fingers over the grill, sniffs that dead air, peers into its maw. The railway track pulls its thin curve into the receding tunnel. Although she strains and strains, her eyes at a certain point reach only a dim envelope, light swallowed. If she could get in there. But it is impossible, the metal gate soldered into the rock face to prevent all explorers of underground, all night children from wandering the myriad tunnels that entrail the mountain.

Arachne peers into the unseeable. Her body pressed against the gate is a body caught in the act of escaping, struggling to get over a last fence. When she releases herself, it is twilight, the lights of Fernie are raptured fireflies. She drives into town, parks the car and sets out on foot. There are only two bars and they are on the same street, their back doors facing one alley. She grins and goes to the Chinaman's for supper, a quiet supper with her back to the wall in a spot where she can watch the door. She drinks two pots of Chinese tea and scrapes her plate clean, then returns to the car and naps until quarter to twelve.

In the alley there is a moon. It quivers above the mountain, the back doors of the taverns, the dented garbage cans. Arachne settles down in a shadow where she can watch both doors, where the moon will not catch the metal of the tire wrench she holds. The spring night is chilly. She draws up her knees and hopes that her instinct is still intact.

She can hear the throat of the bar, a faint vibration in the ground under her buttocks. These men drink long and hard; she's going to have to wait. Still, she's certain that he'll use the back door, push it open and peer out, swing his solid belly in front of him and head for the nearest shadow to urinate. Bar-drinking men hit the outside air and need to piss: it's an irrevocable failing with them.

When the metal exit door screes open, she crouches. He comes out head first, sniffing the air, his black-bearded face perfectly revealed in the light before the door clicks shut behind him. He heads for the overhang of a lilac bush, its smell warning spring. And, yes, he stands, bends his knees and concentrates, watching his urine splatter into the ragged grass at the edge of the alley.

He is letting out a long sigh when Arachne reaches him. He is shaking himself when she raises the wrench. The undeflected descent of the iron, its dull contact with the back of his head, chances to prevent him from tucking himself back into his jeans, from closing his zipper. He falls headfirst into the lilac bush. Arachne hauls him out and stretches him on his back on the gravel. She begins to empty his pockets methodically, putting everything in a pile beside her. String, army knife, a claim tag, a broken pencil, a set of keys which she throws into the bushes, some loose bills which she slides into her own pocket without counting. She tugs his wallet from his hip pocket and sorts through it, taking both the money and his driver's license. She checks his shirt pocket, his jacket. Clean. She has him. She shoves his pile of belongings close to his head and is ready to stand when she sees the soft bud of his penis barely nosing through his open fly. It lolls almost happily, as though in the man's unconscious it takes its leisure, enjoyment. Arachne grins and cups her hand over it, then gently tucks it back inside the man's pants, pulls up his zipper.

"Thanks, sweetie. Stay out of dark alleys."

## Cover

In Cranbrook Arachne goes to the Continental Beauty Shoppe and gets her hair cut and dyed. The result is an awful blond but she's grateful for disguise. She knows that sooner or later they will discover that she has skipped bail. The car is her worst liability, but she cannot abandon it. Where is she going? If she stopped to answer that, she would stop moving, the irrevocable and intractable hum of the tires, the swish of wind through the open window, the hot smell of the car's upholstery and the pedals under her feet providing the impetus, the urgency to continue, continue, follow the carved pavement, the twist of metal guard rails on and on and on. Farther, not toward but away, on the one hand the image of the old man's face as he lifted its grief-stricken nakedness to her, the ascendancy of forced and abrupt decency over the natural; and on the other hand the image of the concrete cell where she spent the night, and all for giving that one old man a small escape. She does not think of where he must be now. She drives relentlessly, driving into and out of herself, a fierce evasion that can bring her nowhere but is itself enough.

She detours to Kimberley, the signs proclaiming the largest lead-zinc-iron mine in the world making her believe that she will garner something beyond that dark at the gated entrance to the coal mine. But Kimberley has been tarted up to resemble a German alpine town and the sign at the mine advertises personalized tours by Haggis Williams, the Scots ex-Japanese prisoner-of-war safety supervisor who functions as public relations man. He takes tourists underground, leads them to distant tunnels and leaves them in darkness; there are always faint calls, stragglers wandering through the maze under the mountain. Some, it is said, never get out and their bones spring to outraged disclosure at given intervals. Arachne does not stop to investigate farther. She turns the car at the gates and drives back down the mountain.

## Double up

She drives on, along the jumbled border towns and into the Okanagan, up to Penticton and Vernon, before turning off on 97 to Kamloops.

At Falkland she sees beside the road a short, chunky woman balanced on one leg, her thumb out, an accordion case at her feet. Arachne cannot tell why she gears down and pulls the Mercedes over, why she opens the passenger door. She should have enough of picking up strangers, McKay should have taught her a lesson. And when the woman turns and sticks two fingers in her mouth, whistles before she trots up to the car, the fat old dog that lumbers from the ditch should warn her. He is blunt-faced and black, a harness with dusty luggage strapped across his shoulders.

The woman pokes her head in the window. "Can Columban ride in your trunk? He won't be any trouble."

Arachne turns off the car and gets out reluctantly. Lifting the trunk lid, she looks down at the black snout nosing her knee and jumps aside. "That's a fucking bear."

The woman clucks and the creature scrambles into the open trunk. "Yup," she says. "It's Iris' bear." She lifts the harness and attached suitcases in beside him, pulls a length of twine from her pocket and ties the trunk lid so that it stays open a few inches, "For air." She bats at the blunt nose that pokes through the opening. "All right, you old fartface, lie down and have a nap."

She settles beside Arachne with the case at her feet. "Where you going?"

"Kamloops."

The woman nods. "And then?"

Arachne shrugs. She does not want that bear in her trunk all the way to Vancouver, although the woman's hands and the cut of her face make Arachne think she's seen her before. "Are you with a circus?"

"No. It's Iris' bear. I'm just taking it for a holiday. Iris is an opera reviewer, she's in Salzburg now. Are you on vacation?"

Arachne considers that. "No," she says finally, "I'm working."

The woman glances at the boxes in the back seat. "Sales?"

Arachne nods.

"Hey, so am I." She begins to unpleat her case, opens it to reveal rows of disc-like boxes. "I sell snoose."

"What?"

"Snuff, you know, chewing tobacco."

Arachne looks at the neat round cases. "People still chew snuff? I haven't seen a spittoon for ages."

"Oh, totally different thing. Whole new method. Look." She twists the lid from a red case and takes out a small brown drop wrapped in what looks like gauze. "No carving it off a plug anymore. Individually wrapped portions, carefully researched in terms of quantity and strength, and no more spitting. The wrapping enables you to chew without the tobacco disintegrating, to dispose of it as easily — more easily — than a wad of gum. You get the full flavor of tobacco without the smoke or messy cigarette butts, and even better, you can keep your habit a secret. Inoffensive to others, and yet the same tobacco high."

Arachne recognizes some of her own passion in the

woman's rapid spiel, in her assurance that her product is desirable.

"And further research has indicated that tobacco can yield additional pleasure – " she twists the lid of another tin – "smell that."

"Hmm, mint."

"Right, and gooseberry, and sage and vanilla, and natural." She opens each flavor and waves it under Arachne's nose. "Good, eh?"

Arachne fights a sneeze.

"Oh, go ahead, gesundheit. See, these can be inhaled." She winks. "We also have research underway on a marijuana version, but of course that won't be available until it's legalized. It has another use too, good as a compress. Cut yourself, apply a plug to the cut. It'll stop bleeding instantly. Tired eyes? Put a couple of damp plugs on your eyelids. Better in no time, wake up next morning bright-eyed and bushy-tailed."

"No kinky sex aids?"

"That's for people to devise on their own."

"I've never seen it advertised."

"Do you advertise your product?"

"No, guess not."

"There you are. Not much difference between panties and snoose. Concealed products."

"Doesn't the bear – uh, interfere with sales?"

"Most people don't even notice he's a bear. I just have to find a motel that takes dogs."

"But why are you hitchhiking? Doesn't your company give you a car?"

"They give me a certain amount of money every month. It's not enough to run a car, but if I hitchhike it's clear profit. This beast must cost you something."

Arachne caresses the steering wheel with her palm. "They pay for it."

"You have influence."

Arachne laughs, thinks of the accountant in Winnipeg. "Maybe."

"Are you staying in Kamloops tonight? The hotel will give us two bills. We could split a room, shave the company."

"Do you keep the bear in the room with you?"

"Of course. He prevents rapists and muggers. You ought to get one. What do you do in these towns?"

"Compile my orders. Pick up an occasional man."

"You know what you need? Someone to read to you."

"That won't put me to sleep."

"It does me. A good voice reading a long slow story." She sighs. "I'm a poet manqué, you know."

"What?"

"A failed poet."

Arachne laughs. "I met a poet once." She names him.

"You met him? Was he any good?"

"I don't know. I don't understand poetry."

"As a lover?"

Arachne shrugs. "Kind of jumpy."

"Shows in his poetry. No eroticism, slurping away without stopping to notice what your response might be. Cannibals." She winks at Arachne.

## Bearing up

The bear smells. Actually, he stinks. His dense, boggy self has permeated the room when Arachne awakens in the darkness of two a.m., awakens with the weight of the woman's leg thrown across her own, the woman's hot skin next to hers. They appear to be curled together in the middle of the one double bed, she and the woman entangled arms and hair and toes within the thrashed sheets. It is hot. It is always hot in Kamloops, thick. The air conditioner rattles. The bear snores and stinks and farts. In the room's dusk the woman sleeps with her eyes half open, pupils green between slitted lids. Arachne blinks down at her. She resembles someone, yet Arachne cannot lay a hand on that furtive recollection. It bothers her more than the grunting bear, the bear that tomorrow will allow the woman to strap the luggage across his back, that will follow her to the highway and stay in the ditch until a car stops to pick her up. Arachne almost allows herself to envy the woman. No kidnapping charge, no car, no uncertain future, but the surety of a case of snoose and a trudging bear and one town that follows another.

"The bear stinks," she says the next morning as the woman scrubs her back in the shower.

"He's allowed. I hose him off once in a while." She

towels Arachne briskly, rubs the terry down the backs of her legs. "Good legs."

"Huh?" Arachne turns to look over her shoulder at the woman. And there, in the steamy mirror, she sees that the face on the other body is hers, if she hadn't dyed her hair this awful brassy blond, she would look exactly like the woman. No, the woman would look exactly like her. She stares. "You look just like me."

The woman nods, buffets Arachne's belly. "I'm your doppelgänger."

"What?"

The woman wraps the towel around her dark hair. "Don't panic. People have looked alike before."

Arachne clenches her shoulder, forces her to stand in front of the mirror, wipes the steam away. Their eyes, meeting each other's, betray the same needling insolence. Without Arachne's bleached hair, they could be identical twins. The woman smiles. "Nice genes. Good sturdy stock. Short, solid. We don't have narrow feet and bad backs. Bet we can carry sixty pounds."

When Arachne rounds the curve at the north end of the lake, the woman is leading the bear into the Thompson River, the luggage and the accordion sample case on shore.

Arachne flees.

# Rerun

When the signs from the highway begin to indicate the suburbs of Vancouver – Agassiz, Chilliwack, Abbotsford, Mission, Langley, Surrey, New Westminster, Burnaby, Richmond, Port Moodie – Arachne finds herself tapping her clutch foot, scratching, chewing her lower lip. It is not the heat through the windshield, the increasing traffic, the damp coastal air, but Arachne driving into her own escaped history. She should not have come west, should have driven toward the open expanse of prairie and shield. This is a dead end; she'll hit the Pacific and have to stop, retract.

She is returning to her gasping, squalid childhood. She should have taken another direction. It was the sun in her eyes; she doesn't like driving with the sun in her eyes. And now, the wash of sea, the Port Mann bridge, she is back where she started; slouching down a street with her shoulders hunched against the drizzle, staring into other people's lighted windows for no reason but to enter a life other than her own.

She had learned the backs of houses intimately, the high bathroom windows and clothesline pulleys. Through the windows facing alleys she saw the hunched shoulders of women pulling on nightgowns, a jaw tensed against a razor, a figure slumped on the edge of a bed. The blue light of television filtered all shape. One house kept unsteady darkness. In another a baby cried and cried; no one picked it up. The shuffle of feet paced the floor. A fridge door clicked. A hanger scraped. A strange sad angry cry from the throat of a woman. And a man's voice, low, urgent, a conjurer's voice. "Whiskey Hotel Echo Romeo Echo Alfa Romeo Echo Yankee Oscar Uniform." Arachne crept closer, trampled a chrysanthemum bush under a window. "Charlie Oscar Mike Echo. India Alfa Mike Whiskey Alfa India Tango India November Golf." The voice was an insistent hand under her elbow. Arachne backed away slowly, fearfully, even as the voice continued, knew she would return. "Charlie Oscar Mike Echo Bravo Alfa Charlie Kilo."

Again and again she crouched under the window listening to the voice. "Charlie Oscar Mike Echo Oscar Uniform Tango." The voice was endless, irrevocable. "Sierra Lima Echo Echo Papa. Delta Romeo Echo Alfa Mike. Delta Echo Lima India Gold Hotel Tango." She began to watch him openly, standing outside the window in the dark.

"Charlie Oscar Mike Foxtrot Oscar Romeo Tango. Charlie Oscar Mike Echo India November."

"Open the window then," she said.

He raised his head, pushed back his chair, turned off his light. He tugged at the wooden sash, the window open as far as it would go, extended his hand to her. She swung in one foot, then squeezed her body through.

The walls of the room were hung with multi-colored flags. The bed was narrow. He helped her take off her leather jacket. Arachne bent to unlace her sneakers.

He knelt, put his face against her stomach so that the words were muffled. "India Whiskey Alfa India Tango Echo Delta Foxtrot Oscar Romeo Yankee Oscar Uniform."

Arachne put her hands on his shoulders. He was wiry, his face lined, his hair greased back. Arachne was fifteen and no one had ever touched her.

## All's fair

She knows that Vancouver will put her back. She needs to get through it, beyond it, as fast as possible. She will head for the ferry, Vancouver Island's lack of habitation, the rain forest. She should have gone the other way, east. Now there is nowhere to go but on, she does not dare to stop here. There is nowhere to hide, no refuge. Rain greases the windshield. She pounds the heel of her hand against the dash. This is simply unfair, she almost managed to escape.

She drives the wet black streets block by block, doggedly retracing their implacable existence, her own terror. At eleven-thirty she needs to gas up, she needs to go to the bathroom, she hasn't eaten since eight o'clock this morning. Kamloops seems centuries past, the snuff woman and the bear a happy dream.

She finds a gas station. "Fill it up. Check the oil." She rests her head against the steering wheel.

"Can't find the dipstick, ma'am."

"Well, look, for Christ's sake." She will not get out of the car.

And she wheels away from the pump with a full bladder and an empty stomach and a hopeless fist at the bottom of her throat, wheels down Broadway until she sees a pink neon sign flickering Sushi. She pulls over and hauls herself out of the car, staggers and has to grab the door. She clings to the handle, straightens slowly. She can't faint now, she needs to eat and piss and get the hell out of this city, go to the island, that's what she'll do, go as far west as the road and the ocean allow, farther than anyone will think of following.

She staggers the few steps down the street to the pink-lit entrance under the sign. Inside is the faint piping of a reed flute, pale-blue walls and paper-divided cubicles, a soft-soled woman in a kimono. The woman, an indeterminate age under black upswept hair, bows. Arachne bows in return, awkwardly. "For one," she says. "Where's your bathroom?"

When Arachne emerges, the kimono beckons her to a high stool against a glass-cased counter, bows again and retreats, returning a moment later with a hot towel on a narrow lacquered tray. The towel is soaked in lime and herbs, and the woman makes a motion of rubbing her hands. Arachne holds it to her face, lets the steam soak into her skin. It erases the dust, the weary lines at the corners of her eyes. "Ahhh," she says and raises her head to the smile of a Japanese man, who stands, knife in hand, behind the glass case. There is a headband tied around his glossy hair, his jacket is snow white. He bows and then stands alert, waiting. Arachne looks at his attentive face. She looks at the chunks of fish in the case in front of her and over her shoulder at the eight or ten tables in the room. They are empty. She's alone, seated directly in front of this smiling Japanese chef with the sharp-edged knife held so carelessly in his hand. He bows again, indicating that he is at her disposal.

The kimono appears at her elbow with a bowl of steaming broth. There is no spoon. Arachne understands that she is to drink from the bowl. She's surprised at her own hunger, how delicious the broth smells and tastes. The chef nods in approval. He begins to wield his knife, taking from the glass case fish pink and gray and white and yellow, chop, chop, chop, his fingers shaping each shiny and transparent piece. The blade flashes, the man's hands are hypnotic. A cup of steaming tea appears at her elbow, a decanter of saki. Arachne curls over the high stool. When the chef stops, she sighs.

"Hocho," he says and puts in front of her a rose of transparent slices and a small dish of brown liquid. He bows and backs away, then in a moment is at her elbow, mixing a green paste into the brown with a pair of chopsticks. He lifts one of the rose pieces from the flower and dips it into the sauce, then hands the chopsticks to her. He bows again. His concern for her is touching; he seems ready to feed her. She takes the chopsticks and lifts the piece to her mouth, its sweetness overwhelming the bile that has been riding in her throat all day. The meat dissolves in her mouth with a strange tang.

He watches every move of the chopsticks to her mouth, every swallow she makes. When she has finished the rose, she puts them down, sighs.

"Fugu?" He bows after the question as though to give her time to consider.

"Yes, yes."

"Fugu." It is a careful ascertaining.

"Yes."

He bows again, his hands clasped in front of him as if praying, then retreats. Arachne sinks back and sips at the tea, the hot saki that slides from her stomach down to her toes, to the tips of her fingers.

He returns, holding in his palms a serving plate the blue of eternity, of innocence, of glacial promise, and presents it to Arachne as if offering her a jeweled crown. Against the peacock plate, the white transparent flesh is overlain into a spider sitting in the middle of its web. Each narrow piece of fish etches a filament, while the spider's eight legs are made of tiny, splayed-out slivers of dark skin. It hangs, trembling in its new-spun web, above the celestial blue. The diamond slivers of fish that compose the spider's body shimmer in the pink light, fine as hoarfrost on a branch.

Arachne looks into his waiting face. "It's too beautiful. I can't eat it."

He lifts a piece from the corner of the web and dips it in the small saucer, raises the chopsticks to her lips. Still watching his face, she opens her mouth, takes the flesh between her teeth. It tastes of distant water, a faint wistfulness in its texture almost like coriander, an emanation that melts away as quickly as the honey she has sucked from the buffalo beans blooming in prairie ditches. She takes the chopsticks from the chef's hand and eats slowly, circling the web inward to the body of the spider in the center of the plate, the Japanese eyes watching her every mouthful. When she has finished, she wants to stand and bow to the chef but her arms and legs feel distant, lethargic. Instead, she bows from her stool, into his bow. "Manna," she says and he nods. She moves her hand to raise the cup of tea, her thoughts like crystal, everything suddenly clear here in the city where she was born, where she grew up, where she left herself behind, all magnified into possibility under the smile of the sushi chef's eyes. Her fingers move around the cup but cannot lift it to her lips. She caresses it instead, feeling its rough glaze with sensory shock. She has only now gained this exquisite awareness. Her arms and legs are warm and numb. She tries to shape the word manna again but finds she cannot speak. Her mouth is swollen with the lingering aftertaste of the fish she has eaten, she is rooted here under his eyes. He bows and backs away, comes around the counter to sit on a high stool beside her. Arachne feels her breathing catch.

The sushi chef smiles. "Fugu," he says, easing her head gently onto his shoulder. "Fugu."

# Ferryman

Arachne finds herself on a ferry crossing the Strait of Georgia. It is dark, she's standing on the bow with the wind buffeting her hair. She does not know how she got here, she has no memory past the infinite languor that engulfed her at the sushi bar, her arms and legs going gradually numb while her thoughts crystallized. I died, she thinks. I'm dead. I was eating fugu. It can kill you.

The light from the bridge is a splash above her and under her feet the deck vibrates. She lays a hand on her own sleeve. She's dressed for rain, in a hooded poncho, at her wrist is a rough woolen sweater. She joins her hands. They are cold, wet with spray. She brings a hand up to her face. It feels the same. On her feet are sturdy hiking boots. The jeans she is wearing are new. She puts her right hand into the pocket. A key chain, she can feel the shape of the keys to the Mercedes. She reaches into the pocket of the poncho; inside is the flat shape of her wallet. She peers into the darkness ahead, a lighthouse over on her right flashing. She can make out the letters on the bulkhead above her: Queen of Alberni. The wind is cold here. She walks toward the stern. Behind the glass windows the passengers are reading, drinking coffee, playing cards, amusing their children, sleeping.

The stern is warmer, out of the wind. A light plays

over the green wash of the ship's wake but the darkness is thick and the air smells like autumn. Arachne breathes deeply, sucking the damp air into her mouth. She had decided to go to the island, go as far west as she could. She leans over the rail, the water's white froth as promising as a thick pillow. She could plunge into that darkness. It's done often, a painless, certain method. A figure flailing on the rail before tumbling away from the ship's vibration, entering the soundlessly cold sea. "She never got off the ferry," they say. And in the flurry of unloading, the intercom squawking: "COULD THE OWNER OF VEHICLE LICENSE NUMBER DOA 000 PLEASE PROCEED TO THE CAR DECK IMMEDIATELY. REPEAT, PLEASE PROCEED TO THE CAR DECK IMMEDIATELY."

A shape looms behind her, the heat of another body. And then a hand on either side of hers. "Not planning to jump, are you, girlie?"

She elbows against his chest but he's solid, unyielding. "Fuck off." She can talk. She remembers her tongue as dead wood in her mouth.

"Mmmmmnnn," he says and brings his lips down against her neck, his cold hands finding their way under her sweater. She can feel him. That is a surprise. She's supposed to be dead, only visible to herself, and she can feel him quite plainly. His rhythm against her is the same convulsive rhythm she has known all men to use. She elbows him again but he refuses to be deterred, only murmurs, "What are you waiting out here for?"

His touch reminds her of warmth and pleasure and anger. Before she can imagine what it might be doing there, her hand closes on the steel hatpin thrust through her poncho like a skewer. He is fondling her breasts now, his lips still mumbling the skin of her neck. She jabs the hatpin into his chest, deep into his heart, her thrust stopped only by the red jewel at the end. The man coughs once and tumbles to the deck, his relentless arms pulling her down. She disentangles herself and straightens her clothes, steps over his body.

The intercom crackles: "WE WILL REACH DEPARTURE BAY IN TEN MINUTES. WOULD ALL PASSENGERS PLEASE PROCEED TO THE CAR DECK. DO NOT START YOUR VEH- ICLES UNTIL THE SHIP HAS DOCKED."

Arachne finds the closest stairway, goes to level B and walks straight to the black hump of her Mercedes. The door clicks as usual, the interior smells of cracked leather and dust. She settles behind the wheel, curves both hands over its cream Bakelite slip. She must be alive.

The cars begin to move and she follows their red taillights over the bulge of the ramp into a wet, fecund rain forest night.

287

## Cedar sleep

She drives north through Lantzville and Nanoose Bay, but at Parksville turns west, her inevitable direction. And then, after Coombs, finds herself dead tired, the warmth inside the car making her eyelids droop. She does not want to stop or sleep, is afraid now that sleep might become permanent. She can tell from the smell in the air that somewhere she has lost three months. She goes through her memory again and again but it is an erased tape, hissing static. She remembers nothing after the delicate taste of fugu and the sushi chef's smile.

The trees overhead grow thicker, blacker, the road winds through a forest of impossible dimension, blotting sky. She meets no car, not an animal stirs. If she pulls over and sleeps, will she wake up or will she be truly dead? She's dropping off at the wheel, she will hit one of those stupendous trees. She slows, turns, pine needles deaden motion. And sleeps, cedar branches soughing above, curled on the wide front seat.

She wakes cautiously, still unsure if she's alive, the sun blinding through the windshield. She tumbles out the door and stretches her arms toward the branches. This is the Cathedral forest, the oldest stand of trees on Vancouver Island. And tests her senses. Smell: yes, cedar; sound: yes, chickadees; sight: yes, green, that impossible green of rain forest; taste: she rummages in the car. Whoever fitted her in new jeans and the sensible rain poncho might have slipped in a few provisions. Under the front seat is a bag of oranges, on the back seat is a box of croissants and a thermos of hot coffee. The oranges smell juicy, the croissants buttery fresh. She sits down on the ground with her back against the front left tire and begins to eat.

# Road control

Most cars turn back at Port Alberni. The highway changes, becomes tight and unnerving, vehicles are rammed against granite cliffs, plunged into the depths of lakes; the road taunts and misleads deliberately, hairpin turns without warning, washed-out bridges and the inevitable impassable pass. The ditches inter abandoned vehicles, half-tons, even tent trailers rusting by degrees. Some of them are upside down, wheels like the folded legs of dying insects.

The Mercedes does not find the road intimidating. It hums at a perfect pitch, even climbing the summit of Sutton Pass. It has obviously been tuned up, the oil changed, the wheels balanced, a chip in the windshield repaired. There is no one to answer her questions but she has the two-hour drive over the pass and along Kennedy Lake to formulate them and then to block them out. Where was she all that time, what was she doing? Smoking opium, sleeping, in jail? Jail. That is still a possibility. She pushes down the gas pedal. The sun glances off the newly polished black hood.

When she reaches the junction, she stops the car and gets out to look at the map. There isn't much more road. South to Ucluelet is only five miles, north to Long Beach and Tofino is twenty-one. She must be almost at the ocean. Twenty-one miles and the road ends. She turns north.

The forest is as green and undiminished as it has been all morning. She slows, her window rolled down. According to the map, she should see open water soon, the Pacific breaking against the shore. She has her eyes on the gas gauge which is hovering close to empty, and this slight incline would seem to be taking the road back into the now gaunter and wind-mauled trees. When the black hood clefts the top of the hill, she's unprepared for the long coast spread in a crash of wind and breaker below her. That first perfect mirage suspends and then disappears as the hill drops. But she can hear it now, the roar thrumming deeper than the car's engine, more insistent than the wind through the open window. And the smell of whipped air, of sand, of bracken, pours into Arachne's ears, her open mouth, brings tears to her eyes.

This is the edge; not end but edge, the border, the brink, the selvage of the world. She can no longer go west. She is going north now but that will end soon; she has retraced her steps into this ultimate impasse and reached not frontier but ocean, only inevitable water. Long Beach, Florencia Bay, Gold Mine, Comber's Beach, Cox Bay, Chesterman; houses, signs begin to sprinkle the side of the road, still winding between the haunted trees, stunted, blunt from the battering of coastal storms. Motels, campgrounds, a gas station, a restaurant, all strung out at a respectful distance along the road, and then suddenly, coming around another bend, a huge sign. Pacific Packing. Docks glisten. Another sign. Tofino. And then a school, a church, more houses, a stop sign, the only one. Arachne stops. To her left a post office, to her right a co-op store, ahead a dead end. She turns right, dips past the hotel to the shack perched at the end of the dock, a floatplane bobbing on the water. She pulls on her hand brake and steps out of the car. The sign is erect and confident, a small square sign that does not need to proclaim itself but says what it has to and leaves it at that. Beneath it is a bench made of a cedar log split in half. A man in a painter's hat is standing on the bench, brush in hand. The sign which once signified something has been painted over with white and he seems about to repaint it. Arachne leans against the hood of her car and watches him, watches the gulls swinging the wind currents, watches the floatplane rev up and take off, watches an Indian cast a line at the end of the dock. She gets out the thermos and drinks what is left of the coffee. She looks at the forest-coated mountains, at old Catface brooding in his film of cloud.

The painter jumps down from the bench. "Good day to you." He waves his brush and ducks into the Pacific Rim Airlines shack, emerging a moment later to begin touching up the sign outside the door. Arachne sits on the bench below his fresh sign. She wishes there were someone with a camera to take her picture. *Pacific Terminus. Trans-Canada highway*. The road runs straight into the deep salt water of Tofino Inlet. From sea to sea, she thinks and laughs, knowing that Victoria, farther east and south, claims the Trans-Canada when it actually ends here.

The sign painter is embellishing a bird-like airplane, the small case of paint pots resting on the dock beside him. He is re-signing the town, all the names growing brighter under his strokes. He paints freehand and with an exuberant confidence that leaves a letter bent here, thickened there.

"Are you the local sign painter?" Arachne asks.

"No, I'm the island sign painter. Pass through every year, patch things up. Paint a few new ones, lose a few old customers who've gone to neon."

He trails the "s" at the end of Airlines. "And you?"

"Just traveling."

"Nice country. Been here before?"

Arachne shakes her head. "Know a good place to stay?"

He gestures. "Resort on open ocean if you go back toward Long Beach. Don't stay here in town when you've got all those beaches."

"Thanks."

"Not at all. Glad to be of service. Want your name on your car door? I do a great sign."

"No, thanks."

"Right." He goes back to the floatplane on his wall.

Arachne finds the resort he suggested, gets a room overlooking the water. There is a suitcase in her trunk and a plastic grocery bag that contains rubber boots. She drags the suitcase up to her room and leaves it unopened, puts on the boots and goes to meet the incoming waves, the suck of sand, the beached logs, the dead seaweed. She breathes and breathes, this edge seductive; she would like to stay balanced here. There is no one around. Early fall, the tourists are back in the city bent over desks, in department stores, on freeways. Arachne walks the miles of sand and rock and scrub, Long Beach itself endless, pure. Later she will go back into town and buy a postcard, send it to Thomas, a postcard of water smashing an offshore rock, of the inflexible lighthouse turning, turning. This is the edge of the world. If only it were easier to fall off.

# The drowned man

There is a full moon that night, hanging low and lantern above the ocean's hiss. Arachne walks the beach until she's cold but still cannot bring herself to enter her room, take off her clothes – who has put them on her, purchased them? – and crawl between the sheets. She cannot remember what it feels like to sleep in a bed, with a pillow and a cover. And there is nothing here to distract her from herself; no television, no radio, no telephone. Only the bed, the window and an ocean of ocean. Clouds trail themselves past the gaudy moon and then drift off again.

Arachne finds herself in the Mercedes, putting the key in the ignition. She'll try the road now, its bends and curves under the moon, go back to her punishment, stick her neck out and pay for the abandoned man, the kidnapped man, the robbed, the murdered man. How did that hat pin get stuck in the front of her rain poncho? She is desirous of peace; the past three months of oblivion have left her longing to return, not to be out here in the world again, driving, endlessly impelled by motion.

The road under the car's wheels is gentle, lulling. She begins to hum softly, turns her interior lights down so that only the headlights compete with the brassy lunar light that pulses through the trees. But she has gone only a few miles when the sign of a telescope makes her hesitate.

So long since she looked through Thomas' telescope at the infinite constellations that he named for her, their incestuous Greek parentage. She presses the brake and shifts down, turns the car sharply. Radar Hill then. One last look over the ocean that she will not likely see again.

For two hundred yards the road is perfectly straight, an avenue linked above by trees in secretive bower. Then it curves sharply and begins to climb, the car labors even in second. And mist, almost impenetrable fog, grabs at the headlights. Arachne is forced to slow to a crawl. But the Mercedes emerges to clear moonlight, as if the fog is a barrier separating the hill from the world below. Arachne sets her brake and gets out into the chill, the sea's echo. She begins to climb the cindered path that must lead to the telescope. She feels no fear, although the moon is satiric and the cedars drip drip drip, her footsteps in the solid hiking boots muffled.

At the top of the hill the sea roils under its lantern moon on one side and the mountains' heave on the other. There are wooden platforms here, a dark concrete hump, and at the very top on a cement block soldered into the glacier-scratched rock, the telescope. The platforms are surrounded with a guide, every hump and bay and mountain ridge named to the three hundred and sixty degrees of world here on the edge: north, Cox Point and Vargas Cove and Wikaninnish Island and Vargas Island and Flores Island, Tofino's scattered lights and Catface and Lone Cone and Meares Island; east, Sea Peak and Tofino Inlet and Indian Island and Grice Bay and Clayoquot Arm and Kennedy Lake and Mount Maitland and the Mackenzie Range and the beacon at Tofino airport (once, a pamphlet in her hotel room informed, the home of four thousand air force men who waited for a Japanese invasion in vain, who chaffed and fretted at the end of that treacherous road unable to come or go, Tofino nothing but an Indian village and Ucluelet the same, only the dripping rain forest and the implacable water, too cold to swim in but teasing, teasing); and then south, Long Beach and Wreck Beach and Box Island and the point of Schooner Cove and Quisistis Point and Florencia Island and farther, farther, Barkley Sound and the Strait of Juan de Fuca. And west, water, water, troughs, billows. The plate edge of water.

This might have prompted a sailor, an explorer: seeing full circle.

Arachne sits down on a flat rock below the cliff's edge and looks west. The broom rustles, the trees sigh. An owl cries. Whoo? Whoo? And then, although she has not heard a car drive up, footsteps up the path, slow, dragging footsteps. Arachne waits. There is nowhere for her to go. Instead of taking the path's circle, the person begins to climb up the rocks directly toward her. Hand over hand, he emerges from the bushes at her feet, panting, and plops down beside her with a sigh. No, not plops, squelches. He is dripping wet, his hair plastered to his forehead, and his clothes, of grayish woolen stuff, run water. It comes off him in rivulets, sliding into the rock's crevasses with a hiss.

He mops his face with a handkerchief that seems as wet as the rest of him. "Nice night."

"Did you walk from the road?"

"No, from there." He points directly below them to the sea. There is no beach, only rocks smoothed by years of hammering ocean.

"From the rocks?"

"Yes. You?"

"I drove."

"Ah. An automobile."

She looks at him and he smiles, nods, his face young and pleasant in the moonlight.

"Do you live here?"

"No." Arachne holds out her line like an old coin. "Just traveling through."

He chuckles. "Care to kidnap an old flyer? I'm getting tired of staying here."

Arachne looks at him sharply but can detect no irony. "Why don't you leave then?"

"Can't. Patriotic duty, you know." He taps open a pack of Players. "Smoke?"

"Sure." Arachne accepts a soggy cigarette. "Have you been swimming?" she says, a jest. "You're completely wet."

"As a matter of fact, I have. Earlier."

"But you can't swim out here. It's dangerous."

He is hunting for matches, turning damp items out of his pockets. Arachne reaches into the pocket of the poncho and finds a small book of matches. She turns them over, sees in the moon's clear light the black letters *Sushi*. "Here." She strikes one, lights his cigarette and then her own.

He inhales deeply. "We're not supposed to. Two of my buddies drowned on July first so we've been forbidden."

"But you do anyway?"

He shrugs. "They were drunk. I'm sober."

"But there's a riptide."

He shrugs again, smiles at her. "The water is soothing. And there's nothing else to do, it's so quiet here. Nothing but regular duty and the water."

"Regular duty?"

"Yes. I like it best when I have watch up here."

"Watch?"

"Yes, watching for the Japs, you know." His lips around the white tube of the cigarette are sensual, curled. "A treat to find someone like you up here. How did you get past them? No civilians allowed. Radar installation."

She stares at him and he laughs.

There is a footstep on the rock some yards behind them and he puts a hand on her arm. They sit motionless until the step retreats, then he leans close to her ear and whispers, "They never look here. Too scared. Spend most of the night in the bunker."

He is so close his breath stirs her hair and she turns suddenly, sprung against him at the same moment as he reaches for her. He is wet through, cold, but the muscles under the soggy clothes are hard and his desire is as fierce and hurried as her own. Astride him, the rock is unbearably hard on her knees, but she has to find out if she's alive, if she inhabits the same body as she always has, if they are more than flies in the amber of time. His mouth is salty and even in the air his skin does not dry. But her body is the same and his too the same, the impulses recognizable, the pleasure familiar.

The poncho, her boots, her new jeans are scattered beside his sodden uniform when he raises himself on his elbows, sits up. He lifts a chilly hand to her cheek, caresses it with his thumb before he stands, a white shape in the whiter moonlight.

"Well, time for a swim." He pushes into the bushes below the rock and she can hear him rustling down the cliff.

Under the pasty moon Arachne pulls on her jeans, laces her boots, picks up the poncho. The heap of clothes belies her solitary watch. She lays a hand on their rough wool, then swings to her feet and goes back to the pointing telescope, the wooden platforms outlining the word. She turns the whole circle once more.

Sitting on the end of the telescope is a feathered shape with large yellow eyes. It blinks at her sleepily and although she passes close to it, does not strike its solemn pose but turns its head to nod after her as she thuds down the path.

In her room Arachne sits down on the bed with the pamphlet. "In 1944," it says, "several men drowned while swimming at night. Subsequently, air force men were forbidden to swim at Long Beach."

## Farther flight

Arachne turns back. Going south from Tofino she sees
the sign painter straddling a scaffold, his brush in his
hand. She honks and he waves.

The only glimpse she gets of the ocean's edge is that
first sweeping panorama reversed in her rearview mirror,
and she doesn't stop, doesn't turn around but turns east
and speeds back on that trickster road, the same Cathedral
forest, Cameron Lake, Coombs or almost-Coombs before
she turns north.

She drives past Cumberland and Courtenay and Black
Creek and Campbell River, Discovery Pass on her right,
until finally, Kelsey Bay, the ferry belching smoke at the
terminal. She gets in line, counts out money for a cabin,
for the car, the cashier shaking her head. "Don't know
if you'll get on." But the deck crew makes a Volkswagen
move and a motor home leave a trailer behind and squeezes
her on, her back bumper barely cleared by the ferry's ramp
so that the orange-vested man hauling it up grins and
says "Tight steal" when she opens her trunk for her suitcase. The ferry is already backing out before it swings
around, its nose north for the inside passage to Prince
Rupert.

# Another direction

East then. Winding beside the Skeena River, she crosses it on the old wooden bridge at Terrace. At Kitwanga she stops before turning north on the Cassiar highway, north to what her map tells her is the Yukon border, up the Nass valley between the coast mountains and the Skeena mountains. She stops for gas, for bacon and eggs in the steamy café next to the gas station. Fall is closing in. The recreational vehicles have turned south. The Indian girls giggle secretly.

Arachne sits, unwilling to go on. If she turns north now, she will be going nowhere, into a lost and limitless world she might not emerge from. But where else is there to go? Back? Retrace her steps into the waiting arms of the RCMP? Back to the home where the old man waits? To Thomas? His square beautiful hands following the undulations of maps, his head bent above a rolled chart. She has been back to Vancouver and died there, one of her lives certainly over.

She wipes her plate clean with a slice of toast, leans back and signals for more coffee. Two hunters compare guns. A gang of rock-toting, backpack-lugging geologists comes in and orders huge hamburgers, sprinkling rye on the meat instead of ketchup. Arachne listens. She drinks another cup of coffee. She waits. The café rattles around her, the coffee gets thicker and stronger, the flies increase. She is steeling herself to enter the blank, the dislocated world of the North. Afraid, she is, afraid. After this there is nothing. What happens when the road comes to an end? After this there is no turning back. What she finds at the end will have to be enough, will have to be enough.

Perhaps she will be able to find a place to settle in, colonize. But what has she to offer to a raw place? Boxes of underwear samples, an excessive car, her third or fourth bootless life? Herself. Bordellos have gone the way of the gold nuggets that were once used as trade. A bar, she thinks, I can start a bar, serve these guys whiskey and rum and cheap vodka. But it seems ludicrous, Arachne in business, trying to make an honest living out of people's drinking habits. So she hesitates, sits on the swivel counter stool and watches the soft-faced Indian waitresses and tries to decide if there are other alternatives, if there are other roads, or if she has reached the last, the final one. Her wallet is stuffed with bills, her car is running smoothly, the boots on her feet fit. She turns the potential roads this way and that until the door swings open and a Mountie swaggers in. The Indian girls stop giggling and straighten up. The Mountie clanks into a stool, raps the counter with his knuckles. He is brought a cup of coffee, which in the girl's shaking hand slops over onto the saucer. He takes a long, derisive slurp. He has a good look at Arachne.

She drains her cup, pulls out her wallet and extracts a bill. She would like to leave the girls a dollar, but he's watching, she cannot do it without drawing attention to herself. Up here tipping means you leave a quarter under your saucer. Arachne does that and picks up her poncho, turns to leave.

"Hey."

Slowly she turns to face the thick face.

"Your car out there?"

"The Mercedes," she nods. The game is over, the police have finally caught up with her. In a moment he'll slap a pair of cuffs on her. She tries to return his look and tense for a bolt to the door at the same time. He takes another slurp of coffee.

"Alberta plates. Going back?"

She nods. His bald statement has made up her mind. If she gets out of here, she will go north, north, north.

Another slurp. "Don't try to go north. Ruin a great car."

"Edmonton," she says faintly. And forces herself to walk slowly, even buy a package of gum as though she's in no hurry, just traveling east on a well-populated highway. The door slams behind her. The Mercedes winks in the fall sunlight. She takes the wheel into her hands like a lover, turns around and drives away, slow, stately, into the north.

## Bluer than the bluest blue

After ten miles the hardtop gives out and becomes gravel, a coarse raucous road that jolts its presence through the body of the car. Her spoor is a balloon of dust, rocks ping against the chassis. Stretched immutable, the road ahead nothing more than a scratch through that skin of tree and rock overwhelming all sense of place, all memory of location. Here the lack of road imposes order, only one way in or out, this noisy slash that might be called a road punishing human and automobile into more than travel. It sinks its teeth into pace and movement so that it becomes impossible not to acknowledge the act of journey. Stupefying as it is, Arachne is happy with the road's intractability. She knows the Mountie won't drive this, no matter who he might have to chase. She clenches her fingers around the quivering wheel and holds the car firm over the potholes.

This entrance into alien territory is not momentous, only a movement from one place to another: a leaving, an arriving. Arachne cannot remember leaving. Her life has become movement without end, the grind of motion wearing itself into her, wearing all else out. Still, Columbus returned even when no one expected him to; he did not sail off the edge of the world. Arachne drives. She pulls over and squats in the bushes. She naps. She drives again.

It grows dark, the dark of the North that each day lengthens itself until it takes over, wraps all.

When she sees the figures gesturing, she imagines fo a moment that they are jesting, their waving only recognition of another person on this lonely stretch. Still, she slows, and they become more insistent, determined. She tells herself not to stop but is gearing down already, the man's gesticulation at her window. He seems familiar.

"What's the matter?"

"Truck breakdown. Have you got room to take us into Stewart?" He's one of the rye-soaked geologists, and before she has time to hesitate, there are four of them in the car, two in the front and two in the back, opening beer bottles on their belt buckles, fondling the upholstery, swearing at their incapacitated truck, checking her out in the blue dashboard light.

"Thanks for stopping, lady," says the one who flagged her down. "Not too many cars traveling at this hour."

She is passed a beer bottle from the back seat, handed a chocolate chip cookie.

"Where you heading for?" one of them asks.

"North." She bites into the cookie. "Homemade?"

"Yeah. Art here is a first-class cook. North where?"

"The Yukon." Cornered already. Why did she pick these jokers up?

"Nahanni, Campbell, Canol or Alaska?"

"What?"

"Which road?"

"Haven't decided yet." She tilts the beer bottle. "Which one should I take?"

"Depends. Want to go to Alaska? Dawson City? Mac Pass?"

"Where's that?"

They laugh. "Macmillan Pass. The end of the fucking road. For everybody."

"I'm not a tourist."

"But we are. And that's where we're going."

"I thought you were geologists."

"We are. We run the great white rock-hunting, scenery-scouting tours of the North. Wanna buy a ticket?"

"No, but I own a share in a coal mine. Want to buy in?"

"Where?"

"Crowsnest."

One of them in the back belches. One of them in the front snores.

"Crowsnest is too close to people."

"Coal dust is hard on my sensitive skin."

The car rocks with them, with their heavy boots and hammers, their clinking bottles. They sing, they tell Arachne jokes both racist and sexist, they take turns sleeping, they offer to drive. They smell. They haven't shaved, they haven't washed or changed their clothes for months.

Arachne almost drives off the road into a creek. "You're going into the bush?"

They agree, that's the idea.

"But it's fall. You're supposed to be coming out of the bush, not going in."

"Oh, we work for a backass company. We go in when everybody else comes out. That way the competition doesn't catch us."

She can see only the shapes of their faces and the white flash of teeth against the necks of bottles.

After a long curve, the two in the back straighten and poke the one who's sleeping. They fall silent, begin to watch out the window with a curious patience.

"Coming up, right around the bend."

"Tommy, sit up. You've never seen this."

"What?" asks Arachne. "What?"

"Wait."

306

"But what is it?"

"Nothing. Keep driving. We're almost in Stewart."

She begins to feel resentful, hijacked, chauffeured; but despite her anger, she is not prepared for Bear Glacier spearing the darkness. It has been misty for so long she cannot take the fist of blue lunging down the mountain, blue shaft flaking thunder to float bluer in the melt, pale blue, electric, icing everything, even the trees crawling up the mountain beside it, even the black rock of the scree.

The geologists are shouting, "Stop, stop, stop."

She manages to slew the car to the side of the road. They pile out. One of them opens her door and she stumbles to where they stand in a silent row facing that terrifying blue. Arachne sinks to her knees. It is the last thing she sees, blue.

## Aerial

They must take her into Stewart and put her to bed because
she wakes the next morning in a room in the King Edward
Hotel, not knowing where she is, her head still aching
from the intensity of glacier her eyes dared to see.

When she stumbles down to the coffee shop, they are
there, sitting at a table eating fried potatoes and scrambled
eggs and drinking gallons of black coffee.

"Here she is."

"Conked out on us."

"Can't drink, eh?"

"I hardy drank anything," she says indignantly.

They howl, they pull sanctimonious faces, they pour
her coffee. And halfway through her breakfast they start
shoving their chairs back. "Hurry up."

"Hurry up."

"Lemme alone."

"No. Hurry up."

"Why?"

"You're coming with us."

"Oh no, I'm not. Where?"

"Flying. Helicopter's waiting."

"I'm not getting into any plane with you guys."

"Helicopter. Hurry up. We're late."

"Fuck off."

"Come on." One takes her elbow, one sandwiches her toast and wraps a napkin around it.

She is out on the street, shoved into the back seat of her own car. The one called Art drives through the shabby, neglected town to a sagging warehouse beside a concrete pad, the blade already spinning, the engine beginning its long whine. They push her head down, pull her arm, stuff her into the back seat, snap her seatbelt, shove the toast into her hand, lock her door. One climbs into the front and two jump in beside her. The pilot mumbles into her microphone, the whine pitches deeper and they lift slowly, lift and turn, the town tilting below them against the long finger of the inlet and the road that ends at Hyder. They leave all that quickly, moving into mountain blackness spangled with glaciation, more blue, the ice like teeth, penetrating. Arachne hides her face in her hands.

After forty minutes they land and she's nudged out, shoved into a crouch while the machine lifts again, lifts and turns away into the endless indifference of wilderness. They are above treeline on a high ridge, with only the wind. The two who have jumped out with her set off toward an outcrop, begin to pound, the huge emptiness around them swallowing the chink of their hammers. Arachne wanders down the slope, sits overlooking a valley untouched, unexplored, uncivilized. Nothing moves.

She has been taken over. Perhaps they would let her stay here, curl up in the lee of a boulder and sleep, without sadness or implication, sleep her last life away.

She wanders farther, and there, before a cliff cuts the slope in half, is a glint. She bends, gets to her knees, puts out her hand. Someone has been here. The bronze marker pin is stamped with an indelible insignia, one that she has seen often on the corners of Thomas' maps. *National Geodetic Survey*. It is buried in the moss, but she digs with her hands and below the insignia can trace with her fingers the double initial she knows so well. T.T.

When the helicopter throbs up the valley, she's ready. They do not have to shove her head down or strap her in. She watches the roadless world below her, knowing she has arrived.

*Notebook on a missing person*

You manage to track down one of the geologists at Watson Lake. It is April. He says he's just come out of the bush. He has certainly been drinking rum, and his eyes are half shut. His first response to your questions is negative. No, he has never heard of Arachne Manteia and he doesn't give a good goddamn what happened to her. When you explain that she was an underwear sales rep driving a Mercedes, his brow furrows and he allows that he might have run into her.

"When?" you prod him.

He half opens his eyes and has a good look at you. "What's it to you?"

You try to explain but he's disparaging.

"You from the police?"

"No," you say and begin at the beginning, your interest in women's underwear and how that led you onto the track of this underwear seller and her life.

He demands more rum.

Which you provide. After two hours he has had nine drinks, told you bear stories, helicopter stories, tornado stories, camp cook stories and staking stories, without any reference to Arachne Manteia.

You make one last effort. His head drops to his chest and he looks almost shy.

"Last I saw her," he says, "she was heading for the Yukon border in that fat old car. Going north." And he passes out.

She must have taken the Cassiar highway from Stewart, past the Skeena Mountains and Dease Lake and into the Cassiar mountains. Although by that time she would have been sick of mountains, would not have cared about differentiating them, simply driven that long slow road that continues and continues forever until you hit the Yukon border and Watson Lake.

You are in Watson Lake. There must be a clue, more than this geologist who is now snoring, his head tipped back over the edge of the chair. Soon the bouncer will come and throw him out. You leave a bill and emerge into the chill of a Yukon spring, the muddy road that the town strings itself along. You decide to check everywhere, miss no one.

You start at the end of town with all the lost signs, all the places in the world gathered together. Vienna, 16 km. Washington, 101 miles. Pretoria. Passetto-Fernandes. Argentina-Rosario. People steal signs and bring them to Watson Lake, reminding them of the world outside, the world so far beyond their borders.

You try the Watson Lake Hotel, Watson Lake Motors, but in one you are offered a drink and in the other a lube job. No Arachne. The drugstore and the jewelry store and the food store and the post office too are futile, but then, you don't expect that Arachne went into them. After trailing one side of town and then the other, you return to your hotel, even check the bar for the geologist, but he too has vanished. You ask the desk for a place to buy film, you intend to take pictures of the signs, and are directed next door to a log-structured store that seems to sell everything, a conglomeration of junk and necessities.

You take one look at the sharp-faced man behind the

*counter and recognize possibility. "Women's underwear,"*
*you say steadily, clearly.*

*He points.*

*The panties lie in a luscious heap, ice-cream colors.*
*You smell one, touch your tongue to another.*

*Very slowly you find the label and scrutinize it. It is*
*clear, indelible.* Ladies' Comfort, *Winnipeg, Manitoba.*

*You buy the lot.*

*There are two roads to choose from here. You can cross*
*over to Whitehorse on the Alaska highway or take the*
*Campbell highway that joins the Canol Road. Highway*
*is a misnomer. These are gravel roads. You decide on*
*the route to Whitehorse. It is by far the better road and*
*you're sure Arachne would have considered the Mercedes.*
*She loves that car more than herself.*

*And so you take that meandering ribbon that passes*
*Rancheria and Swift River and dips back into B.C. before*
*reluctantly hoisting itself up to Teslin and Johnson's*
*Crossing, where you stop trying to investigate further.*

*It is a hopeless business. At Johnson's Crossing, at Jake's*
*Corner, in Whitehorse, when you mention Arachne Man-*
*teia, they shake their heads. It's not a name they know,*
*not a name they care to remember. And when you mention*
*the time, the fall that she passed through, they begin to*
*talk about the comet, that night in September when they*
*were lying peacefully in bed, when they were having a*
*quiet drink or a solitary walk, when they were visited*
*by the comet, its glowing blue tail spread wide across*
*the sky, so wide and so low its hissing that some thought*
*it was the northern lights come late or early, some thought*
*it was cloud, or the end of the world. It was, they say,*
*impossible to escape, a conversion, a momentous occasion.*
*They talk about the way it felt as though they bathed*
*in its tail, its audible blue hiss.*

*You keep trying to steer them back to Arachne Manteia,*

*underwear sales rep, driver of an antique Mercedes, gloomy, glowering Arachne Manteia. They speak of death and deliverance.*

*Exasperated, you leave the White Pass, the incoming tourists and the Robert Service souvenirs, and drive on. You can go up to Dawson, you can go on to Alaska, cross the border. You have found only one clue, a sled-dog trainer who insists he heard a helicopter pilot talking about an old Mercedes in a strange place. He insists also that you watch him feed his dogs, a brutal noisy ritual, and then he allows that the helicopter pilot is stationed at Mac Pass. You look on the map and decide that you better get going. The Canol Road up to Ross River and Macmillan Pass is summer traffic only.*

*The Canol Road is hell. It is not a road but a track, a pair of cat marks over rock and muskeg and fallen stumps. It jars your teeth, your vertebrae, your eyeballs, your arches. You are in a four-wheel-drive rented truck. You cannot believe that Arachne took her Mercedes up here, but it's the only clue you have. You decide that in the last few months of her life, in the period after she left Calgary, she became a different person.*

*You are relieved to reach Ross River, although it consists of only a few impermanent aluminum trailers. It reeks of decay. Although it is summer and the beginning of field season, there are only a few geologists and surveyors, and the regular residents of Ross River are inebriated, cross-eyed and shy.*

*This is the ultimate frontier, a place where the civilized melt away and the meaning of mutiny is unknown, where manners never existed and family backgrounds are erased. It is exactly the kind of place for Arachne. You search the town from end to end, check the Alcan coffee shop and the bar and the hotel, but she is not here.*

*And so you drive on.*

*Now the road begins to frighten you. There is nothing anymore, no promise of a town or a place. You are heading for the Mackenzie Mountains that separate the Yukon and the Northwest Territories; and if you reach them, you'll be nowhere, at the end of a road built by the American army in the middle of the war, officially opened, then abandoned, never resurrected.*

*You have fallen off the edge. There is no ocean or continent beyond, only the enormity of spectrum and range and latitude, of, dear God, four-dimensional nothingness.*

*You are crying as you drive. The potholes shake your cheekbones, you are wiping away tears. Although you know you must turn back, you continue, no longer on a quest for an ill-defined traveler but for the infinite anguish of uncivilized territory. You've lit out and now you can't stop.*

*There is no sign to tell you when you reach Mac Pass, nothing but a trailer and the beaked shape of an electric-blue helicopter. You stop the truck and stumble into the dust, the moss. You are carrying your own gas and you begin to refuel, afraid to look up at the mountains, afraid to look toward the trailer.*

*The pilot comes out, saunters over like a cowboy without his horse, his boots stirring up puffs of dust, his one-piece flying uniform snug and racy.*

"Howdy."

"Hello."

*He grins.* "Need a hand?"

"No, thanks."

*He looks over the truck, looks you over at the same time.* "Lost?"

"No."

"You're up here on purpose?"

*You nod.*

*"Cup of coffee?"*

*He stalks back to the trailer and after you cap the gas can, you follow the imprint of his heels.*

*He waves you to a chair. "Bit rough," he says, "but I've got everything I need here." He sets the coffee down in front of you, sits across the table and leans forward. "What are you after?"*

*For once you hesitate. For once you do not launch into your spiel about a chunky, dark-haired woman driving a Mercedes. Instead, you begin to explain your research, how it all began with the history of women's clothing, but that was so confused, Parisian fashions and Italian fashions and the English influence, that you began to investigate what went underneath, what women wore to bolster themselves, protect themselves, what made them sweat and itch and grind their teeth. You began to understand the connection between the inner and the outer appearance, began to comprehend the philosophy of the accoutrements of women.*

*You launch into the idea of underwear, its significance, as metaphor, as reality.*

*He listens without interrupting. When you get to your question hours later, he stands up and refills your coffee cup, sets it in front of you and says quietly, "Yes."*

*You gape. No one has answered you so directly.*

*And now it is his turn to talk, to tell you about the travelers up that endless and abandoned road, what he sees passing his trailer, the dust that billows behind wheels. A circus, a car carrier; sports cars and station wagons, landaus and jeeps; a white Cadillac with California plates. And Arachne in her black Mercedes, driving slow and steady, face forward and absorbed, headed into nowhere.*

*"She didn't stop?"*

*He shakes his head.*

*You ask where the road ends.*

*"There is no end."*

*You have to swallow before you ask the next question.*
*"Do they ever come back?"*

*He shakes his head. "Never."*

*You thank him for the coffee, you step out into the*
*wind and walk to your rented truck. When you settle into*
*your seat and fasten your seat belt, you understand that*
*there can be no going back.*

*A few miles up the road a flash of color makes you*
*slam on your brakes. You slide out and step into the ditch,*
*bend to retrieve it. The panties are gray with dust but*
*their scarlet invitation has not faded. Ladies' Comfort.*
*Another few miles and you find a peach pair, then a tur-*
*quoise, then sunshine yellow. Each time you stop, shake*
*the dust from their silky surface and toss them on the*
*seat beside you. There is no end to the panties; there will*
*be no end to this road.*

# ABOUT THE AUTHOR

Aritha van Herk was born in 1954 in central Alberta. She grew up on a farm near the village of Edberg, just a few miles from the Battle River, an area that she still writes about. She published her first poem when she was twelve, and her first published story won the Miss Chatelaine Short Fiction Award in 1976. In 1978 she won the Seal First Novel Award for *Judith*, and in 1981 she published her second novel, *The Tent Peg*. In 1986 she was selected as one of the ten best fiction writers in Canada under forty-five years of age.

She has been a secretary, a hired hand, a bush cook, an editor and a teacher, and she has lived in several western Canadian cities. As a child of immigrant parents, she has always inhabited multiple worlds; she is interested in the unexplored landscapes of Canada, as well as the unexplored areas of human myth and possibility. A regionalist and a feminist, she works through her fiction to rediscover lost stories and myths within contemporary time and space.

Her work has been published in eleven countries and nine languages, and she has traveled extensively, giving lectures and readings from her work. She has also co-edited two anthologies of fiction, *More Stories from Western Canada* and *West of Fiction*.

Ms. van Herk received her M.A. in English from the University of Alberta in 1978. She is currently Associate Professor of English and Creative Writing at the University of Calgary. She is married to Robert Sharp, who is an exploration geologist.